Chaos and Night

Also by Henry de Montherlant

SELECTED ESSAYS (edited by Peter Quennell; translated
by John Weightman)

THE BACHELORS (translated by Terence Kilmartin)

THE DREAM (translated by Terence Kilmartin)

CHAOS AND NIGHT

A NOVEL BY

Henry de Montherlant

Translated from the French by Terence Kilmartin

The Universal Library

Grosset & Dunlap   NEW YORK

Author's Note

In my *Textes sous une occupation* (p. 51) I wrote: "Napoleon once said that of all the peoples of Europe the Spaniards disgusted him least."

I wanted to make this the epigraph for *Chaos and Night*, and looking through my manuscript notebooks in order to check the exact wording I found that it was one of a series of notes I had made while reading the *Memorial of Saint Helena*.

I therefore asked two experts on Napoleon, and particularly on the *Memorial*, to give me the necessary page reference. They both assured me that no such observation occurs in the *Memorial*.

I find it difficult to believe that I could have dreamed up such a quotation, with those inverted commas seeming to guarantee its authenticity: that would be grave indeed! Perhaps the phrase comes from another work, which I read at the same time as the *Memorial*.

I am writing this only in order to make it known that I would have liked these words to be the epigraph of the present book. The uninhibited tone in which the characters and I speak of the Spaniards here is no different from the tone in which my characters and I speak of everything, especially the French. The same tone is to be found in my other novels. It in no way affects the profound blood-friendship which has bound me to the Spanish people ever since my adolescence, and of which I have given countless proofs. I would like to make this clear on the first page of this book.

Preface

At the beginning of April 1952 I outlined in two pages of my *Carnets* the idea which emerges at the end of Chapter VII of this novel as it stands now.

Waking up in the middle of the night of January 13–14, 1954—three weeks after the opening of my play *Port-Royal* at the Comédie-Française—I worked out a fictional plot that might express the idea. I wrote down eight pages which summarized this narrative.

I had some hesitation about the civil status I should give my hero. A Spaniard living in Spain? I do not possess the knowledge of Spanish society that would have been required. Living in France, then? In this case it seemed reasonable to make him a political refugee rather than a supporter of the present régime: it was the feelings natural to an exile belonging to a defeated party which brought him to the situation around which I wrote the book.

Thus I was led quite accidentally to an attempt to create a Spanish republican. This decision once made, I found it tempting to make him "a bogus leftist," a man who calls himself an anarchist but really belongs to that strange, bitter, ingenuous world of people who are perpetually on the fringe of society, cultivating their own eccentricity, not to say their absurdity—a world which seems to me peculiarly Spanish, the patron saint of which is Don Quixote. In the same way I was obliged to evoke here and there throughout the book the Spanish Civil War, about which I was ill equipped to speak. The novelist sometimes resembles a hunter who is drawn on by his prey and eventually finds himself lost he knows not where.

Which is to say that the sentiments attributed to the hero of this book have been invented solely in response to the needs of the book. The tendency to saddle an author with the sentiments of those of his characters who are most "alive" is a widespread one, and comprehensible enough. It is even more so when the novel in question is one which is obliged to touch on politics, in an age when people are, with good reason, worried and obsessed by politics.

It is therefore more than ever necessary for the author to repeat as emphatically as possible what he has often said before. A writer of fiction puts something of himself not only into one but into all the characters of a given book, however different, however opposed they may be. And if he puts something of himself into a principal character, he puts just as much that is the opposite of himself: thus he is *in* the character, but the character is not he. To go back to an image I have used before on several occasions: if you look at yourself in a dark metal bowl full of water, you will see your reflection more or less exact; stir the water with your hand, and everything becomes blurred: it is no longer you. I should like the reader to keep this image constantly in mind when he recalls his impressions of *Chaos and Night*.

Another thing. The number of anarchists or pseudo-anarchists in Spain in 1936 is usually estimated at two million, and this without counting those who were never registered. It is more than likely that there existed a Celestino among these two million-odd, and Spanish friends, both left-wing and right-wing, to whom I have shown my manuscript, confirm this. Moreover, as I have never ceased pointing out, Celestino is an exceptional case, ill at ease even with his own party. To suggest that I wanted him to

represent the whole of the Spanish Left would be tanta-
mount to saying that I wanted Coantré (in *Les Célibataires*)
to represent all bachelors and Andrée Hacquebaut (in *Les
Jeunes Filles*) to represent all young women. Indeed in the
latter case this has been suggested. But not for a second
will it hold water.

Meanwhile I should like to say this: while I was writing
Chaos and Night—between July 1961 and May 1962—the
idea which is developed at the end of Chapter VII and
which was originally the germ of the book became sec-
ondary and almost anecdotal by comparison with the ideas
developed at the end of Chapter VIII, which is also the
end of the book.

H. M.

"TO THE NORTH, there's England, an incomprehensible country, and the Scandinavian states, incomprehensible countries. To the south there's the Vatican. The dome of St. Peter's is the candle-snuffer of Western thought: like this dome here" (he pointed to the Sacré-Coeur nearby on their left) "only on a larger scale. Around the Vatican there is Italy, and Italy means the aeroplanes that protected Franco's reinforcements when the game was almost up."

He stopped, and seized his companion by the arm. The other stopped too.

"To the west, there's the United States. The United States is the canker of the world. On the one side Good, on the other, Evil: that is obvious, I learnt it from the good Fathers. The United States is Evil . . . I even prefer the Pope to the United States," he concluded, his eyes gleaming.

"Let's go and have a drink," said the shorter of the two gentlemen (both of them spoke in Spanish, the little one with a strong Valencian accent). "I should have offered you something at home, but it will be cooler in the *posada*."

They were in the rue d'Orsel. They turned into the rue Briquet, a narrow passage between the rue d'Orsel and the boulevard Rochechouart. There were bollards at either end, put there in an earlier age to prevent carriages from entering; yet there were motorcars in this so-called street, which was deserted on this late July day, one of the hottest of the boiling summer of 1959. At the far end it led into

Africa; the natives of that continent could be seen walking past the opening, with now and then a few rare Frenchmen, no doubt captives and slaves; some of the blacks carrying enormous spades, to bury the corpses.

No sooner had they entered the street than the taller of the two men stopped again, and put his hand on the forearm of the little one, who stopped docilely. The tall one said:

"To the east there's Germany, an incomprehensible country . . ."

"And Switzerland," said the little one with a sly, mischievous look, as though he were setting a trap for the tall one. The latter did not flinch.

"Switzerland is a very, very important country. The only civilized country where there are no decorations. In this, Switzerland sets an example to the world. Nobody realizes it, and if they did they wouldn't understand, or rather they would find it blameworthy. To think that even the U.S.S.R. has decorations!"

"Yes, there's the U.S.S.R. . . ."

"We owe an immense debt to the U.S.S.R. And yet, it has to be admitted, reservations must be made."

"More than reservations," said the little one, trying to walk on. But the tall one hung on to his arm, immobilizing him, and continued:

"I have in my pocket an article of mine about the United States. It has by way of epigraph a phrase of Trotsky's: 'The pillars of Hercules of the United States are vulgarity and stupidity.' You know how much there is to alienate me from Trotsky; he could not abide either anarchists or adventurers, 'those who express the revolt of the masses only fortuitously.' He went so far as to talk of 'the cretinism of the anarchists' . . . And yet he was an intellectual, a deviationist, an outcast and a failure, and that makes a kind of bond between us. In my article I have written quite categorically that the United States is 'a nation without honour.'—However, I shall omit this phrase."

"Even if it were true, there are other nations without honour."

"You mean the Spain of today?"

The little man made a vague gesture, which seemed to mean that it was not Spain he had in mind. As the gesture was more or less circular, one might, assuming the worst, have taken it to mean the France of today.

The tall man tried to open one of the three newspapers he was holding in his hand, but in doing so he dropped them. As he stooped to pick them up, his companion took the opportunity of walking on, and said:

"I like this street. It has something of an alleyway that reminds me of home. These bollards are similar to those of our Calle de Madrid, which is seventeenth century. And look at this!"

To their left, in the Passage Briquet, narrower still, washing hung from windows, bright and multicoloured, evoking a Mediterranean town.

"And the *posada*! Purely French, and yet with something Spanish about it. The only thing missing is a poster on the wall announcing six *hermosos toros*. Can't you feel the coolness of it? A haven of coolness . . ."

It was true; a puff of cool air came from a little café on the left-hand side of the street; a modest tavern without a terrace, almost without furniture, a sort of hole in the wall which brought to mind the recesses made in the porches of certain old houses in Madrid into which a man could withdraw when a barouche passed through.

They were at the door, through which the air now felt

almost cold; they had only to go in. But the temptation to speak again was too strong for the tall man. Once again he stopped the little one, holding him back by the sleeve. . . .

"Twice, the workers and peasants brought the Republicans to power, in April '31 and February '36. Each time, the traitors of the Popular Front betrayed the victory of the people to the serpents of democracy. When I spoke to you about Trotsky, it was apropos of the United States, but it was also because Trotsky . . ."

The little one took a step forward. The other followed him into the café.

"The *posada*!" said the little man. "The darkness and the cold, and the drinkers, not so much workers as rustics. One might be in another world. And only ten yards away —ten yards exactly—is the torrid boulevard with its profusion of squalid dives. Less than a hundred years ago, I believe, this would have been just beyond the *Barrière*, which was in the boulevard Rochechouart—one would have been outside Paris already. On the other side there was the slaughterhouse . . ."

"Ah!" said the tall man delightedly, "the slaughterhouse! So it really is the *Posada de la Sangre*."*

Close by, in the boulevard Rochechouart, there was a particular narrow point—at the bottom of the rue Séveste—from which the walls of the Sacré-Coeur, framed by the perspective of the two blocks of houses on either side of the street, took on the unlikely appearance of a section of a bullring seen from the outside: a white bullring such as did not exist in Spain but which the tall man seemed to remember having seen in the south of France. Often he

---

* Inn in Toledo made famous by *Don Quixote*.

would stop at the bottom of the rue Séveste and contemplate it with emotion. But just now, between the bullring and the site of the slaughterhouse, the *posada* thoroughly deserved to be christened *de la Sangre*.

They sat down and ordered two *anis*.

The tall man looked rather less than seventy: he had a short black beard, black hair cut straight across the forehead, a deep-lined, leathery complexion, tufts of hair in his ears, the backs of his hands black with hair, a black, glittering, austere look. His name was Celestino Marcilla and he was from Madrid, but he had been a refugee in France for twenty years because of his active participation in the civil war. He had lived in Paris for eighteen years with his daughter Pascualita, now twenty years old. He did nothing, or rather we shall see what he did in the next chapter, if we are still alive to write it.

The little man was about fifty, plump, hairless, a little greasy. From his glasses one could see at once that he was an intelligent fellow. A Valencian, he also had been living in France for twenty years, but more from choice; at any rate for less pressing reasons than Celestino Marcilla. Don Celestino's wife had died in giving birth to Pascualita. M. Ruiz—as the little man was called—lived with his wife and daughter, the latter a year younger than Pascualita; he had a son studying in Lyon. M. Ruiz worked at *les Halles* in import-export, specializing in bananas, on the exact site of Labienus's camp during the battle of Lutetia, 52 B.C. He also imported entire families from the Valencia region along with the bananas. M. Ruiz was seriously thinking of leaving the banana business and opening a picture gallery.

Celestino spread out the newspapers on the table. His right shirtcuff, impeccably white on top, was black with printer's ink underneath: he had been carrying the papers around for hours.

"Always newspapers!" exclaimed Ruiz. "Always newspapers!"

"Newspapers are more important than machine guns."

"Lucky you're such a resolute enemy of the freedom of the Press!"

"Newspapers are more important than machine guns provided there is no freedom of the Press."

"If only you were kept in touch by really well-informed people!"

"Well-informed people merely repeat what they have read in the newspapers."

"And an evening paper, when you're still carrying around the morning ones!"

"One cannot understand the evening papers if one hasn't read the morning ones. It's like a serial: if you miss a single number, you're lost."

"What if you are?"

"To be unaware of what's happening in our time, what's coming in, what's changing, is to sin against progress, to show that you despise it." He gave a quick glance at one of the papers. "There! They're talking about *juntas*. . . . Ah, no! it's about the *young*." It was a habit of his to transform words in this way according to his obsessions. A *police d'assurance* became simply the *police*, a *garçon d'étage* became a *garçon d'otage*, a *fusilier marin* a *marin fusillé*, an *avion de tourisme* an *avion de terrorisme*, etc.

Another glance at one of the newspapers:

"Missiles, pluviometers, Pakistan, yams: everything, I must keep up with everything! Always at the listening-post, always on the lookout. Initials are a problem, but I have my code, and I keep it up to date." He opened his wallet and brought out several visiting cards covered with groups of capital letters with the full meaning opposite.

"In other words, for you a newspaper is a bit like a crossword puzzle."

"No, but one has to know one's way around—no doubt about it."

Celestino opened an evening paper with a huge circulation and read some of the headlines under his breath—which led him to exclaim:

"Man has never been so intelligent as he is today!"

"You talk like Jean-Claude, our charwoman's son. He's at the Lycée Voltaire. An excellent child I may say: eleven years old and he hasn't slit anyone's throat yet. This very morning I heard him say in an unanswerable tone of voice: 'Man is more intelligent today than fifty years ago, even thirty years ago.' "

"Absolutely right."

Don Celestino held forth at length on the subject of intelligence, with so many gesticulations that one might have been reminded of the story, whether true or false, that Napoleon forced himself to keep his fingers in his waistcoat to combat his Latin tendency to gesticulate too much. Celestino did not know that a Frenchman, who had met him with Ruiz, had nicknamed him "the machine gun"; he had indeed the violent, crackling, inexhaustible delivery of a machine gun. From time to time, encouraged by the heat, Ruiz's eyelids drooped. Finally he said:

"You talk like a book. After all this time with nothing to do, why haven't you written your book yet?"

"I can't write my book because I have too many ideas."

"If you had a job, you wouldn't have time to have ideas. *I* work, which is why I have no more ideas than are strictly necessary. In any case, ideas. . . ." He lowered his voice:

"Listen, I'll tell you something; the world of today is governed by fools; but they are fools with ideas, that is to say deadly fools, for ideas are always deadly. . . ."

"Even if you have no ideas, I hope that at least you have, deep down, some political opinions," Celestino said in a severe tone.

"I have no political opinions, because I don't read the newspapers. Besides, there are feelings, and even sensations. . . . Look, if the newspapers, at this moment, weren't carrying headlines about the heat, we wouldn't feel hot."

Ruiz looked down at the unfolded newspaper and began to laugh.

"Uncle Sam and the Pope joining in a mad race in order not to be overtaken on the left by anyone—a race lost before it has begun—what a spectacle! What a subject for caricature in a comic paper! The modern world is an explosive mixture of the tragic and the grotesque. The tragic everyone sees, but few people see the grotesque, especially few among those who help to create it. Jean-Claude thinks that man has never been so intelligent as he is today, because this is an idea which a schoolmaster is bound to hold and which his master has pronounced from his rostrum as an article of faith. But you have made up your mind to believe it, even though in your heart of hearts you don't. You only believe in the past."

"So I'm insincere, am I? When my brain is bulging out of my head with sincerity!"

"Your will aspires towards the future, perhaps, but your innermost being belongs to the past; all anarchists belong to the past, because they only believe in death."

"And you go around saying that anarchists are phrasemongers! You're a fine one to talk."

"Actually, you don't belong to the past or the future.

You're not even an anarchist. I don't know what you are. I don't even know if you're a man of the Left. . . . Let's go into the square for a bit. The worst of the heat is over."

They went back up the rue Briquet, Celestino protesting and still holding forth. One might have wondered how it was that there were cars in this street, since the bollards at either end contracted the entrances to prevent them from getting in. Now people could be seen climbing into them, whereupon they rose perpendicularly into the air, like lifts. They came down again by the same means beyond the rue Briquet, and having landed, drove off. It was simple, once you thought of it.

As soon as he had spotted the Sacré-Coeur, Celestino burst out:

"Political attitudes must be determined solely by the following question: does such and such an event contribute or not towards the destruction of Christianity?"

"The revolution had nothing to do with the religious question. It was to do with private property."

"The first act of the revolution should have been to see to the destruction of Christianity. By the hair on my legs, no half-measures! Pitiless and total destruction! The ancient Romans, who are regarded as a narrow-minded lot, were one of the most intelligent peoples who have ever lived, because they believed less in their gods than almost any other people. But in their struggle against the Christians, they behaved like children."

"You people only know how to destroy! When you have destroyed everything, then will you be happy?"

"What a question! The pleasures of destruction. . . . If things had turned out differently, there is only one post I would have accepted: that of Minister for the Destruction of Religion. Spain is not Catholic; in 1936, there was not

a single Spanish writer who claimed to be Catholic, except
Bergamin. No other nation, except Russia, has done so
much for atheism as we have. When the Communists come
to power in France, they must first of all blow up that
candle-snuffer (he pointed to the dome of the Sacré-
Coeur). As for the rest of the building, they could turn
it into a swimming pool."

"A swimming pool with red snappers," murmured Ruiz,
rather pleased with himself. But one might have noticed on
Don Celestino's face a bovine inaptitude for understanding
any witticism whatever. He neither laughed nor smiled,
ever. As soon as he gave the ghost of a smile, his mouth
puckered up in an ugly way—the smile of a plesiosaurus—
whereas, so long as it remained serious, his face had a certain beauty. If Ruiz told him, for example, with great excitement, that Franco had been put up for the Nobel Peace
Prize, first he would believe him and then, when Ruiz
roared with laughter, he would give him a black look.
Ruiz's jokes shocked and offended him.

They reentered the rue d'Orsel, where Ruiz lived. Fifty
yards from the boulevard Rochechouart, it is a small provincial street, full of homely charm—the counterpart, morally and materially, of the avenue Trudaine, to the south
of the boulevard, which is, however, wide and prosperous-
looking, full of retired "artistes" and ladies of easy virtue
who have migrated from the dubious quarters of Pigalle
and Clichy to end their lives in modest respectability.

"If I had had a son," said Celestino, "and he had wanted
to be a priest, I would have killed him."

"Cigarette?" Ruiz suggested.

"No, my convictions are enough for me."

By which he meant that he was just then so taken up
with his passion, and so intent on giving it expression, that

a cigarette would only have been a distraction. There is a story that Pope John XXIII, when a Nuncio, once said to Edouard Herriot: "After all, what is it that divides us? Our ideas? You must admit that's not much." This was certainly not Celestino's attitude.

They had entered the square Willette, which Don Celestino used obstinately to call first "le square de la Villette," then "le square Notre-Dame de Willette," for, after twenty years, he was still unable either entirely to understand spoken French or to speak it himself correctly. He read it without difficulty, but whenever he spoke or wrote, it was indescribable. For this reason he communicated with Frenchmen as little as possible. When he was forced to do so, in order to overcome the feeling of inferiority which it induced in him, he was liable suddenly to become ill-mannered, although by nature he was courtesy itself. He would suddenly decide not to answer a letter, or to arrive twenty-five minutes late for an appointment without apologizing, or to ask someone to telephone him the next day at such and such a time and then deliberately not answer. At such moments as these he felt he had risen to the civilizational* level of the French. But soon nature would reassert itself; it was so painful to him to be rude that he was obliged to revert to his customary politeness at the risk of feeling inferior to the French.

The square was very busy in spite of the time of year, Climbing precipitously, since it follows the slope of the Butte, with streams that flow only on Sundays and holidays, the lower part of its steep lawns was bordered with human beings, like the froth left by waves on a beach. A neat and placid little race, somewhat overpowered by the

---

* Since we have "cultural," such an indispensable word nowadays, why not "civilizational"?

heat, but invigorated by social promotion. The two men sat down in chairs on the edge of a path. There passed a Chink, dreaming of acupuncture; some mongoloid children awaiting the age when mongols die, which is fourteen; venerable old men avidly licking ice-cream cornets, sticking out their long tongues with a purposeful expression; and pretty girls whose escorts occasionally happened to be French (technicians, of course). Exhausted butterflies fluttered low over the lawns, where cats lay prostrate here and there like cows. Children shouted to one another—they were all called Jean-Claude—and showed one another how eventually they would be able to pick their noses while driving a car and bite their nails while riding a motor-scooter. This apprenticeship was well on the way.

Celestino was on the point of bringing out from his pocket the typescript of his article against the United States, in order to show it to Ruiz or to read him a few passages. But Ruiz's "atmosphere" was not favourable. The article remained in his pocket.

A pale young man with circles under his eyes, a ghost of a young man, was sidling up to people and offering them a newspaper. Almost without stopping, he would say to them: "Read *Là-Haut*, the paper published by the Will of God," and pass on.

There was an old couple sitting beside the two Spaniards. The old grandma said: "He comes here every day. I've never seen him sell a paper. In fact, he doesn't look as if he even wants to sell them."

"He's a madman," said the grandpa.

"One must respect all sincere beliefs," said Ruiz, very Import-Export.

"Read *Là-Haut*, the paper published by the Will of God." The wraithlike young man went off, scarcely offer-

ing his wares. People watched him with blank, expressionless faces.

"One of these days they'll be hunting priests in these
bushes with dogs," said Celestino.

"Please God!" said Ruiz sarcastically.

"One day I went up to the top of the hill where that
barbaric monument stands. Near the church there are long
white walls without a single gap, like the walls of convents
at home, except that these are white and ours are yellow.
I wonder what goes on behind them. All those imprisoned
women, or men, or children, in these Bastilles of hypocrisy
dominating the whole of Paris—it's heart-rending. . . ."

The faintest breath of wind imperceptibly stirred a few
shrivelled leaves, then dropped again.

"It's getting windy," said the grandpa anxiously.

"Oh yes, it *is* windy," agreed the grandma. "I'm not
staying here." She got up, and they both went off.

"Before I leave you, I shall go and meditate for a while
at *Caballero de la Barra* . . ."

"*Caballero de la Barra?*"

"The *caballero* who was beheaded and burnt for muti-
lating a crucifix."

"Oh yes! The Chevalier de la Barre."

"It's a long way," sighed Celestino, "but I shall go nevertheless." (It was two hundred yards away, but distance is
relative.) "This story of the *caballero* has a Spanish flavour,
like the *posada*. Mutilate a crucifix! What sort of mutila-
tion? Ours,* I suppose. And this *auto-da-fé* reminds me
of something else. It took place in France less than two
hundred years ago. The great-grandparents of these Parisians could have witnessed it."

---

* During the Spanish Civil War, both sides castrated enemy corpses,
in Arab fashion.

"But the Parisians don't care a damn. You're the only person in France who takes freethinking seriously. Your secularism is as anachronistic as your anarchism. You know the French: they have no opinions, no convictions, they simply decide that a thing is 'done' or 'not done' and that's all there is to it. Freemasons have themselves buried by the Church. The clergy swish their skirts all over the place. No newspaper will print a word against the Pope; no writer will criticize the Church. You cannot breathe a word against Catholicism without some notorious atheist eyeing you with disapproval and putting you in your place. Nobody "believes" but everyone pretends to. Why? Because the big-circulation magazines celebrate the miracles at Lourdes, and because to go through the motions of believing is supposed to exorcise Communism."

"By the hair on my legs! I may be the only one, but I shall go and commune with myself at *Caballero de la Barra*! France, the cradle of the Revolution! Bakunin was quite right: the French love the State and hate liberty."

"Don't talk so loud. You know quite well you must be under surveillance."

A young mother with scarlet nails had settled down beside them, and was feeding a baby calf—her son—with a bottle. A little boy with smooth legs, but forearms covered with hairs so long that he could almost have plaited them, was wiping his sweaty palms in his hair from time to time.

Ruiz went on:

"You have never understood a thing about anything—which is why you became an anarchist. It would be too much to say that you don't know where you're going, because you aren't going anywhere. You're a living symbol of mental confusion, the characteristic sickness of our age. You're an ideological throwback, yes, that's what you are:

an ideological throwback. It's all very well to talk of the
stupidity of the Americans, but one ought to examine oneself a bit. You've never thought anything out in your life,
and you never discriminate. If one neither reasons nor dis-
criminates, what is there left? Isn't it true, yes or no, that
your anarchist pals told you that unless you held your
tongue a bit they would settle your hash, and that that
very same day you obtained a permit to carry a gun? And
a permit from whom? From the State, the accursed State!"

"I didn't need a permit from anyone to . . ." began
Celestino weakly.

"If you were capable of compromising anything, you
would compromise your own party. What is more, it's
because of men like you that we lost our war. You're always going on about Don Quixote. Don Quixote was the
first anarchist; he was irrational and pig-headed, which is
why he lost his battles nine times out of ten. You're a caricature of a man of the Left, just as Don Quixote was a
caricature of a knight-errant."

Celestino opened his mouth to speak. No sound came
out. Ruiz went on talking, and Celestino could smell his bad
breath, which he had never noticed before.

"As I say, you're incapable of compromise. But you're
also provocative, and that will get you into trouble. If the
Americans, knowing what you think of them, were to take
over here, they would arrest you. If the Communists came,
they would take you out and shoot you. If the priests were
in power, they would roast you. You're lucky your life
is nearly over. Don't put it off too long, otherwise you'll
be back in the dangerous world of your forties, but this
time with a decrepit body and a deliquescent mind, which
will make you much more vulnerable."

Don Celestino stood up stiffly, like a man who has to make

an enormous effort, and walked away with the taut, rapid, mechanical gait of one who does not trust the strength of his legs. Although his skin was naturally dry, and moreover the heat of the day was a dry heat, a wave of sweat had broken out over his body, from the shock. In a second, his Aertex vest was soaked.

It was from Ruiz, a friend of twenty years' standing, it was from Orselito—as he called him, after the pleasant Spanish fashion for diminutives: little Orsel, or the little man from the rue d'Orsel—that he had received this quiverful of insults. But why, almost from the beginning of their conversation, had Ruiz been so sour and bad-tempered? He could not understand it. Unless it was for this reason: three weeks before, Celestino had had an inkling that Ruiz, as a result of his wife having had a long illness and an operation, was in financial difficulties. Celestino had very discreetly made it known to him that, if necessary, he was ready to oblige. Ruiz had refused, insisting that he had never been so well off in his life. And, since then, something had changed in him. He had been colder, more distant, until, today, he had become openly hostile.

Celestino climbed the steep path through the square. He was aiming automatically for the rue Chevalier de la Barre. When he realized where he was going, he no longer felt the desire to go and "commune with himself" in the street of the *caballero*. Ruiz had extinguished a tiny flame within him. An ideological throwback. Perhaps he *was* an ideological throwback. Perhaps it was an anachronistic gesture to go to the rue Chevalier de la Barre. In any case, his heart was no longer in it. When he had reached the top of the square, he turned sharp south down the rue Ronsard.

He would never see the rue d'Orsel again, for he would never see Ruiz again. Never again the *Posada de la Sangre*.

Perhaps this was what he regretted, more than he regretted Ruiz: the neighbourhood where Ruiz lived—and perhaps also a habit.

Now there was only Pineda for him to talk to, to unburden himself to. With his daughter, everything went in one ear and out the other; she was utterly indifferent and frivolous, at least as regards important matters. But Pineda listened to Celestino, and did not tease him all the time like Ruiz. And he was loyal.

Apart from Ruiz and Moragas (his solicitor), Marcial Pineda was the only Spaniard, or rather the only person, whom Celestino had anything to do with. A youngish man —he was about forty—a decorator and a bachelor, Celestino would have had little inclination to make an intimate of him, having a horror worthy of a Desert Father for everything to do with art, theatre, literature, etc., were it not for a kind of all-round competence in Pineda, combined with a rare degree of loyalty and good nature. For information of every sort, practical, political, intellectual, or whenever anything difficult had to be done, it was always: "Let's ask Pineda." Celestino had only known Pineda for five years, but those five years, in terms of active friendship, were worth twenty years of Ruiz. Where Ruiz's political opinions were as changeable as the plumage of the cock-pheasant, Pineda appeared, quite genuinely, to have none. He used to say that anyone who enjoyed his work had no time to spare for political opinions.

The taxi rank opposite the square d'Anvers was taxiless. A little travelling roundabout, all on its own, was revolving there, empty and silent as death. When a taxi arrived, Celestino stood aside for a woman who had arrived after him, because one must always give way to women. Then a Negro arrived, and when the next taxi drew up he stood aside once more, because his political convictions demanded that one should give way to Negroes. Then came a vicious-looking individual with enormous shoulders, and this time Celestino walked away, because he did not feel strong enough.

He walked down the rue du Delta into the boulevard Magenta.

The boulevard Magenta was as indescribable as ever, with its bearded women, its denizens of Aulnay-sous-Bois, its technicians, its red lights like monkeys' behinds, its squalid, stinking market, and its church, so unexpected, so incongruous, set down slap in the middle of a world so alien to it that one could only assume it was deconsecrated. The greatest genius in the world would be powerless to distill a drop of literature from the boulevard Magenta.

Nor was the boulevard Magenta a place where it was easy to think. Celestino was so preoccupied with avoiding the cars and the passersby that he did not give a thought to Ruiz until he found shelter, for a moment, under a covered bus stop. There, a thought struck him: he would never again have to go down the boulevard Magenta, since he was dropping his old friend. He was pleased at the thought.

As he came within sight of his own street, the rue de Lancry, he had a second thought, which instantly cheered him up and straightened his bearing and his legs. He had found his revenge. Under some pretext or other, he would break with Pineda. Pineda would pay for Ruiz.

The implacable asphalt was reflected in the sky. Not a leaf stirred in the trees, still as death against the asphalt sky.

THE FIRST THING Don Celestino did on arriving home was to telephone Pineda and arrange a meeting in the course of which he would break with him. This meeting was fixed for the following day.

Pascualita was dining with the family of one of her friends; so the old gentleman could reflect at leisure on what had happened.

In the first place, still no regrets at having discarded Ruiz. Total indifference. They had known each other for twenty years, and for the past four had met every week and spent hours together "machine-gunning." Their daughters were friends; Pascualita had twice spent the summer in the country with the Ruiz family. Yet it was all based on nothing, as this incident had proved. They had continued to meet because, having once begun to meet, there was never any particular reason why they should stop. Now, thank heaven, there was. "Friendship, that shadow of a shadow," as a character in Aeschylus called it, in an age which nonetheless made a cult of friendship to the point of drivelling nonsense.

Similarly, the married state as a rule is based on a habit fraught with lassitude. But that is well known. It is less well known of friendship, still less of parental or filial ties. Yet our own experience, as well as history, shows us with frightening force how fragile they are. In Paris, and doubtless elsewhere, it is a general rule that twenty years of conversation, of familiarity, of kindness, of intimacy or of what passes for intimacy, with one's wife, one's mistress, one's friends, one's secretary, one's servant, creates nothing and is nothing: one parts for ever in an instant, as though one had never met. The more one thinks of it, the more extraordinary it seems, the more it gives food for thought. Separation without continuous pain means indifference, no matter in what tender colours this indifference is painted. This is not to say that every relationship, between parents and children, between husband and wife, between friends, is a matter of indifference, but that it is a matter of indifference if not in a majority of cases then at least in a very substantial minority.

Don Celestino went even further. He told himself that if, in a new civil war, there was the slightest suspicion about Ruiz, he would have him shot. And he asked himself: "Why such a hurry?" And he could only answer: "Because he was my friend."

"It's because of men like me that the revolution was defeated! There's my reward. It takes a long time to find out if a man is your friend: twenty years is notoriously insufficient. By what aberration has it taken me twenty years to recognize the odious side of this man, otherwise so genial and pleasant? He doesn't know if I'm a man of the Left! I must be a feudalist—yes, that's it. And he calls me an idiot. I certainly was an idiot to trust him. I've talked too much to him. He made me talk."

Ruiz used to claim that a moment always came when wars and revolutions turned into sombre farces, and that he was glad the Left had been defeated in Spain, because it would have been corrupted by victory, whereas now it was still a potentiality and therefore something pure and good. At the time, Celestino had failed to react as he should to these pernicious theories. Now this dilettantism filled

him with disgust. In fact everything about Ruiz filled him
with disgust; not only his character, but his face and his
whole manner. Come to think of it, he had felt like this
about Ruiz for a long time. How long? Five or six years,
perhaps. . . .

"When we were discussing the causes of the civil war,
he used to say: 'It was because the Spaniards needed to
kill. Ideology was only an excuse.' Fancy reducing the
revolution to that! At once Franco-ist and progressive,
freethinking and clerical, he's another case of muddled
thinking, but this time deliberate and venal. False to the
core. I suspected as much, and yet I went on seeing him
and telling him everything. Why? Because I didn't know
anyone else, except Pineda, and you . . ."

For this solitary monologue was addressed, aloud, to the
absent Pascualita. For the past year or so Celestino had
taken to talking to himself, at home or in the street.

"When he told me I was probably being watched, was
he making fun of me or was he trying to scare me? For
example, when he warned me that I'd be shot by all the
parties (which could have been more delicately expressed).
If *I* were in charge, I'd have him shot for scepticism. Or
perhaps, when he said that, it was because he knew something? Maybe it was *he* who was watching me. Maybe he
has been, I don't say for twenty years but at least for some
considerable time, an informer and an *agent provocateur*."

Celestino was forgetting that he himself during the civil
war had sometimes seemed like an *agent provocateur* in the
eyes of his party, on account of his verbal extremism and
the ill-considered violence of some of his actions.

"What a fool I was! He hardly ever used to telephone
me; it was I who had to chase him; he managed to impose
it as a sort of rule. And he used to hang up on me in the

middle of our conversations." (This grievance was imaginary: on two occasions their calls had been interrupted by a technical hitch.) "And he was already being insolent last winter. He thinks friendship gives him the right to insult you: 'I can't stand on ceremony with you. You upset me very much by being so touchy. I wouldn't have expected it of you.' The weapon of the Spanish Left is dynamite; the weapon of the Right, insult and calumny. I should have realized he was a fascist. Now he had made it clear: to betray the man is to betray the cause. I carried on. I needed to talk. . . . Luckily I have you."

He turned on the radio. With rapt attention, straining not to miss a syllable, he listened to the news which he had already read in the evening paper.

When Pascualita came home, he told her—without going into the humiliating details—that Ruiz had insulted him and that he was breaking with him. Pascualita did not ask for the details. She too, for longer than her father, had been shocked by Ruiz's scepticism.

"I shall never forgive Ruiz. I shall be in-ex-orable. Besides, this incident has given me some ideas of a more general nature. Get a pencil, I want to dictate an article to you."

"Dictate? Usually you write them. . . ."

"This time I don't want it to go cold on me."

He dictated:

It is strange that men should be willing to break the law but at the same time unwilling to suffer the consequences. They transgress; and then everyone has to do his utmost to protect them from the consequences of their actions. Every time a man is condemned to death, two groups of people—always the same—intercede on his behalf: the "tender-hearted" (underline "tender-hearted"), that is to

say stupid idiots, and the "socially conscious" (underline
"socially conscious"), *that is to say thumping crooks. In a
civil war there must be no reprieve. The death sentence
cannot be regarded as an administrative formula which
automatically means life imprisonment, in other words am-
nesty after five years, or escape. In all circumstances words
should correspond to a reality; otherwise they are nothing
but garbage.*

Pascualita showed no reaction. When she had read back
her shorthand aloud, Celestino thought for a moment, and
then asked her:

"Do you think I can publish that?"

"Why not? You know quite well that one can write
anything in France."

"I won't publish it."

There was a silence.

"Very well. Shall I type it out anyway?"

"Of course. It will go into my archives."

Later that night, Pascualita heard someone talking in her
father's room. She knocked, and getting no reply, went in.
He was asleep, his arm resting against his forehead in an
attitude familiar among the larger apes, and he was saying
in his sleep: "Leave us alone with your democracy. . . ."

When Ruiz insulted him, Celestino Marcilla did not
reply: "So you think I don't know what I'm doing? They
knew what I was doing when I had an automatic in my
hand." He had never spoken, either to Pascualita, or to
Pineda, or to Ruiz, of the role he had played during the
civil war, and he was equally ignorant of Ruiz's role in it.
Ruiz had fought with the government troops, or so he said.
That was all his friend knew about it.

The Marcilla family, who called themselves Marcilla Hernandez on grand occasions, came from Teruel, Maestrazgo de Montesa, bordering on Castile, Aragon and Catalonia, but family legend had it that they were of pure Castilian stock. Having moved to Madrid because he could no longer get on with his *cacique,* Celestino's father had raised himself up unaided to the post of departmental head in the Ministry of *Fomento,* an untranslatable word which means, roughly, the activation of various things. A sincere monarchist, with liberal leanings, he activated as much as he could for thirty years, from 10 to 11:30 in the morning (his working hours), eventually receiving the customary ribbon, which was his only pride and joy. Celestino, a pupil of the Jesuit college of La Flor, later embarked on a long and idle period of law studies, occupied mainly in political discussion in cafés and culminating in failure in his final examinations. He in his turn entered the Ministry of *Fomento.* Despised by his colleagues for his lack of social standing, through awkwardness and indolence he failed to exploit his comparative affluence (estates near Saragossa inherited from his mother) to make his presence felt. Eventually, recognizing his inability to get ahead, he began to pretend that he had no desire to do so, and veered imperceptibly towards socialism, the more easily because his work brought him into contact with the miseries of the working class. He steadily refused, however, to join a party. He did not like Fourier, a scatter-brain and a deist. His heroes were the Encyclopaedists and Proudhon, Bible and Gospel of nineteenth century Spanish socialism; Tolstoy, for whom he had a filial affection (for a time he played the landowner who is ashamed of his estates); and Bakunin, so intelligent and such a good atheist. As for *Das Kapital,* he had had several stabs at it with little success, and many of the pages remained uncut. Ruiz would have said that this was because of all these doctrinaires Marx was the most alive, or rather the only one who was alive at all, and that "anarchists are only interested in death." Hating the Spanish State, which had provided first of all his father and now himself with a paltry living, he came to hate the State in itself and authority in any shape or form. As a conscript, his rebelliousness and his military incompetence, deliberately cultivated, had caused him to be blacklisted and frequently confined to barracks. His only sister had married a Madrid businessman (in scent); both of them were sly and *bien pensants*.

The proclamation of the Republic left him pretty cold. Whatever the regime, it still spelt tyranny: the only serious difference was its atheism. In May 1931, he got his hand in by helping to set fire to the college of La Flor: burning down one's old school, what an intoxicating sensation! In '34, events in the Asturias gave him for the first time an inkling of the possibilities of revolutionary solidarity; he was bowled over, and from then on he never looked back. From the beginning of '36 it was nothing but *juerga** in the streets; the decline of the Republic was the last thing he worried about; the aim was to have a good time; and to hell with "solidarity": he shot at the socialists too.

Then came July and he set out enthusiastically for the front with the militia, the red-and-black scarf of the anarchists round his neck—his only concession to party disci-

* How translate *juerga*? The nearest English equivalent is "spree" or "binge," but here of course a spree of violence is meant. Perhaps the word *fantasia* would be more suitable, because of the gunpowder. To sum up, rather loosely, *juerga* can be said to consist, in peacetime, of shooting at anyone impartially in the street.

pline. In effect, what had been revealed to him was that the State acquires some meaning when it allows you to kill legally those of your compatriots who do not think as you do. So, long live the Republic! And long live solidarity, once more! (Until it was time to return to passionate discriminations.)

For two and a half years Celestino went through the civil war mill, doing the routine things as well as the exceptional. When everyone else in the Fifth Column had his union card, he, for two and a half years, was desperately "uncontrollable"—and yet so loyal and so lucky that he never got into trouble: the unions vouched for his integrity. In 1937, when the Government took the army in hand, he was made a Captain, as much for his conduct under fire as for his law diploma. He donned his old private's uniform which he had kept to play the fool in at private *charlotades*,* and drew three stars on the sleeves in pen and ink. His style in battle was personal and suicidal: that was how he liked it. If anyone expressed astonishment at his always escaping without a scratch, "God protected me," he would quietly reply. Something of a devotee of the stews in his youth, he had remained a bachelor, for fear that a wife might bully him. In May 1938, on leave from the Ebro front, he got married on the spur of the moment, because his father had told him that he wasn't afraid of shells but he was afraid of women: "Ah! So I'm afraid of women, am I?" In January 1939, he was one of the two hundred and fifty thousand men of the Republican army who took refuge in France, and he spent six weeks in the internment camp at Argelès. When he was released, his wife, crossing the border through a village in French Cer-

* Small burlesque bullfights.

dagne, joined him in Carcassonne, and died soon after while giving birth to Pascualita, who was born no bigger than a bottle (they bought her a doll's layette).

His sister and his brother-in-law had never left Madrid. The brother-in-law was of very middling intelligence; but when it came to surviving at any price, he was very intelligent indeed.

Celestino lived very uncomfortably in the Aude for three months—a damnable country where at first he did not even know how to ask for a glass of water! The republican functionaries of the French Republic had at first treated him as a beggar, if not a delinquent, but when they realized that he was a bourgeois astray in the red army they began to pander to him. When people saw that he was not kept under house arrest or forced to work for starvation wages like the unfortunate majority, a shopkeeper and a functionary even advanced him some money. Eventually, when his income began to reach him regularly through another country—a very, very important country—he moved to Paris, which he had not left for a single day ever since. Having made one "exodus" he fought shy of another, in spite of the risks facing the Spanish refugees (though in fact only the "heads" were arrested). On the night of June 13-14, 1940, when he was living in a very modest hotel off the Grands Boulevards, he heard a great trampling of feet in the distance. Was it the French army leaving, or the German army arriving? He had gone back to sleep. At eight o'clock next morning, hearing the same noise, he went out and saw what it was: the German heavy artillery, with armoured cars and motorcyclists. He did not look for long, but returned with his eyes full of tears. The Spanish Republican army had been defeated for the second time. "And yet *we* are in the right."

Little Pascualita had been left in the care of a religious community in Carcassonne, for lack of any alternative (the schools in the unoccupied zone being overrun by refugees). Celestino guaranteed to de-Christianize her without difficulty when the time came: it would give him something to do. When she was six he sent her to a lay boarding school near Paris; at fifteen, he brought her home, and put her into a *lycée*. She was very serious, firmly disapproving of anything she regarded as "bad form." She had not become Christianized; he was frustrated on that score.

For twenty years Don Celestino lived a bachelor existence, his only contact with life being through the newspapers, the radio and television and, during the last five years, his daughter. It was not an oppressive life: time passes quickly when it contains nothing, or when it contains only an obsession, and an extraordinary capacity for eliminating everything except this obsession. Alone, or almost alone, taking part in nothing, to some extent he had achieved the anarchist ideal: he was independent. (In addition, his health was magnificent: in twenty years he had spent two days in bed.) He had lived in the rue Daubenton, then the avenue des Gobelins, then the rue de Lancry; he was pleased to discover this final abode, which brought him closer to Orselito. He read almost nonstop—newspapers, magazines, and reviews, Spanish as well as French, glued to them like a fly to a piece of dung, until one wondered how he could breathe.

He read about everything: the whole planet was his concern. But preferably about Spain—whenever he could, for Spain at the time was practically blotted out of the French press. Every morning he would pounce on the French newspaper to which he subscribed, and tear it open in the hope of finding that General Franco had had a heart attack. He

searched for articles and news about his country as greedily
as a writer looking through a newspaper which he thinks
may have an article about him, and often flung the paper
away with the same bitterness and fury as the writer when
he has drawn a blank. Blackout over Spain! Still a blackout over Spain! If there was no mention of Spain he was
mortified. If Spain was criticized, he was mortified. If Spain
was praised, he was mortified, because it meant praise for
the Franco regime.

He took notes on newspaper articles, then cut them out
and filed them. The notes were also filed. His pockets were
always full of scraps of paper, which fell out whenever he
took out his cigarettes. He was supposed to be writing a
book, and whenever he was asked about it he would say:
"I'm clearing the ground." Mostly he wrote political articles, about which we shall have more to say later on, if we
are still alive. He refused to do anything whatsoever to
earn money. By working, he could have increased Pascualita's dowry. But time spent working would have been
time taken away from armchair politics and he preferred
politics to money, and his disinterestedness to his daughter's
welfare: somebody always has to pay the cost of noble sentiments. Upright, and so scrupulously honest that many
people would doubtless have regarded it as verging on
neurosis, he could not even conceive of guile and intrigue,
however innocent, in a world that lives on guile and intrigue, and was stupefied and appalled when they were
pointed out to him. Just to the point of inhumanity, as
long as politics were not involved, whereupon he became
human once more, he had a private maxim: "Justice through
injustice."

On no account would Celestino have allowed his daughter to work, and she herself had no wish to work in Paris,

since this would have obliged her to mix with French society and—horror of horrors!—take orders from Frenchmen.

The house in the rue de Lancry was one of the four or five bourgeois houses in the street, the rest being more modest. Don Celestino's flat consisted of three rooms: a sitting room-cum-dining room, of which the most one can say is that it was respectably furnished; Pascualita's small bedroom, furnished haphazardly, full of girlish knick-knacks thrown together in the most unbelievably bad taste (or perhaps in a taste unbelievably different from French taste); and Don Celestino's spacious room, which contained only five or six pieces of antiquated furniture, also bought at random in junk shops. Like most Spaniards, Celestino was indifferent to his domestic surroundings. The floor of his room was piled high with newspapers, magazines, and reviews going back as far as 1941, meticulously sorted in chronological order, year by year, and even day by day, but stacked in such a way that he could never find the one he wanted except by chance. The whole flat was very clean —they had an excellent maid—but these stacks of papers collected great quantities of dust, for the maid was forbidden to touch them. The floor was also strewn with files and card indexes. Plain deal shelves, which no one had bothered to paint, contained books, far fewer in quantity than the newspapers and magazines. Each of these books had been summarized and card-indexed. It was the study of a thinker, but a thinker who did not think. Celestino was not in the least worried by the bareness and disorder of his room: anarchists and monks have a great deal in common.* He had also inherited from his race—through the

* "Why do monks and anarchists fight one another? They are very alike. . . . Anarchism is the monasticism of the atheist." (Unamuno).

Muslim tradition—a tendency towards privacy and seclu-
sion. No one was allowed into his room except his daughter
and the maid. *Har'm* also applied to Pascualita's room. Even
Ruiz and Pineda were only received in the sitting room, a
circumstance that had once provoked some acid remarks
from Ruiz.

Don Celestino did not associate with any Frenchmen,
both because—as we have said—he could neither understand
them properly nor make himself properly understood by
them, which humiliated and exasperated him, and because
he did not like Frenchmen. They were for him (not without good historical reasons, stretching from the Middle
Ages to the recent civil war) the hereditary enemy. But he
had made it a point of honour never to speak ill of them,
not even to Ruiz, Pineda, or his daughter. They had given
him asylum; they had allowed him to live a life that was
on the whole bearable, whereas all the other countries of
Europe were "impossible" for one reason or another. Only
South America was at all possible, but South America, like
the rue Chevalier de la Barre, was so far away, and then
there was seasickness, and Don Celestino, like Cicero, preferred death to seasickness. As for aeroplanes, the less said
the better; they were a triumph of human ingenuity, but
only on condition that one didn't use them.

His tolerance of everything that could be said to divide
Spain from France, especially the refusal to send arms to
the republicans during the civil war, was not the genuine
and astonishing tolerance of noble natures, who forget indiscriminately both the good and the evil that is done to
them; it was a deliberate, tight-lipped, self-complacent
tolerance: a bad kind of tolerance.

He also avoided conversations with the French because
he never knew where they would lead. For example he had

once met a Frenchman with Ruiz—a banana Frenchman—
who had started making fun of Franco. After listening to
him for some time Celestino had taken umbrage and proceeded to defend the Caudillo, recalling, among other
things in his favour, the story of "the Hendaye siesta,"*
and hinting that no one but a Spaniard would have shown
such style in similar circumstances.

If he did not associate with Frenchmen, neither did he
associate with Spaniards, with the exception of his two
friends and his lawyer. Neither with the whites, because
he hated them, nor with the reds, because he was afraid
of being compromised by them. He had been their com-
rade in arms, but the *camarillas* of exiles, with their gossip
and their indiscretions, their illusions and their grievances,
all under the beady eye of the police of the protecting
country, displeased and frightened him. Moreover, as might
be expected, he had nothing but aversion for anything to
do with association, solidarity, mutual aid. He was annoyed
when he was put automatically on the mailing list of an
anarchist sheet published in Paris (and there was no question of writing to ask them to discontinue the service: they
would have laughed at his pusillanimity). Only once, at
the beginning of his life in Paris, had he been to a left-
wing meeting. Thereafter he had avoided like the plague
anything remotely connected with politics, even the act of
eating in a Spanish restaurant, for fear of being addressed
by a stranger. Only one thing mattered, and it was all-
important: to keep in with the French government. Sometimes, in his worst moments, he was haunted by the spectre

* Franco, on meeting Hitler at Hendaye in 1940, wanted to have a
siesta after lunch and made Hitler—who had just conquered the whole
of France—wait half an hour until he had finished sleeping or pretending to. The authenticity of this anecdote is guaranteed.

of having his residence permit withdrawn, or simply being interrogated about his means of livelihood. But nothing ever happened. "How nice to have a government that shuts its eyes," he thought to himself. The accursed State had found its justification at last: to shut its eyes. He would even have granted extenuating circumstances to Napoleon for the invasion of Spain, had he known the great man's remark: "The policeman's art lies in not seeing what he does not need to see."*

During the war, his enemy number one had been, according to the mood of the moment, now the Communists, now the Socialists, most often the Falangists. His attitude towards the Communists was a very personal one. By nature he was too egoistic and too undisciplined to be anything but scandalized by collectivist notions. As an anarchist or pseudo-anarchist, he could not but detest communism, with an antipathy that dated from the First International. Added to which there was his resentment at the behaviour of the party during the civil war. Stalin despised not only the Spaniards but the Spanish Left; he had refused to send aircraft to Catalonia; the Republicans had had to fight against the Communists more than against the Fascists; the Communists had throttled the anarchists in '37 and had declared that once Franco had been beaten they would annihilate them utterly.

However, since coming to Paris his attitude had gradually changed. Anarchism, though still alive in his heart, seemed from Paris to have no real European existence; and socialism being unacceptable because of its bias towards democracy, the Communists alone seemed both effectual and uncorrupt—even, looking back in all fairness, during

* Letter to Fouché, May 24, 1800. Napoleon, *Pensées sur l'action*. Presses universitaires de France, p. 39. Paris, 1943.

the Spanish war. Finally, the climate of Paris had managed
to convince Celestino that communism—whether he liked it
or not—represented the future of the proletariat, in fact *the*
future pure and simple.

He had always had an inferiority complex vis-à-vis the
Communists. In Spain, when he talked to one of them, he
used literally to lose his way in the Marxist dialectic. "Yes,
yes," he would say, pretending to understand. But he did
not understand; darkness filled his mind. Anarchism, like
celibacy, is simple; it was because they are simple that
Celestino had clung to both of them. In Paris, having re-
jected the anarchists, and despising the Socialists, he decided
to try a cautious rapprochement with the Communists. His
first step was to send an article, under a pseudonym, to a
left-wing French review. The article failed to get through,
but the review, in an editorial comment, made a pointed
allusion to it, referring to "certain Spaniards of today, out-
of-date anarchists, who reveal the same fatal lack of understanding of the laws and the tasks of the revolution as their
fathers," and going on to show these same fathers "sabotag-
ing the workers' insurrection in 1937 and helping to save
the dictatorship of the bourgeoisie, in other words proving
themselves, at the most critical moment, counter-revolution-
ary." So that was their reward for having sacrificed so
much in a terrible war! That was the price of their blood!
Celestino did not understand that blood only counts if it
can be made use of, and if it cannot be used it does not
count.

Celestino retreated into his shell: his sensitivity was
acute. And perhaps in his heart of hearts he preferred to
remain anonymous. Besides, convinced that communism in
the not so long run would triumph in Europe as well as in
Spain, he was not sorry to refrain, out of self-respect and

out of a more subtle respect for the victor of tomorrow, from "trimming his sails to the wind," when so many others were trimming theirs. He had often wondered whether, for instance, the French Resistance in 1943-44, or the Communists of today, had much respect for those who did not trim their sails. He was afraid not.

One day when her father was sitting alone in his study with the door half-open, Pascualita had heard him heave a great sigh, the sigh of a small boy who has quite given up hope of understanding his sums, or the sigh of a small boy who feels he is not loved as much as he should be. She was surprised by this sigh, so uncharacteristic of her acrimonious father. She would have been even more surprised had she known the cause of it. Celestino's heart was heavy, and he was sighing, because he could not understand and because he felt unloved: exactly like the small boy. But *what* could he not understand, and *who* did not love him? He was sighing because he realized that he would never really be able to understand Marxism. And he was sighing because he had been rebuffed by the Communists and would never be accepted by them, even though, deep down, he was not all that keen on it. He was exiled from communism just as he had been exiled from his country, because he was with them without being wholeheartedly with them: they would have been closer to each other if he had been a Fascist.

All of which goes to show that he had never perceived the true nature of the conflict. But the reader must already have discovered that it was Celestino's specialty never to see reality for what it is.

Celestino's virtues during the war had been loyalty, bravery, and self-sacrifice; his faults, individualism, with all its questionable exertions, military ignorance, and, of course, the somewhat half-baked condition of his political ideas. He was not a man of hope, any more than he was a man of love. He had waged war out of hatred—as good a reason as the next man's. Of the various stages in the development of the human race predicted by Bakunin, the day of judgment attracted him more than the day of brotherhood. A future society without social antagonisms, in other words without violence and civil war, quite frankly did not interest him. Scorched earth, rather than the Promised Land.

However, if he did not love his fellow-men enough, he was at least very fond of children (like all his compatriots, and like the Moslems). Until she had reached the age of fifteen, he adored his daughter—no doubt for two reasons: first, that he saw very little of her since she was at a boarding school in the country, and secondly, that he could not scold her for anything because all is forgiven at that age. When, at fifteen, she came to live with him, things became less rosy. For a long time she had kept up her childish, inconsequential "why's"; until one day she grew out of them. . . . At thirteen or so, she had astonished her father by the apparent enthusiasm she showed for social questions, the rudiments of which he used to teach her. Of course, when she declared vehemently: "I'm against the trusts," he smiled to himself. But still, it was a positive reaction. Now, if Celestino gave her a heartrending description of the present state of Spain—"Of all the countries of Western Europe the one in which men have been worst exploited"—all she could think of saying was: "How sad it all is!" Whereupon she would skip to another branch like a little bird that cannot keep still. Moreover, she laughed; and when Celestino saw anyone laugh, he glared at them with hostility and indignation. Adolescents of both sexes have souls that are as changeable as the sky; within a few months they are utterly transformed, for good or ill; it is almost impossible for those who know them best to foresee how they will develop.

Once when he was explaining to Pascualita how the various forms of Popular Front were nothing but devices for cheating the workers (this was a hobbyhorse of his), Celestino saw her cheeks swell in an odd way round her grimacing mouth. Goodness, how plain she looked! What did it mean? Well, she was yawning "inside her mouth," or, if you like, she was trying not to yawn. He remembered the man he had asked the way when he was trying to cross the Spanish frontier, who had yawned his head off while Celestino was telling him things that were a matter of life and death to him. Celestino had noticed it and suddenly stopped talking as though he had received—already—a mortal blow; then, without another word, he had wandered off into the mountains. Nobody really understands the human condition unless he realizes that, apart from one or two persons, there is not one soul who is interested in whether he lives or dies.

Sometimes, when he was about to see her, a brilliant idea would come to him and he looked forward to expounding it to her. Of course there was now no question of educating her; they had gone beyond that; it was simply a subject of conversation. And then, when they met, finding her so uninterested, he would stop short and rapidly switch the subject to broken-down refrigerators or lifts out of order. It was like dealing with somebody senile: one thinks of something to say to them; then one realizes that they will not understand and will start drivelling, and so one keeps quiet. She seemed to have decided that social questions were meaningless and no concern of hers. She reminded Celestino of some people he had met in Barcelona during the war, who, in the middle of the most grave and tragic events, showed little interest in what was at stake and were only waiting for it all to finish, no matter how, as long as it was quick.

Apart from this, she was always very helpful, translating and typing his articles, and coping with everything. This "everything" was a great deal, for Celestino Marcilla did not want—in fact strenuously refused—to cope with anything. Anything, that is, except the most elevated things. His fundamental impracticality was inextricably mixed up with a genuine contempt for material things, under which he contrived to camouflage it. Since, like a good Spaniard, he knew *Don Quixote* by heart, he was always quoting from it, and never failed to remind his daughter, apropos of household problems, of the words of Don Quixote to Sancho: "Do you think a man like me can be bothered to know the difference between a fulling mill and an ordinary windmill?" She was useful to him, too, in proving to everyone that he was not a bachelor, a state which in France is a sort of crime.

Among the things that were not sufficiently elevated was Pascualita's future. She was now twenty. Marry her off? First of all, it was terrifying to imagine having to do without her. And then, marry her to whom? To a Francoist Spaniard? Out of the question. To a red Spaniard? Out of the question. To a Frenchman? She would reject this even more strongly than he. And "this man" would turn his life upside down, criticize him, disagree with him. To have to reckon with "this man"! To have to give him some of his precious time! Moreover, Celestino was capable at one and the same time of liking children and hating young people. If he had seen a young man flirting with his daughter, his mouth would immediately have gone dry. Nothing

in the world was more of a closed book to him than a girl
of twenty, nothing more tedious than what happened inside her head. As a youth he had taken some interest when
he was courting one of them. But even then, any other
girl was scarcely a human being in his eyes. Faced with a
problem such as this, Celestino Marcilla, who had proved
himself determined and courageous and might have done so
again in similar circumstances, could imagine no other attitude but to ignore it: "Never think about the next fight."*
Accustomed as he was to postponing everything, whether
tedious or not, to the day after tomorrow, systematically,
this attitude came easily to him. But soon he saw the gravity
of it, and though he persisted in it, he did so with a mixture
of shame and rage and horror.

Even if he had really wanted to, he was incapable of
marrying his daughter on his own. Everybody would have
had to take a hand in it. But who was "everybody"? Only
the Ruizs. Pineda was a bachelor of no social standing;
Moragas, his lawyer, was not a friend.

To make her life pleasanter, and to discourage her from
dreaming of other things, he thought up the most childish
schemes: trebly childish, for they showed the childishness
of the male in his relations with women, particularly young
women, the childishness of the parent, and the childishness
of the intellectual. He had her room recarpeted, he offered
her presents, a fountain pen, a handbag, a pottery lion, and
what have you, always the sort of things that gave her little
pleasure—and in any case a pottery lion is a dubious substitute for a husband. She wore or kept these objects out of
politeness, and they piled up in her unprepossessing little
room. Celestino, far from realizing that his presents were

* A maxim familiar among matadors.

an embarrassment to his daughter, and if anything aggra-vated their mutual lack of comprehension, sometimes won-dered if she had seen through his game and was taking advantage of it for the indiscriminate acquisition of other things she coveted. The whole thing made him feel a little ashamed. But he told himself rather naïvely that he was also a mother to her, and mothers always spoil their daugh-ters—which is true only if they get on well together; if they do not get on well the mother becomes too hard on her daughter, and Celestino and his daughter did not get on well.

After all this, we have not yet described what she looked like. Her hair clustered thick over her temples, and an old-fashioned bun, as heavy as a bunch of grapes, hung down over the nape of her neck; her eyebrows were thick and straight, her wonderful eyelashes like black rays cast by her eyes, her tiny ears pressed close to her head, shiny as ivy leaves. And her face smelled good on days when the weather was warm.

A word about Don Celestino's articles. Ever since the end of the German occupation, he had been sending politi-cal articles under pseudonyms to various Parisian journals, articles which he tried to make as temperate as possible because of his residence permit. Most of the time they were neither acknowledged nor printed. This forced him to buy the paper in question for some time in the hope of finding his "piece," and he would crumple it up and throw it down in disgust in the middle of the street when he failed to do so. One day a middle-of-the-road paper published one, and sent a cheque for 1,000 francs. Full of childish joy, he reread his printed article seven times, succumbing every ten minutes, irresistibly. But the succeeding articles, with two exceptions, suffered the same fate as the first ones. So then he thought of the idea of simply writing letters to newspaper editors, and some of them, or extracts from some of them, were published. Each time this happened, he would cut them out and send them to Ruiz, Pineda, and Moragas. He constantly alluded to his articles, whether published or not. To such and such a question from Ruiz he would say: "I've already answered that in my article on Bakunin which I gave you to read a year ago. Don't you remember?"

At this moment he had just written, very discreetly, an article entitled "Dancing before the Bear." The dance before the Bear was the dance executed by the bourgeoisie of various countries in front of the Russian bear with the object of currying favour with him: it was a far cry from the days when it was the bear that danced in the middle of a ring of spectators. This article had been weighed word by word, and it had taken him four days to write. But after these four days he decided it was unpublishable. Nevertheless, like all the rest, it was translated and typed by Pascualita—not without some unfavourable comment from her father on the quality of her work—and tucked away in a file along with a dozen other cautious and unpublishable articles.

Thus did Don Celestino's days go by, fulfilling Marx's dictum to the effect that an anarchist inevitably ends up a petty bourgeois.

Two days after the scene in the Square Willette, Don Celestino received a letter from Ruiz. He did not open it, but tore up the envelope and its contents into small pieces which he placed in another envelope and sent back to Ruiz.

It was on the very same day that he was to break with Pineda. A meeting had been arranged with this object in view at a café in the boulevard Saint-Martin, at the corner of the rue de Bondy, only thirty yards from the Place de la République, but to him as far away as the Puerta del Sol. There was a small terrace there, steeped in shade all day long (in summer) and therefore dear to Don Celestino, practised as he was, like all Spaniards, in the subtleties of sun and shade, which they sample judiciously according to the hour and the season.

This café was at the extreme eastern point of a star traced out by Celestino's daily walk, the spine of which was the boulevard Saint-Martin. The extreme northern point was his house, a point he would sometimes overlap when he went to Orselito's. The western point was the Porte Saint-Martin, a point often overlapped when he went to buy the Spanish newspapers on the boulevards. The southern point was the rue Vaucanson, in a rather peculiar district of which more later. Don Celestino hardly ever deviated from the spokes of this star: a man of thought—whether real or not—is a man of habit, because automatism does not distract him from his thinking. Moreover, in his case an inordinate curiosity for social, economic, and political facts was accompanied by an inordinate lack of curiosity for everything to do with art, beauty, and life. And his socialist universalism was combined with something narrow and insular in his makeup: the population of the Faubourg du Temple, as well as that of the rue Turbigo, close though they were, he would have regarded with hatred had he chanced to stray among them.

The Grands Boulevards are well-to-do commercial from the Madeleine to the Opéra, less well-to-do commercial from the Opéra to the Rex cinema, petty bourgeois turning to proletarian from the Rex to Strasbourg-Saint-Denis, proletarian from Strasbourg-Saint-Denis as far as the Porte Saint-Martin, only to become once more mysteriously petty bourgeois, almost nonproletarian, between the Porte Saint-

Martin and the Place de la République, which is itself
eighty per cent proletarian.

This last sector is the boulevard Saint-Martin, the characteristic of which, as compared to the other sectors of the
boulevards, is emptiness. Fewer pedestrians, fewer cinemas,
less thriving shops, very few cafés. And—for exactly five
hundred yards—not a single policeman, not a single taxi-
rank, not a single urinal, not even one of those containers
ostensibly for people to throw their refuse into but in
reality for respectable old gentlemen to rummage round in
and fish out, ecstatically, all sorts of treasures. And the only
underground station in the boulevard Saint-Martin has
been closed for years, as though to emphasize the abandoned, run-down, almost plague-stricken atmosphere of
the boulevard, a sort of no man's land before the proletarian
districts which begin in the Place de la République. Added
to which, as though to reinforce its oddity, over these five
hundred yards not a single street leads into it from the
south, except for two private alleyways tunnelling between
the houses, scarcely wider than a gateway, the despair of
the murder victims of the rue du Vertbois and the rue
Notre-Dame de Nazareth, who, fleeing their pursuers (before becoming victims) four steps at a time up the Pont-
aux-Biches steps, try to penetrate these alleyways only to
stumble against their barred gates, closed at night, at the
foot of which they meet their fate.

If you are seen to stop for a few moments between the
Opéra and "Richelieu-Drouot," you will be asked the way
to the Opéra. If between "Richelieu-Drouot" and the rue
Montmartre, you will be asked the way to the Musée
Grévin (this is so much a matter of form that if you are
asked, for instance, the way to the rue de l'Echiquier you
scream blue murder and run for your life). If between the

rue Montmartre and the Porte Saint-Denis, you will be asked the way to the Basilica of Montmartre (many foreigners and provincials assume that the Basilica of Montmartre is near the boulevard Montmartre, which after all is not so silly). If you are seen to stop in the boulevard Saint-Martin you will be asked nothing, because the boulevard Saint-Martin represents nothing. And this perhaps explains, if we are to believe those French writers who hold that the Spaniards adore Nothingness, why Don Celestino had made it the favourite, or rather, to all intents and purposes the sole orbit of his peregrinations.

As for the southern point of Celestino's star, it demands an explanation. Whenever his light sleep was interrupted by the hooting of a van of the *Santa Hermandad** (it was thus, out of Quixotism, that he referred to the police) which had succeeded the drums and tocsins of old, or if the concierge, bringing up the morning mail, announced that there had been a murder in the night, it had always happened either in the Faubourg Saint-Martin or on the southern frontier of the boulevard. Celestino disregarded the Faubourg; he specialized in the southern streets, where he used to go to hear the gossip, sniff the blood, and sometimes see the traces of it. There he had rediscovered his old life, and on his very doorstep; for there were plenty of other scenes of crime, but so far away!

Running parallel to the boulevard Saint-Martin on the south side are, first the rue Meslay, a fairly quiet street situated on the site of the old wall of Paris (under Louis XIII), then the rue Notre-Dame de Nazareth, less quiet, then the rue du Vertbois, consisting almost entirely, in the

* *La Santa Hermandad,* or Holy Brotherhood, a police organization which existed in Spain under various forms between the 14th and 17th centuries.

sector which concerns us, of small lodging houses occupied by Arabs.

The rue du Vertbois runs alongside the north front of the Conservatoire des Arts et Métiers, and is met perpendicularly by the rue Vaucanson, which runs along its east front. Celestino was a man who revelled in street-fighting: hatred is more at home on a pavement than in the open countryside. From the very first day he had entered this district, the old gentleman had been struck by several features which seemed to make it an ideal spot for a brawl. The police station in the rue Notre-Dame de Nazareth, the underground flight of steps in the Passage Pont-aux-Biches, leading from the rue Nazareth to the rue Meslay; the narrow alleyways, not even the width of a gateway, like those which lead from the boulevard to the rue Meslay, but the width of a man, which pierce certain houses (two) and connect the rue Nazareth with the rue du Vertbois—at least for those who know of their existence, since they are not easily detectable by a stranger to the district; and finally the Conservatoire building, which on the rue Vaucanson side was bounded by wide, deep ditches, themselves fortified by railings, as though it had long been conceived with a view to withstanding a siege. All this constituted a strategic system which set Celestino's mind working, the more so since the powerful Conservatoire building flaunted on its pediment, opposite the rue Vaucanson, in the most provocative way, a royal escutcheon bearing the three fleurs-de-lis and surmounted with a coronet! From thence to imagining that the Conservatoire was, as its name implied, a citadel of conservatism besieged by popular forces, was only a short step, which Celestino took on the very first morning he had set off, at eight o'clock, to sniff the blood of a fresh murder victim in the rue Vaucanson.

The sole denizens of the rue Vaucanson at eight in the morning were old crones feeding hordes of haggard and emaciated cats and old men waiting for overfed dogs to relieve themselves. So much so that Celestino at once, performing prodigies of French, christened it rue Pissechiens (Dogpiss Street) or rue Bouffechats (Guzzlecat Street). It was there that he first conceived his battle plan, a plan he was to touch up and develop during the course of his innumerable subsequent visits. These did not attract attention: with his black suit and tie, his black beard, his black, broad-brimmed felt hat (similar to the one which Léon Blum used to wear in 1936), he was taken for a Jew, and Jews are numerous in the neighbourhood.

So the Conservatoire des Arts et Métiers was held by reactionary cadets, like the Alcazar in Toledo. This was of course an imaginary notion, for Celestino had no doubt that its students were in fact all Communists—but in every game somebody has to play the policeman! The people's militia came pouring in from the Place de la République in lorries, via the rue Meslay, whose petty bourgeois population dug themselves in, the rue Nazareth, actively sympathetic, and the rue du Vertbois, wildly enthusiastic. The police station in the rue Nazareth had been swiftly neutralized. But from the east and the west came powerful contingents of C.R.S.* from the barracks in the Faubourg Saint-Denis, Gardes Républicains from the barracks in the Place de la République, and firemen from the Château d'Eau and Landon barracks. Celestino had set up his headquarters in the patio of a house which, being traversed by an alleyway, was at once 49, rue Nazareth and 54, rue du Vertbois. There he was under cover from enemy fire, and through the door of

* Compagnie Républicaine de Sécurité.

No. 54, where he had placed a machine gun, he commanded the rue Pissechiens in its entirety, a segment of the rue du Vertbois, and two sides of the Alcazar, while through the door of No. 49 he received reinforcements from the rue Nazareth and could retreat if too hard pressed. The fight lasted three hours. Obviously we are not going to describe it in detail, but Celestino had it all worked out down to the most minor incident until the final outcome, which he had the grace to leave in doubt. With what profound satisfaction, whenever he came back to the neighbourhood, did he "see" the Alcazar entirely demolished, in places razed to the ground, its moat filled with debris, the houses in the rue du Vertbois gaping open. Only the madwoman of Chaillot, pink-hatted and belaced, continued to feed among the ruins the still emaciated cats, and the old men to watch their overfed and immovable dogs relieve themselves. But whenever he returned from the rue Pissechiens his heart beat fast, his nostrils quivered, and he felt exhausted, as though he had really fought for three hours.

Don Celestino, as we know, had his little habits at the Café de Bondy. With his Spanish mania for not staying at home, he spent whole afternoons there, in the back room, reading and annotating newspapers, and writing his articles or his letters to the Press. On his table was a briefcase stuffed with papers—unusual contents for a briefcase: the briefcases of Parisians are stuffed with sausages and loaves of bread, since it is the men who do the shopping instead of their wives. On Sunday he had his meals there. Country girls, much bespangled, drank sweet vermouth with an earnest air. Mothers ordered aperitifs for their five-year-olds and scolded them if they refused them. Other cus-

tomers settled down to sauerkraut and beer, and Celestino
cast murderous glances in their direction, for he hated both.
In the whole crowded room, the only person of any distinction was a Negro. Distinguished and melancholy. Distinguished because only he was lunching alone; melancholy
because he knew that, whatever apocalyptic changes the
future might bring, he would always be black. Celestino
had made himself famous in the Café de Bondy because
one day, enraged at not being served quickly enough, he
had spectacularly set fire to his paper napkin. "I cannot
express myself on social and political matters," he had explained furiously, "so I relieve my feelings by setting
restaurant napkins ablaze." For all this, if one of the waitresses arrived at a door at the same time as he, he would
give way to her, raising his hat; his politeness exasperated
them; he was the only one who was polite, apart from the
Negro, but while Celestino's politeness exasperated the
waitresses, the Negro's politeness delighted them. If the bill
seemed stiff to our hero, he would take his revenge by
peeing in the washbasin. What a book one could write
under the title: *The Joys of Secret Revenge!* When he
peed in the basin, with his tall and dignified bearing he cut
a splendid figure.

On the terrace of the café Celestino awaited his victim.
A century before, he would have seen water flowing and
flowers lifting their young faces: there had been a fountain
here, and a flower market. Now there was a stone bust, and
a cinema. The cinema was showing *New Adventures of
Tarzan*, and there was a notice saying "No admittance
under 18." The under-18's went in nonetheless, having
painted moustaches on their upper lips with charcoal.

There was only one other customer on the terrace: an

overwrought technician who only stopped gnawing his thumb in order to look at his wristwatch: "time is money." From the way his nostrils dilated, you could tell at once that he was an educated technician.

Later, three chattering cicadas settled down at the next table: a mother and two little girls, the older one about eleven, her features already as formed as those of a young woman, the other resembling Pascualita as a child. Celestino thought the little girls were so sweet that, having unpacked a box of chocolates he had just bought for Pascualita and overcome his shyness about speaking French, he offered them to the whole family. "They're so good," he explained naïvely, almost stupidly. A scrap of meaningless conversation ensued: Draguignan, the father an engineer, etc. The chocolates were so popular that Celestino begged them to accept the whole box. After putting on an elaborate show of reluctance, in the way provincials do, they gave in. Then off they went, Celestino forcing his most ravishing plesiosaurian smile.

For some time he was to dream of meeting another little girl on a café terrace, accompanied by her mother and looking like Pascualita, to whom he could offer another box of chocolates. The nuisance was to have to walk around carrying a box of chocolates the whole time. This problem got the better of his little dream, which took flight . . . like so many others.

The French regard one as a scoundrel if, having been invited to dinner at eight o'clock, one arrives at eight o'clock. Spaniards, tired of being continually accused of unpunctuality, pride themselves on arriving on time. Pineda, five minutes late, mumbled profuse apologies. Celestino remembered the man during the civil war who came to tell a prisoner that he had been condemned to death, and before doing so, apologized for being late. Here it was the other way round: it was the condemned man who was apologizing for being late.

Pineda, who was rather unimpressive in appearance, had a thin moustache shaved above and below which was intended to give him an aristocratic air, a constant preoccupation among Spaniards of the lower middle class. He had just come back from a visit to the châteaux of the Loire. He described the châteaux of the Loire. The curious thing was that he repeated every sentence, or practically every sentence, twice or even three times in exactly the same words at intervals of thirty seconds. Naturally it took a long time. As he spoke, Celestino muttered to himself: "I couldn't care less. If he only knew how little I cared. Why can't he understand that I couldn't care less." The technician gnawed his thumb, then looked at his wristwatch. Celestino waited for an opening—for Pineda to lower his guard so that he could start making the blood flow.

A waiter brought two of those gadgets which the French call *filtres*. They are affiliated to the grenade, the locomotive, and the missile. It is impossible to handle them oneself, the mechanism is so complicated and the metal so burning hot; one has to get a waiter to manipulate them, otherwise one is likely to get hurt, and the table flooded with spurting coffee. The coffee trickles through interminably, and when the cup is full, or rather half-full—for a cup of coffee in a French café is a half-cup—the coffee is no longer hot and tastes insipid; since there is nothing to drink in the cup—two mouthfuls—this hardly matters. This account of the *filtre* is strictly Celestino's: he called it "one of those French monstrosities." The author, for his part, might point out that the Spaniards too have monstrosities of a similar sort, but we are not writing a treatise on comparative monstrosity.

"You drink your coffee without sugar because you want to be different," said Celestino, watching Pineda with an ugly look. "A decorator, an artist, are we? Art against the people. I've watched you drinking coffee without sugar for five years, and it has always struck me that you would much prefer it with sugar, but you want to be different from the rest of us. You're antisocial."

"And you who haven't got a motorcar, you're antisocial too."

"I haven't a car because I can't afford one. And anyway, if I did have one I wouldn't use it because it's too inconvenient."

"You might at least have one of those fashionable little cars. It would show that you didn't despise the future."

"The advent of socialism is more important than the conquest of the moon, let alone motorcars."

Nevertheless Pineda had found Celestino's weak spot. Ruiz also used to tell him that he did not like progress, that he was a bogus left-winger. Celestino-the-despiser-of-the-future and Pineda-the-antisocial looked at each other, or rather their two guilt complexes faced each other, gazing sadly out of their clear blue eyes. Pineda was the first to turn away his eyes. Celestino had won *dominio*.* He struck.

"And you eat the rind of your cheese, also to make yourself different. I've seen you. You ate the rind of a Camembert when you dined with me in May, and the rind of a Reblochon when you came last October."

"Yes, because of the vitamins. Forgive me, but it's a habit I caught when I was starving. I can't get rid of it."

* Power of domination. A bull-fighting term. A matador has or does not have *dominio* over a given bull.

Celestino said nothing. It was the misery of the manual workers he had fought against. The misery of an intellectual or an artist left him cold.

"Anyway, why are you bullying me like this, Celestino? Is that why you asked me here?"

Pineda was very upset. His voice trembled. The technician gnawed his thumb and looked at his wristwatch.

"And when you order an ice, you want it to be warm! Again just to be different, to divorce yourself from the rest of humanity."

"I'm fond of ices, but I don't like them too cold. They make my teeth hurt."

"No, you like warm ices. When one is a decorator, one has to like one's ices warm. One has to *épater les bourgeois*, as the French say. By the hair on my legs, you'll see if they give you warm ices in the society of tomorrow!"

"I don't understand, Celestino. What have I done to you? What have you got against me? I know what it is! We're so dependent on the wage earners nowadays that the only people left to insult are our friends."

"What? What are you saying about the wage earners?" Celestino bellowed.

In his bitterness and humility Pineda had somehow shrivelled up until he was scarcely larger than a cottage loaf. There had once been a whole period when he swelled or shrank in this way, but that was according to whether or not he was eating enough. The tiny figure perched on the edge of his chair aroused a mixture of pity and horror in Celestino, in whose brain the real and the imaginary were so closely intertwined that often he could not distinguish between them. The pity and the horror rendered him cruel, but it was above all Pineda's sweetness and modesty that maddened him. Like all anarchists, Celestino felt himself to be in a perpetual state of legitimate self-defence against anything and everything.

"Warm ices liquefy. But there is also such a thing as the liquefaction of the mind. Forgive me, it's too much for me, I cannot speak to you any more. We'll meet again another day. Good-bye."

Celestino stood up, as though galvanized into new life. First of all, he had taken his revenge. Then, by breaking with Ruiz as well as Pineda, he had revived the civil war, on the personal plane. An extraordinary sensation of power, of reckless defiance, had come over him. He passed by the statue of Baron Taylor. The baron has an extremely vicious look in his eye, and Celestino winked at him before making his way towards the group of pigeons stationed in front of the peristyle of the Théâtre de l'Ambigu. Usually he avoided the pigeons, even with his eyes. This time he took up a firm stand on the edge of the flock.

The pigeons had one thing in common with Celestino: an obsession, which in their case was eating, as in his case it was thinking about politics. In spite of this common characteristic, they exasperated the old gentleman. On the ground, they were so fat and heavy that one could have kicked them like a football. In flight, weighed down by their paunches, they almost flung themselves in your face (one of them had flung itself against the windscreen of a car, causing an accident). They covered the pavement and the benches with droppings the merest particle of which, burning through the stuff it fell on, would irreparably ruin an expensive suit—sacred droppings which were never cleaned up and which had come to form a thick white crust on the pavement. And Celestino, little though he loved, and with good reason, the French marshals of the Empire, wondered what sort of people it was that could

allow the statues of its victorious marshals (on the façade
of the Louvre in the rue de Rivoli) to be completely covered with pigeon dung, to the extent that their names were
obliterated from the plinths. (And as if the pigeons were
not enough, there were also their shadows.)

But what exasperated him most of all was the misguided
sentimentality which the pigeons aroused. The pigeons were
as sacred as the monkeys of Benares. It was their scruffiness
which endeared them to people; had they been beautiful
or noble, nobody would have given them bread. There was
never a word of protest against the foulest infamy. Indeed,
if anyone spoke of interfering with the pigeons of Paris
there was a flood of letters to the newspapers and a universal howl of indignation. The most inhuman race in
Europe,* callous to the old, brutal to children, ungrateful
to its heroes, tyrannical at the slightest opportunity, soft-
hearted only when people were looking, so as to be able to
show off about it, was moved, quite sincerely, to tears when
it came to these pigeons. And to think that one night would
have been enough to rid the whole of Paris of these stupid,
bloated, disgusting creatures!

On the edge of the pigeon walk stood a little boy, half-
bourgeois, half-plebeian, a young plebeian woman, and an
old bourgeois gentleman, all of whom were feeding the
pigeons. The entire nation was represented, every class and
every age, partaking in the cult of the pigeon. The ritual
of the cult, like all such rituals, had become quasi-auto-
matic: it was performed half-consciously, as some people
masturbate. The woman, who was eating something, threw
the pigeons whatever remained between her teeth; when
there was nothing left, she threw them her teeth. Don

* Had Celestino read Chateaubriand? "Of all peoples, the French are
the most inhuman." (*Mémoires d'outre-tombe.*)

Celestino stepped forward, like a matador leaving the *barrera* to face the bull, and crossed the whole length of the pigeon walk. He had adopted the attitude of studied nobility affected by matadors in these circumstances. The pigeons rose in the air and flew at Celestino's face with the hiss and speed and power of a group of racing cyclists, so much so that he was forced to half-close his eyes. But he knew what he was doing. He sensed rather than saw the malevolent looks. The old man, the young woman and the child, each one of them eaten up with passionate hatred of something or somebody, present or future, were enraged that anyone should dare to disturb the pigeons.

Celestino paused for a moment on the other side, savouring his pleasure and audacity. Then, once more, he strode across the pigeon walk, and once more the pigeons took wing, in such a dense cloud that he thought they were going to knock him down, as the crows which emerged from the entrance to the cave of Montesinos knocked down Don Quixote.

"Leave 'em alone. Pore little fings. A proper shame it is."

The woman who had challenged him glared at him with hatred in her eyes. There was hatred, too, on other faces. Celestino did not reply, because he knew that they would realize at once, from his accent, that he was a Spaniard, and then: "Ah, so that's it! You're the people who torture bulls. Savage!" So he stood stockstill, mute and imperturbable, while the pigeons settled again and people started once more to throw them crusts which were enough to strangle them, being ill-adapted to their throats, but which in their hysterical voracity they swallowed nonetheless.

He allowed a long time to elapse. This time he hesitated —let's face it, he was afraid. A matador can bring off two daring passes without a qualm, but when it comes to a third, he is overcome with apprehension. And yet, as with the matador, there was a look of implacable willpower on the old gentleman's face that was not entirely proportionate to its object. He must have realized this, for he said to himself: "I would walk like this if I were walking to the scaffold."

For a third time, his nerves stretched tight, he crossed the pigeon walk diagonally. He expected to be lynched. There was merely a storm of abuse, with people advancing towards him, shouting:

"So you're doing it on purpose!"

"We're not going to allow this to go on!"

"Isn't there a policeman? Jean-Claude," (this was one of the small boys) "run along to the Porte" (the Porte Saint-Martin) "and see if there's a policeman."

The word "policeman" had an immediate effect on Celestino. You begin with a traffic policeman and you end up by being extradited. After all, there comes a moment even for a matador when discretion is the better part of valour. Besides, "to retreat is not to flee": we have the authority of our own Don Quixote for that. Full of dignity, Don Celestino made his way slowly towards his concrete box.

There was a sign beside some roadworks which read: "Crossing prohibited," and an arrow indicating a new temporary crossing. Celestino went fifteen yards out of his way in order deliberately to cross at the forbidden point. There is legality and illegality even in the smallest things.

As he arrived in the rue de Lancry, he thought to himself: no regrets at dropping Ruiz, no regrets at dropping Pineda. He savoured to the full the intoxicating feeling of being self-sufficient (which was quite untrue, for two people were indispensable to him, Pascualita for the household,

Moragas for money). He looked forward to recounting to Pascualita the stirring episodes of Pineda and the pigeons. However, when he arrived she talked about the irregularity of the post and the excessive amount of space taken up by advertisements in certain magazines; and then, after a silence: "Well, any news?" She had completely forgotten, although he had warned her, that her father was to have liquidated Pineda that afternoon. Celestino swallowed hard and let it go at that. Forty-eight hours later, his daughter had still made no allusion to the promised scene. More than ever Celestino let it go at that. He was silent about the civil war. He could also be silent about everything else.

ONE SUMMER NIGHT when he had left his bedroom window half-open—with the shutters closed—to admit the invigorating effluvia of the Faubourg Saint-Martin, a strange thing happened which was to remain one of the most painful memories of his last years. Only his daughter was sleeping in the flat, the best and the worst of him. (The maid slept on the top floor.) In his sleep, Ruiz's phrase came back to him—"a bogus left-winger"—and suddenly it took on a considerable, almost monstrous importance in his mind. Was he, after all, an unconscious fascist? Were there not hundreds of traits in him that showed he was a fascist, or rather that fragments of fascism were embedded in his socialism? In the grip of this nightmare, he turned and twisted on his bed, where, because of the heat, he was sleeping without either blankets or top sheet, struggling to get rid of his fascism, which was in reality an enormous bumblebee that had come in through the window and was buzzing around knocking against the walls and making a great deal of noise.

The bumbleblee was irresistibly attracted to Celestino's perspiring face, especially the more questionable features of this face, the face of an old man asleep—the nostrils, the open mouth, the moist patches at the corners of the eyes—and kept on coming back to it again and again, like a boy irresistibly attracted by the more squalid aspects of a fruit machine. The closer the bumblebee came to his face and the louder it buzzed, the more Celestino felt the threat of his inner fascism and the more terrified he was of it. He cried out silently (for the whole of this scene, unlike his customary nocturnal scenes, occurred without his raising his voice): "I'm not a fascist! I'm not a fascist! I gave my blood!" (By pure chance, as we know, he had not spilled his blood, but his failure to do so remained a sore point, as her short stature was a sore point with Pascualita.) When the bumblebee touched his forehead, Celestino felt he was going mad. He put his hand to his forehead, thinking to ward off the fascist menace but in fact because it was the natural reflex action provoked by the bumblebee's touch, and in doing so he awoke. He switched on the light, got up, and instinctively, in his long nightshirt, from which emerged his lean and hairy calves, went towards the window to fling it wide open and free himself from his nightmare fancies. His heart was beating fast, as on the day when he had led the assault on the Conservatoire des Arts et Métiers. His face, hardened by vigour and severity during the day, had sunk in his sleep, and wore a sad, almost tragic expression. On his way to the window, half-awake, he knocked over the alarm clock on his bedside table. He opened the window. Outside, the warm night brooded over the roofs, dotted with a few uninteresting stars. Suddenly Celestino realized what a target his window presented, all lit up—for a bazooka, for example—and swiftly he turned off the light. Then he went back to the window, this time upsetting the telephone. At the same moment the bumblebee, which was completely idiotic, and would never have sensed from any distance that the open window was the road to freedom, came upon it by chance and flew away. Once the bumblebee had gone, Celestino felt released; he had exorcised the traitor's words. No, he was not a self-deceiving fascist. The alarm clock was de-

ranged; the telephone was deranged, but *he* was not deranged. His self-doubt had vanished.

At breakfast, he said not a word about all this to his
daughter. Pascualita did not notice the rings under his
eyes, just as he had not noticed the bumblebee. Such is life.

Summer drew on. For the past two summers, Pascualita
had gone to spend three weeks in the country with the
Ruizs. They invited her as usual.

"I won't go and stay with somebody who has insulted
you."

"And what about Isabelle [the Ruiz daughter], won't
you see her again?"

"No."

Ruiz had invited Pascualita. Therefore he considered
that nothing had happened. A man insults you, but that is
of no importance, and it is you, the insulted one, if you
get annoyed, who are "impossible"!

Pascualita, like her father, had little difficulty in deciding
not to see the Ruizs any more. As for Pineda, he had telephoned once, and Pascualita, alone in the flat, had answered vaguely. Pineda had given no further sign of life.
Pineda, the "so nice," the "obliging," the "devoted" Pineda
—he was even worse than Ruiz! Really, what a curious thing
friendship was! Enmity was more reliable.

Pascualita did not want to go anywhere alone. And
Celestino did not want to go anywhere either alone or
with her: holidays and fresh air were a European fad.
Pascualita stayed in Paris, and went to libraries to do the
chores which Celestino did not wish to do himself. Besides,
as he did not fail to point out to her, libraries are fairly
cool in summer.

Nevertheless he was touched by her self-sacrifice, and

the fact that he was doing nothing about getting her married, that he refused to do anything about it because he had "no time to waste on that sort of thing," weighed more heavily on his conscience. There was a sort of spectre in his life, the spectre of what he ought to have done but did not and would not do. Sometimes he found himself beginning to dislike her because of the guilt she induced in him, and sometimes this guilt brought him closer to her, although he was determined to overcome it.

A Buddhist saint lived with his wife in a forest. There he met an old tiger which, no longer having the strength to hunt, was on the point of dying of hunger. Moved to pity, he gave the tiger his wife to eat. Celestino gave his daughter to the tiger of his political speculations, and the deep and silent labours which these speculations inspired him to.

He wanted to make a sacrifice for her in return, and this sacrifice was to invite Moragas to dinner on his return to Paris in September. The Ruizs and Pineda having gone, Moragas was the only one left who might, on occasion, attend to Pascualita and break the evil spell of isolation which her father had cast upon her. At certain periods of our lives we feel so many hostile forces piling up around us that we take fright and settle down with almost anyone out of an instinct of self-preservation. Moragas was not "anyone," but in the fifteen years during which he had been looking after Celestino Marcilla's affairs, the latter had only twice invited him to dinner. He always used to explain: "I haven't the time to be nice. I have my work to do." Moreover, they had nothing to say to each other: integrity was their only bond, right-wing integrity in one case, left-wing in the other. Moragas loved only Jesus Christ (he had, incidentally, a job in a Jewish bank), and handling other people's money, for personally he was not at all rapacious. Although Moragas was tactful enough not to let his political opinions leak out in front of Celestino, the latter had speedily smelt him out and pigeon-holed him. But on a number of points Moragas was extremely liberal, almost as advanced as a man of the extreme Left. Yet even if Celestino had heard from his lips the very phrases—even the most explosive—which made up his own habitual repertoire, it would have made no difference: Moragas was classified once and for all. In fact, Celestino was acutely irritated when he heard Moragas talking in these terms or telling him, for instance, about the representations he had made to the directors of the bank on behalf of the employees. His reaction was: "What right has he? Hands off! That's our business." The Left was for him a private preserve. Just as personal attraction between person and person across the class barrier (notably sexual) was an odious thing, so any agreement between the bourgeoisie and the proletariat, even on a minor question, entirely temporary and tactical, was always a double betrayal of the proletariat, a betrayal both by the bourgeoisie and by the proletariat itself.

Celestino invited him early in September, and was astonished not to receive a reply for ten days, because he knew through the bank that he was there. On the eleventh day, Moragas replied saying that he was very sorry but that he was "just off to the country." Don Celestino choked back the dinner. "Obviously I'm not very amusing." Snubbed by Moragas, the man of Christ!

One day in September, Celestino came home in a very sombre mood from the boulevards, where he had bought two Madrid newspapers and a Barcelona one, newspapers which always displayed a dithyrambic fervour on what-

ever subject they dealt with—religion, bullfighting, eco-
nomics—and which he had read and annotated with different coloured pencils in the back room of a café in the
boulevard Montmartre. He ran into his daughter, who was
also on the way home, and they walked along together.

"Stop dragging your feet," said Pascualita, looking over
her shoulder like a cruel little bird.

"I drag my feet when I like, and when I don't like I
don't drag them. I can be senile at will."

They sat down on a bench in the boulevard Saint-
Martin, before returning to the concrete box.

This bench was familiar to Don Celestino because it
was situated opposite a shop which encouraged him to
daydream. He had christened it "M. Houyou's shop,"
although its owner, whose name was written above the
door, was not called Houyou at all. This shop reminded
him of a number of shops in Madrid. It was an optician's,
obviously very old, probably a hundred years or more.
Its age could be guessed from the decayed condition of the
paint on the shop-front, where, under the word "Optician,"
an earlier inscription could still be made out, together with
enlargements in gilt relief of the obverse and reverse sides
of a medal won at an exhibition, such as shopkeepers were
wont to display during the last century. The archaic aspect
of the shop was accentuated by two stone steps, also more
than a century old, leading from the pavement to the door
and covered with a carpet held down by brass stair-rods.
It was the only establishment in the boulevard which had
steps or carpet or rods of this kind. The shop itself was
very well-kept, both inside and outside; but it was its great
age that arrested one's attention. As for the proprietor, we
shall speak of him when he makes his appearance.

Two doors away from M. Houyou's, there was a house

which bore a plaque in memory of Georges Méliès, "inventor of many illusions." He was not alone in this.

"You know who Lyautey was?" Celestino inquired.

"Lioté?"

"The French marshal."

"No."

"You spent five years in a French lycée, and you never heard the name Lyautey?"

"No."

Celestino was pleased. He hated his daughter's lycée, as he hated all State education. When she was at the lycée, he had spent many an evening maligning her teachers.

"Lyautey was a French general, then a marshal, who died about twenty-five years ago. He conquered Morocco. He did it more intelligently and more humanely than others would have done, but he was nonetheless the kind of man I cannot abide. The crucifix, the coat of arms, the snobbery, the publicity, all that French bombast. With his red burnous and "sabre-across-the-saddle," he claimed it was meant to impress the Arabs but it was just as much to impress the French—like those priests who let their hair down ostensibly to make themselves popular with unbelievers but in fact because it comes naturally to them. And the whole thing, in Lyautey's case, concealed a dishonesty both of principle—because Morocco belongs to the Moroccans—and of practice—every time he wanted to invade a territory he falsely asserted that its tribes had attacked him. Later on, having conquered the Moroccans, he was defeated by the French, disavowed, and persecuted. When he was recalled from Morocco, only a British warship was there to do him honour. Finally he died when everything he had built up was beginning to crumble, when the cause in which he believed was beginning to be undermined, and

I have heard that on his death-bed he said: "I am dying because of France." He did not mean that he was dying because of what France had done to him, but because of what France had become. There is an element of the Passion, in the Christian sense of the word, in Lyautey's fate, including his posthumous fate, to which a man who has undergone what I have undergone cannot be indifferent. That death-bed remark of his reconciles me to him up to a point; I never think of it without being moved. For one can pay tribute to an enemy, even a hereditary enemy, whereas civil wars are always too serious for such whims. Why does that remark of Lyautey's move me: "I am dying because of France?" Because *I*, for the past twenty years, have been dying because of Spain. You know Don Quixote's saying: "I was born to a lifetime of dying."* Either it's a statement of the obvious: we die a little every day. Or else it's the strangest remark in the whole book— a staggering remark. What exactly did Cervantes mean? I don't know, but I, like Don Quixote, die as I live. I always used to say that I wanted a better life for humanity, but really I only wanted it for Spain. It's Spain that has been bleeding inside me for the past twenty years, Spain this clot of blood that I feel in my left side...."

"Was it the Spanish papers that gave you these gloomy ideas?"

"Yes. ... To be continually immersed in grief; immersed in indignation; immersed in silence! It's a terrible thing to be defeated, but it's worse to live in cowardice

---

* Is this taken from the poem which Don Quixote sings in Chapter LXVIII, Book 2: *Asi el vivir me mata*: "Thus living kills me"? If so, the phrase probably does not have the profound and tragic significance Celestino ascribes to it. The little poem, as it happens, is not Castilian but translated from Cardinal Bembo.

for twenty years. There are days when one cannot bear it any longer, this silent shame. It wears one down terribly, you've no idea."

"I can't understand this need men have to express their political opinions, much less write them. Can't they keep them to themselves? Can't they keep quiet?"

"No, it chokes them; it poisons them."

Pascualita thought to herself that having survived a terrifying ordeal, with nothing to fear, plenty to live on, smoking the best cigars, doing, literally, only what came into his head, he must find the poison bearable.

"What would you like to do?"

"Fight. Do something, however small, to bring that government down. I've read somewhere that there's a law in France whereby a man can be put in prison for not helping a person who is in danger of death. I am a man who does nothing for his dying country. To know that *that* exists, and to go on living!"

"You've done enough."

"There are others who are exiled like me who continue to do something. I suffer from not suffering."

He meant, taking his inspiration from Saint Teresa: I suffer (in my soul) from not suffering (in my body, i.e., from not being persecuted by the fascist beasts like other members of my party). There was always, too, another source of guilt: he had not been wounded and he had not been in prison.

"But you avoid all the others like the plague."

He was silent.

"In any case they're younger than you. You have to be careful."

"Nothing that interests you or gives you pleasure tires you, and anything disagreeable does. For example, as you know, I have such a horror of domestic chores that making up the day's menus is enough to exhaust me, whereas working eight hours at a stretch not only does not tire me but actually refreshes me."

"You get things off your chest in those articles of yours, but you don't know how to go about getting them published."

"They can't be published because I tell the truth in them. Not that I tell much, even in the notes I write for myself, because one's always in danger of being searched."

"Searched! I can't think why anyone would want to search *your* house. But you're always afraid. . . ."

We know how brave Celestino had been during the war. And yet in his daughter's eyes he was a man who was always afraid. It was like an old friend who accuses you of "going gaga," or a mistress whom you treat with the utmost generosity and who thanks you by saying: "You're always throwing money down the drain," or a man on whose behalf you have moved heaven and earth to get him out of trouble and who thanks you three months later by saying: "Could you do me a favour, I know you hate doing people favours, but . . ." At first we accept these little remarks with good grace. But when the old friend or the mistress eventually goes too far, it is remarks such as these that press the button, as it were, which controls the iron curtain. The iron shutter comes crashing down, never to rise again. Old friend, little mistress, your fate is sealed! All's well that ends well.

Pascualita went on:

"There's also the fact that you aren't cut out to be an exile. None of us Spaniards are. We're too different, and too intent on asserting our difference. We love what we are and we suffer for it, but there's no question of our

changing. Do you think *I* like living with the French?"
"What you haven't said is that the Spaniards are all mad:
it's a well-known fact. I'm not mad, but I'm one of the
rare exceptions."

Yet he was surprised. She had spoken in an unfamiliar
tone; it was not often that she expressed a personal opinion.
Before answering her, he looked around him. The boulevard, the houses, the people: their looks, their clothes, their
voices, and all he knew about them. Never had he been
so aware of the gulf that separated him from this race
among which he had lived for twenty years, or of the
acute uneasiness he had always felt at being involved with
them and dependent on them. Frenchmen remained for
him like the inhabitants of another planet, just as, he well
knew, he and his compatriots were in the eyes of the
French. The Place de la République was a mere thirty-
yards away from the Café de Bondy. In four years, he
had only twice "ventured" as far as the Place, and one of
these times only very fleetingly. In fact, the French proletariat did not interest him; what interested him was the
Spanish proletariat (similarly, the Spanish Catholics were
not interested in the Church, only in the Church of Spain.)
Yes, as he had said, he was uniquely Spanish. He could
never imagine himself shooting a Frenchman, or an Eng-
lishman, or having them shot: indeed, such an idea would
have shocked him. Whereas a Spaniard at once produced
in him the reaction: "Is he one of ours, or ought we to
have him shot?"

Just at that moment they noticed a number of passers-by
stop and look up in the air. Beyond the boulevard Sebas-
topol, dense plumes of grey-white smoke billowed upwards
to the sky.

"It's a bomb from an Italian plane," said Celestino.

Gradually the smoke subsided. It was a neighbourhood where fires often broke out, and whenever they were brought under control without too much delay, Don Celestino was rather piqued. He would have liked the conflagrations to spread. Not out of malevolence towards the French. Just simple pleasure. . . .

M. Houyou had come out of his shop to look at the smoke. M. Houyou was the positive to Celestino's negative (which is no doubt what had struck the Spaniard about him). He was roughly the same age—sixty-five—he had a short beard, but a white one, whereas Celestino's was black, a pink, smooth face, whereas Celestino's was swarthy and wrinkled. But the most striking contrast was in their expressions. M. Houyou's was bursting with honesty and radiated an extraordinary sweetness, whereas Celestino's was hard and forceful (although he was no less honest). M. Houyou was dressed in an old-fashioned shopkeeper's overall.

"Look at M. Houyou," said Celestino. "In appearance he belongs to the France of yesterday, and so does his shop. But observe the objects in his window: they are all of the best quality and the most modern manufacture. France has kept the best of her past, and is being led boldly and skillfully towards revolution: although defeated, she has managed not to be treated as one of the defeated. We who had all the cards in our hands in 1936 have rejoined the ranks of the defeated, where we had been for the past three hundred years. An undernourished, unintelligent, illiterate country. . . ."

"In fifteen years' time France will be just as illiterate as Spain—and a great deal more pretentious."

"Look at Spain, known throughout the world as a failure, the only country in the world (except Portugal) where our ideas have been defeated. And look at me, a man who belongs to an intellectual lineage that has been continually defeated for the past hundred and fifty years, who has been personally defeated during the past twenty years, and who will never know—*never*—what it is to be anything else but a failure. As a Spaniard, a suspect European, a second-class European; as an anarchist, an object of opprobrium (luckily as far as these people here are concerned I'm supposed to be merely a 'republican'), and as a man, an exile who hardly dares to open his mouth in case he is told: "After all, what are you doing in our country?"

"Spain is not a second-class country. It belongs to the UN, to UNESCO, and I don't know what else. It's become a great tourist country." (Celestino grimaced sourly: Spain defiled by those . . . !) "Spanish football is internationally famous. The new Spanish cinema is recognized everywhere . . ."

"Have you seen *Calabuig*? They say it's a good film."

"I don't like going to the cinema, because Frenchmen behave improperly in the cinema."

"You should give them a good scratch. . . . No, perhaps not, because the manager might call the *Hermandad*. You could always change your seat. . . . They say *Calabuig* is really a very good film."

Pascualita said nothing. Celestino was surprised because only a week before Moragas had told him: "I was in my car and I saw your daughter coming out of a cinema on the Grands Boulevards with another girl. *Calabuig* was the film that was on there." So he returned to the charge.

"Really, you ought to go and see it."

"I don't want to."

Silence. Celestino was flabbergasted. Why was Pascualita

refusing to admit that she had seen *Calabuig?* Why this
secrecy? He had never forbidden her to go to the cinema,
or even advised her against a particular film. He had
not even blamed her for going to see *Welcome, Mr.
Marshall,** although from all accounts this film would have
been a dagger in his heart. He had merely suffered in
silence when he heard her maintain that it was a very
amusing film, which was not at all derogatory to the
Spaniards.

So, she was lying to him. At first he was speechless.
Then he muttered a few words at random. He had only
one thought: to get rid of his daughter and go to a near-by
café to telephone Moragas and ask him if he was *sure* he
had recognized Pascualita.

Pascualita left him. He went to a café. Moragas, at the
other end of the line, said to him:

"I saw her as clearly as I can see you. She was wearing. . . ." (He described one of Pascualita's dresses.)

"But are you sure she was coming out of the cinema?"

"I saw her charging out of the foyer like a bull from
the toril."

"With a girl friend only? Not a young man?"

"Only another girl. Very small, with rather square
shoulders."

"I know the one: an old school friend. Perhaps they had
gone into the foyer to look at the stills."

"They were coming out with a large group of people:
evidently the big film had just finished. And in any case
I remember seeing her throw the tickets away."

Celestino felt obliged to explain why he was telephoning.

"Don't worry," said Moragas. "Girls are mysterious

---

* A Spanish film in which idiotic Spaniards are shown crawling to
the Americans.

creatures. My own is the same. They learn secrecy in the convents we shut them up in."

Returning to the bench in front of M. Houyou's—he could not face being alone with his daughter in the concrete box—Celestino hesitated: the bench was irrevocably marked by the transfiguration which he had seen her undergo there: he would never sit on it again.

He wandered off towards Strasbourg-Saint-Denis. He could not understand it. He could no more understand it than he had when Ruiz had turned on him. Five years of cohabitation, of shared anxieties, of intimacy (how he had talked! how he had tried to educate her!), had yielded nothing—five years between father and daughter no more than twenty years between friends. She was like a piece of ground occupied easily in wartime and then gradually yielded, inch by inch, inexorably. Pascualita, seemingly so open, Pascualita so clear of brow, an *enigma*! Ridiculous. As though it were not enough to have to worry about Spain, he would now have to worry about his daughter. And why had Ruiz betrayed him? Why had Pineda, "good, kind" Pineda, given up trying to see him after one telephone call? Why had Moragas refused his invitation to dinner? Why did articles as remarkable as his never appear? Why had the left-wing review suspected him and snubbed him as soon as he approached them? All these questions fluttered about in front of him, cruelly, and he stared at them with doleful eyes, like an ox, trying to understand. And his head was full of darkness. Don Celestino had no difficulty in combining an awareness of being continually mistaken with the conviction that he was always right. Muddle and eccentricity were his natural state of mind.

He felt so weak, morally and physically, that he did not dare to brush against a passer-by in case he was jostled and his legs gave way underneath him. So he sat down on the first bench in the boulevard Saint-Denis, almost opposite the Porte Saint-Martin.

There was a tramp on the bench, indescribably filthy, scarcely human, respected by all, as sacred as the pigeons, and for the same reason: because he was so filthy. On the opposite pavement there was another pigeon walk, even more excremental than the one in front of the Ambigu: a milky way of excrement. Here the tramp, there the pigeons: in a tiny space, everything that makes the heart of Paris beat. (Celestino's ideas; nothing to do with the author.) However, for the Parisian the love of tramps forms part of an ideology and he will soon get up and go if a tramp comes and sits beside him on a bench. Celestino, on the other hand, had sat down beside the tramp without the slightest embarrassment, as a Moslem notable or dignitary rubs shoulders quite happily with the most ragged of his coreligionists.

The tramp was talking to himself. His words were unintelligible, except when he said: "I am a patriot" (he was about the only one). Celestino was following his own train of thought: "For years there was complete trust between us, and trust is a honeycomb. And suddenly I find her lying to me, like a maid one catches going through one's wallet; yes, like a maid. . . ."

"What you shouting at me for, guv'nor?" asked the tramp, turning towards him with irritation.

"I wasn't shouting at you, Méssié," said Celestino in his Spanish accent, "I was talking to myself." He realized that as he had grown more excited he had spoken his thoughts aloud: he was speaking to the Void.

The tramp went off muttering to himself, leaving behind a hideous stench of stale wine, urine, and filth. A young woman put down on the bench a little boy of about two or three with the wide-open eyes of a cat.

"You love mummy?"

"No."

"At least you love Grandpa?"

"No."

"Shall I buy you a lollipop?"

"No."

"Wait here, I'm going to buy a lottery ticket. You'll be good, won't you?"

"No."

The mother did not seem affected by this unconstructive attitude and went off to gossip with the ticket-seller, who was dangling a ticket at the end of a stick out of her cabin by way of a bait, to save herself the trouble of stretching her arm. The infant, looking at a plastic horse it was carrying, said:

"That's right. Very good, Jean-Clau! Nice horsie. Horsie no bye-bye."

He went on in this way. Celestino was pleased that everyone was talking to himself. He had a family after all, Pascualita or no Pascualita.

Ruiz had told him one day that his daughter had kept something from him which he had found out afterwards, and when he reproached her she had said: "I can't tell you everything." Ruiz had explained: "She wants her little private preserve. It's only natural." And if Pascualita had given him, Celestino, the same answer, he would have had to agree: "I too have my private preserve: our war, about which I've never told her a thing." Such is life. We accuse others of concealing things from us and lying to us, and nobody conceals or lies more than we do ourselves.

There was of course Pascualita's diary. . . . But he remembered it only to thrust it aside at once. We shall speak of this diary later, if we are still alive.

The mother with the lottery ticket returned and removed her child. Immediately two old ladies of provincial appearance, in bonnets, sat down in his place, after having unfolded beneath them, one a handkerchief, the other a newspaper.

As evening began to fall the pigeons went off to nest in the frieze of the Porte Saint-Martin, and their droppings could be seen descending from a height of thirty feet, a touching sight: pale, along the pavement, spread this sprinkling of evening stars. On either side of the arch were statues in high relief, one of which represented Louis XIV dressed only in a wig, with a piece of drapery veiling the best of his royal person. One of the old ladies said: "It's St. Michael giving half his cloak to the beggar. But they've made a mistake. St. Michael was on horseback."

Don Celestino thought: "The man is not St. Michael, but Louis XIV. It wasn't St. Michael who divided his cloak, it was St. Martin. Everything is false. Pascualita is false: she lies to me. The frieze on the Porte is false: it's been restored, brand-new from one end to the other. So everything is false. Let's go home to dinner." Taking care once again to go via the forbidden crossing, he returned to the concrete box.

Two policemen walked in front of him, linked to each other by handcuffs attached to their wrists. At least that is what Celestino saw. It was strange.

☙

One thinks one cannot bear something any longer, but one does bear it. For years and years one finds a person "perfect"; then the person ceases to be "perfect," and yet one adapts oneself to the fact without too much difficulty. In Don Celestino's mind, the fact that his daughter had deceived him gradually lost its force, became diluted. What remained was the need to talk to someone about political matters, and also about his own little affairs, and now that Ruiz and Pineda had been swallowed up, there was nobody to talk to but her. So he went back to using her as the outlet for his lamentations, his indignations, and his vehement dogmatisms. They would be chatting away placidly about the dangers of flueless stoves, when suddenly he would "take off": to refuse to have your eyes bandaged in front of the firing squad was utterly meaningless, it was schoolboy heroics. . . . He was aware that he bored her, but he did not care. After all, if he bored her, she deceived him, so they were quits. The rites of courtesy remained; he would say to her: "I'm boring you with my stories," or: "Stop me if I've told you this before," and she would invariably reply: "No, no, of course not," and hold out her hand to him; and he would stroke it affectionately. He no longer had complete confidence in her; but this was of less consequence than he had thought at first, and everything had more or less returned to normal.

After a week or so he even began to trust her again without noticing it. He needed to talk. He was also like everyone else: there came a point when he needed to trust someone.

And, without giving it another thought, he went back to sitting on M. Houyou's bench.

IV

LOVE MAKES people soft; hatred makes them stupid; bitterness makes them mad. Twenty years of political bitterness and private bitterness had brought Celestino Marcilla to a state bordering on madness. However, the sudden decline that overcame him in December 1959 was not provoked by any grave worry of a personal kind, or by anything particularly upsetting in the "international situation," which he tended to take to heart as though it were a family affair. The circumstances in which it occurred were as follows.

Their maid had left in October, at the end of her month's holiday. Give people a change of air, and they acquire a taste for another sort of life and become sick of the life they have enjoyed up to then: October, not August, is the month of departure; it is in October that our servants and our mistresses leave us.

Another maid succeeded her, and left. Thereafter, in the absence of a maid, there was a succession of daily women, who also left, always because of Pascualita: they were prepared to be polite to an old gentleman, but not to a slip of a girl. In mid-December Pascualita engaged yet another. Everything was agreed; she was to come the following morning at nine o'clock. By ten minutes to nine Don Celestino had already "guessed." At a quarter past nine she was still not there. She never came.

There were plenty of Spaniards at the employment agencies. But when one of them had been interviewed by

Celestino and in reply to his question: "Why did you come to France?" had answered, "I don't like the Spain of today because the men are cowards," Celestino had trembled. She had spoken like a true Spaniard; she had said what he would have liked to hear from Pascualita; but he had enjoined his daughter to exclude all Spaniards, without exception, from his ancillary enterprises. It would only mean trouble.

The cumulative effect of all these days of having *nobody* and of Pascualita having to do everything, including trailing round the employment agencies, had gradually undermined Celestino. He seemed intact, but the crack was there and was slowly widening. This time, when he realized that "the new one" was not going to come, he collapsed into an armchair, prostrate, like a more or less innocent man when he is told he is going to be charged. The fact was that he had been mistaken "once too often." Mistaken about Ruiz, about Pineda, about Pascualita. But mistaken also about all the maids who had made up their minds to leave next day but behaved as though they were delighted with the job, and about the charwomen who swore they would turn up on a certain day, knowing very well that they would not. On top of everything else it was "too much."

His eyes had lost their lustre. His heart beat furiously. His voice, when he spoke, was so feeble that Pascualita could not help laughing. She pretended to take it all as a joke. "At least we'll be able to talk in peace without having a stranger listening in." Moreover she was full of zest in canvassing the employment agencies, putting advertisements in the papers, and badgering the dairywoman, who had some addresses. But Celestino had been completely laid low. Now he could hardly speak at all; his voice was incapable of uttering a sound, apart from a brief and almost inaudible "It won't do any good. . . . There's nothing to be done. . . ." If at that moment the postman had brought a cheque, however modest a cheque, a cheque for two thousand francs, Celestino would have found his voice again. But no postman, no cheque. And he remained shrivelled up in his armchair, all bent and bowed, his eyes empty of expression, aged ten years in a few minutes.

Pascualita took her string bag and once more made the rounds of the food shops. Celestino remained shrivelled in his armchair. When he tried to light a cigarette, his hand trembled.

This time Pascualita could not even find a charwoman. She herself had to do the shopping and the cooking. Celestino did nothing. He had never in his life been inside a food shop except during the civil war and for the first few days after he came out of the French internment camp; but then anything can happen in wartime. Now it was peacetime, and he simply could not go into a food shop when things were normal. On no account would he have anything to do with such degrading things. Moreover he had sometimes noticed that there were queues outside some of these shops. He would sooner stay in bed, without food, wasting away, perhaps dying, than queue for anything—and behind Frenchmen, what was more! In this utterly sublime behaviour, suggestive though it was, and more than suggestive, of fascism, the example of Don Quixote sustained him.

They were three weeks without either a maid or a charwoman. Pascualita tired herself out making the two beds, and eventually asked her father to help. But he excused himself on the grounds of incompetence, and pointed out that making beds was only a bourgeois convention:

nothing happened if a bed was never made. Watching her turn the mattresses, his exhaustion was such that he had to go and revive himself with iced water from the refrigerator and then collapse into his chair, worn out by his daughter's efforts. Of course, if it had been a question of storming a fascist stronghold, or reinforcing a barricade with mattresses, he would have found his feet again —up to a point at least. He did however, pick up a dish cloth from time to time, but only to wipe with studious care something she had already dried. And sometimes he would inspect with a critical eye a plate which she had put before him, to show her that he had doubts about its cleanliness. For he considered that her work was bad, and this annoyed him, as it humiliated him that she should be working at all. He was also annoyed, at mealtimes, by her continually getting up to fetch some dish or utensil. He even told her once that she was too restless. She replied with a laugh. Then a gleam of commonsense flashed across his mind "How patient she is to put up with me!" When he looked at one of his buttons which she had sewn on again, he was at once irritated and rather touched.

In order to give her a rest, they often had meals at the Café de Bondy. There he would make her sit beside him, so as not to have to look at her, because when they ate at home she sat opposite him and he noticed that her face looked tired (presumably as a result of her household chores). She had begun to droop; there were lines at the corners of her mouth; because of the shape of her jaw, the contours of one of her cheeks was rounder and less accentuated than the other, and this was now more obvious because her face was thinner. He pointed this out to her. "What can I do about it?" she retorted, with obvious displeasure. All this did not please him either. There is a horrible and implacable law of nature, in accordance with which this almost imperceptible loss of looks estranged him a little from his daughter.

❧

There are at this moment on our planet five hundred and fifty million Catholics . . . Protestants . . . Moslems . . . of other religions. And there has probably always been a more or less equal quantity of believers ever since the world began.

The man who believes in the fables on which these religions are based—fables so absurd that the most elementary commonsense should suffice to reject them with a shrug of the shoulders—is more often than not totally unintelligent, though sometimes, on matters other than his religious beliefs, he may be intelligent. He may even be, in what is called his "line," a man of distinction.

This gap in the intellect—the result of two very widespread instincts, both petty: the need to believe in the miraculous, and reluctance to face up to the finality of death—makes it impossible for us to respect the great majority of the human race. Moreover, the believing mass has, as it were, secreted alongside itself a mass of unbelievers who pretend to believe, because they regard it as the "done" thing and because they judge it to be to their advantage. This group cannot be respected either, because of their baseness in upholding, by flabby complaisance and self-interest, something which they know to be a fraud.

Now love, the will to progress, the building up of the society of the future, in short, socialism, cannot be exercised for the benefit of anyone who is unworthy of it either by his stupidity (the believer) or by his baseness (the unbeliever professing to believe). Neither the believer nor his accomplices have a right to the socialist future.

It follows, therefore, I repeat it yet again, that the basis of the revolution must be the ruthless elimination, without the slightest compunction, of everything to do with any religious faith whatsoever. This must be carried to the point of physical destruction of the recalcitrant. When man is finally cleansed of the last trace of religiosity, then and only then will he deserve our respect and our love, and in consequence we will devote our lives to him, to the extent of sacrificing them if need be, in order to make his condition happier.

Pascualita, having translated and typed out the article by her father of which we have just given the first few paragraphs, silently handed him the typescript. He scrutinized her face to see what it might reflect (signs of revolt?): her face reflected nothing. Nothing. And she returned to her chores. She had nearly always been like this, especially of late, but then the articles were usually political, and it was permissible for her to have no opinions on them. About this article she might at least have said: "When you were risking your life for the proletariat during the civil war, you didn't make any distinction between believing proletarians and unbelieving ones." (And it was true that Celestino contradicted himself a little: every author, however honest, now and then writes things that are not directly in line with what he feels or what he is, and knows it.) But no: nothing—she said nothing, and very probably she thought nothing. If she had merely typed the article. . . . But no, she had translated it, that is to say, weighed it word by word. And yet nothing.

Pascualita's silence had struck her father with particular

force on that occasion, but now he noticed it with every article he gave her. Celestino's articles were always full of ideas. These ideas were expressed without the slightest qualification (as Ruiz had pointed out), but the paradoxes and the question-begging often concealed truths, courageous truths. On every one of them that he gave her to type, Pascualita ought to have been able to hold forth for an hour. And in the old days she did. But now that she was grown up, far from taking a greater interest in them, she would return them to her father without a word, as though she were handing him the sugar tongs. Or with one word, just one, which seemed to suggest that her attention had been caught by a minor detail, and that what was really important aroused no reaction in her, either for or against, nor even the slightest curiosity.

As a result, these articles, instead of being a source of animation and life for Celestino, became a source of pain. It was like a lukewarm bath gradually going cold. With each succeeding article Celestino's enthusiasm grew cooler, and he said to himself: "She seemed intelligent, but she isn't, or she isn't any longer." Yet he suffered from not having these opinions of hers by which he set so little store.

Such behaviour on Pascualita's part, evincing neither intelligence nor kindness nor even simple politeness, alienated her from her father ever more steadily. He felt so strongly about it that he toyed with the idea of sending his articles to an outside typist and not even showing them to Pascualita any more. But he no longer had enough enthusiasm for them to put himself to this inconvenience. And he continued to give them to her, knowing that each one of them drew them a little further apart.

In all this, to be honest, Celestino was not being entirely realistic. He did not realize that in those years ninety-five per cent of Frenchmen, and no doubt the same proportion of other civilized peoples, would have reacted, or rather would have failed to react in exactly the same way as Pascualita. Not the ghost of a personal opinion: thought reduced to following—thoughtlessly—the ideologies of the Right and the Left, or not even that: following the received ideas of the day. The best conversation between Goethe and Eckermann, appearing as an interview under contemporary names, however well-known, would have no more impact than if it had never appeared, because it would not be "committed," or at any rate not directly related to current events.

If he told her that he had sent his article on Lenin to such and such a newspaper, the days would go by without her ever asking: "Haven't they answered?" It had gone out of her head. In the old days she would listen to him holding forth, huddled up in a corner gazing at him with the look of a panther gazing at its trainer (her pupils full of crushed respect). That was to concede some importance to what he said. Now nothing that he said seemed to be of any importance, and she even went so far as to put on a superior air when he started talking about Proudhon or the October Revolution, an air that seemed to signify: "He's off on one of his hobbyhorses again." So he wanted to play Don Quixote? Well, *she* would play Don Quixote's housekeeper and niece—the one who, whenever the "ancient" is mentioned, puts her index finger to her temple and shakes her head in commiseration. She had made a resolve, and in this resolve she was as firm and unshakable as the mules of her native country. This resolve was to give her father, with untiring patience and devotion, all the help he might need in the material domain, and to refuse him all the help he needed in the intellectual domain

which, however infinitesimal it might be in his case, was
the one he regarded as his *raison d'être*. And that is how
it was for this inverted Antigone.

🚩

From the moment they found themselves without either
a maid or a charwoman, politics, the social problem, the
situation of Spain, the future of the world, everything had
been devoured by this calamity. It all vanished at a single
stroke, like sexual passion in a bitch that has been in heat,
and meals and evenings were henceforth occupied solely
with household questions and Celestino's lamentations on
his fate. He was annoyed that Pascualita showed so little
pity for him, and that she took their domestic troubles with
a certain amount of good humour. "You don't care about
me, any more than you care about the condition of our
country. . . ." She would answer him amicably, and Celestino was even more annoyed by the fact that she was not.
One evening, however, provoked beyond endurance, she
told him: "You only think of yourself!" To which he
replied, quite simply: "What else is there to think about?"
Next day, the first thing she said to him when she kissed
him good morning was: "You know I share all your
worries." He took it that she had realized how bad-tempered she had been, and as a result her bad temper became
even more real to him; her remark disturbed him instead
of consoling him. He also found the word "worries" far
too mild as far as he was concerned.

An idea (anarchism) which has to struggle against the
entire social system, against the Left as well as the Right,
creates obsessional reflexes of anxiety and defensiveness.
On no account would he have had it known in France
that he had fought with the *anars*. Detested in Spain, even

under the Republic, in France the word "anarchist," very nineteenth century, evoked the idea of fanatics hurling bombs into crowds, or criminals using the label as an excuse for indulging in larceny. To the natural obsessions of the misfit, his additional afflictions added a sense of humiliation. Telephone calls, rare though they were, hitherto had irritated him; now he waited eagerly for them; sometimes, when the bell started ringing, he would almost run to the telephone, licking his lips with pleasure, but it was always a wrong number. In the street (apart from the fact that his overcoat weighed him down, depriving him of the feeling of youth he had in summer when he went without one), it seemed to him that people looked askance at him or else deliberately avoided him. At the barber's, in restaurants, he handed out large tips or expensive cigars so that people would not despise him. He pulled himself up straight when he arrived in sight of his house. As he passed the concierge's door he would cast an eager eye inside to see if there was a letter in his pigeon-hole. He began to think that the concierge despised him, because for two days running his letters had not been brought up to him. He sent Pascualita down to soft-soap the concierge. Later he addressed some empty envelopes to himself, adding under his name, in a feigned hand: "Past Vice-President of the Spanish National Society for the Social Sciences" (a nonexistent society, needless to say; he had put "past" and "vice" so as not to exaggerate). Then he posted them in a box some distance away, in case the concierge, if he looked at the postmark, was surprised by all these letters coming from round the corner. Soon it seemed to him that the concierge no longer despised him.

"They would respect me," he thought, "if they knew how many men I've killed."

At that very moment, throughout the civilized world, powerful and ruthless old men, bowed down with dignities and responsibilities and decorations, in cabinets, congresses, assemblies, committees and subcommittees, were writing reports or making speeches on which millions of people depended, and then, more than half-dead, the worms already alerted under their testicles or at the backs of their throats, intriguing for another sinecure, another promotion, another "honour"; and in all this, after seventy or eighty years of existence, they showed the same puerility as Celestino in his petty affairs: the puerility of self-deception, the puerility of conception (conception without awareness), the puerility of ostentation. Only, these old men had "arrived," whereas Celestino had not. Which goes to show, once again, how worthy of esteem Don Celestino was.

Old age had descended on him like a cloak as he waited for the charwoman who would not come, and it was old age that had shrivelled him up in his armchair. The days without a visitor, without a letter, without a telephone call, became interminable: they gave him a feeling of death. Frequently his eyes would stray to the clock. How slowly the hands advanced! What an age five minutes were! Not so long ago he used to say to himself that in old age one must pay more attention to time because there is so much less of it left. But now, on the contrary, he saw that old age was the period of wasted time. Since he had become indifferent to everything, did it matter what he did with his time, or even if he did nothing? And so, from morning till night—rather like the soldiers in Lucullus's army of whom Plutarch writes, who, stupefied by the heat, shifted stones about at random in the African desert—he frittered away his time until he could go to bed early and bury himself in the oblivion of sleep. This decline, of which he himself was so acutely aware, was complacently described by the old gentleman to his daughter. There was an exchange between them very similar to the one which had already occurred. "You're always thinking how old you are," Pascualita said. "How can I think of anything else?" was his reply.

For the first time in his life, he realized that he was on the downward path; careering down at a speed he could no longer control; about to stumble any moment and finally crash to the bottom. This headlong rush towards death was felt at the same time as a flight from death. His panic in the face of death might have been checked or slowed down had he been keenly religious, or a keen womaniser, or a keen stamp collector. But he was none of these things. And as for his political passion, he needed to be able to talk about it. He would have thought less about death if he had been able to talk politics. But he had no one left to talk to. Talk politics to Pascualita? No, the spring had broken at last. Talk to her about maids, yes. But that was not much of an antidote against death. He had nothing to talk to her about except his death, and that was what he did.

The days cheered up a little towards evening; there were plans in the evening which introduced a sort of energy. But whenever he woke up in the night, and when he woke up in the morning, the first thing that appeared to him was death, as if it had stood there all night, at the foot of his bed, waiting for him. Waking up in the morning was the moment of greatest anguish. "Am I going to wake up at all? And if so, how many more times is this miracle going to happen? What am I waking *for*?" When he awoke during the night, his hands were numb and inert, as though death had been practising on them for its great final assault.

It was because he was going to die that Ruiz . . . that
Pineda . . . that Moragas . . . that Pascualita . . . that the
concierge had failed to bring up his letters, that the charwomen had flouted him, that the telephone company had
refused to accept his complaint, that the electricity inspector had been rude. Now he understood: there was no
point in bothering about him since he would soon have
ceased to exist. And what a mockery it was to complain to
someone who was deserting you (Pascualita) about being
deserted! All these insults clung to him like *banderillas* in
the neck of a bull. He was given no credit for all that he
had done (and for him this meant his articles, his famous
articles, far more than his record in action). Defeated from
the very start because he was a Spaniard, defeated because
he belonged to a party that had been defeated in the war,
defeated because an anarchist is always defeated, defeated
because he was a refugee, defeated because in twenty years
he had failed to learn French. Defeated because he would
soon have ceased to exist.

The stronger and more virile a man is, the more painful
his physical decline as a result of age or infirmity: he has
to pay for it. Celestino was by nature authoritarian, given
to harsh and violent reactions. Moreover, by ideological
inclination he was averse to taking orders. All his life, more
or less, he had imposed his will on others, and now he
was at the mercy of everyone.

Reality had become for him another world: his own
world was the world of death. As he dressed or undressed,
he would glance at his black and yellow body, and think:
"Where will it start?" just as, during the war, surveying
a still virgin countryside, he used to wonder: "Where will
the first shell fall?" When his daughter said to him on her
way out: "See you tonight," he never failed to answer:

"If I'm still alive." One day, alone in his room, he said to himself out loud: "I saw Primo de Rivero, when he was dictator, with a carnation in his buttonhole having a good time. He died all the same." And always he would hark back to the same questions: "How will I die? How will I behave in the face of death?" He reflected that the moment one said to oneself: "This is the end," there was no other power but steadfastness of soul. Philosophy was humbug; religion, of course, was humbug; memories were humbug, too. What was wanted was courage; courage alone mattered. All the rest meant nothing. Alone with one's courage, held tight against one's breast, like the kings on their tombs clasping their long swords. . . . But why courage? Why not quite simply be a coward?

And why was it that the fear of death was a fairly recent phenomenon, unknown or little known before the nineteenth century? Did people fear death only since they had ceased to believe in God?

"And why is it that I cannot bear the thought of my death when myriads and myriads of men and women have borne the thought of theirs? Why, when only twenty years ago I was renowned, even among the fighting men of a very courageous people, for my indifference to death? If it's purely a question of age, could it be said that 'Celestino Marcilla is a "brave" man' when I was brave yesterday and no longer brave today? What date should I be judged on? And are there not men who were brave in their youth and who remained just as brave up to the age of sixty-seven and beyond? Why am I a coward? And why am I the only one who is a coward?"

Sometimes his clothes and his personal possessions, which he had had for too long, encouraged his appetite for death. Sometimes, looking at his clothes, he would have the opposite reaction: "How many more times will I be wearing them?" or at his possessions: "I shall never see them again!" Why did he want to keep death at bay, since it would deprive him of nothing worthwhile? Trapped between a horror of living and a horror of dying.

In this condition, the arrival of a cheque was still the only thing that might have galvanized him a little. Or a word of encouragement about his journalistic work: "Say but the word, and my soul shall be saved."—But no, perhaps if the word had been said, he would have thought he was being made fun of. So abandoned, and never a moment of abandon.

One evening, at the end of February, Pascualita came home beaming with joy.

"I've found a very nice French girl. A Breton. She's coming tomorrow morning."

"Yes, on the stroke of nine!" said Don Celestino, moistening his lips, for his mouth had immediately gone dry at the prospect of waiting in vain once more. He ridiculed Pascualita's optimism, and repeated the national dictum: *Lo peor es siempre cierto*, "the worst is always certain."

Next morning he went out for a walk at a quarter to nine: no more agony in the armchair! When he returned, he found a young woman, somewhat ill-favoured by nature but apparently willing, already wielding the vacuum cleaner.

He asked her name. "Marie-France," she replied. Celestino gave a start: in three syllables, no more, the hereditary enemy and the Immaculate Conception—it was too much! And then, besides, it was neither very Catholic nor very French: so at least Celestino, within whose breast the

auto-da-fés of history secretly smouldered, at once suspected. He asked her to produce her identity papers: she
was a hundred per cent French, but her only Christian
name was Marie. "Why Marie-France, then?"—"My father
added 'France' last year."

Celestino was shattered. The thought of pronouncing or
hearing this name a hundred times a day! They suggested
calling her Marie, or Françoise. Her face began to pucker
and her eyes to fill with tears: no, her father had wanted
her to be Marie-France, and she wasn't going to disown
either her father or her country. They had to swallow it.

"We'll call her Marie-France when we speak to her, but
between ourselves we'll call her Mendoza," said Celestino,
thinking of Mendès-France.

Marie-France stayed. As she did everything to perfec-
tion, they took no notice of her and were hardly aware of
her existence—it was only the difficult ones who made their
presence felt. She was a little simple-minded, which was a
guarantee of honesty. Domestic life was transformed, but
Don Celestino was not. Whatever happened now, it was
too late: the blow had fallen.

In any case he began to live in the constant belief that
Marie-France was going to leave—hanging on the whims
of this chit of a girl as though on a branch above an abyss.
Now there were two abysses below him: the abyss of
death, and, a little nearer, the abyss of Marie-France's departure. For two and a half years he had had the courage
to slaughter his compatriots and to risk being slaughtered
by them. But faced with the prospect of Marie-France's
departure, his spirits failed him. He had cut Ruiz and
Pineda out of his life, even though they could be helpful
if occasion arose, and he would have cut out others who
were even more useful to him. But one hesitates to describe

the depths to which he sank in order to humour the little maid, he who would not have paid the slightest attention, even out of politeness, to a king.

On the twenty-ninth of February Don Celestino sat down in front of two blank sheets of paper and, with a cigarette between his lips and a glass of *anis* at his side, wrote out his last will and testament in a majestic hand— *Yo, el Rey*—which was intended to show the posthumous reader that he was in no way affected by what he wrote.

1. *My last hours will be attended exclusively by my daughter, with the exception, of course, of any members of the medical profession who may be called upon to attend, and of the person in our service, who is known as Marie-France, if she is still with us, which is extremely doubtful. Señores Ruiz and Pineda, in particular, will be emphatically excluded. No priest will be admitted, under any pretext whatsoever.*

2. *When I have expired, no one will be admitted to see my body, except for the above-mentioned persons and those whose professional obligation it is.*

3. *The coffin will be carried straight from the place of my decease to a cemetery, where my body will be cremated without any ceremony either civil or religious.*

4. *My death will not be announced in the newspapers, and no one will be informed except my sister and my brother-in-law in Madrid.*

5. *If it is possible for my ashes to be thrown to the winds, or into the dustbin, that is what I would wish. I do not know whether this is possible in France; I shall make inquiries. If it is impossible, and the ashes must remain in the cemetery, in an urn or a casket, it is my wish that this urn or this casket should bear neither name, nor date, nor any sign whatsoever. If, after a certain time, my ashes can be*

restored to my daughter, it is my wish that the latter should throw them to the winds or into the dustbin, as I have already stated.

I call upon my beloved daughter, Pascualita, to carry out these my final wishes, without let or hindrance, and with the firmness of character I know her to possess.

Celestino drained his glass of *anis*. He was delighted most of all with the thought that no one (except his daughter) would accompany him to his "last resting place." He showed the text to Pascualita and said to her:

"What I want, you understand, is to avoid society in dying as I have avoided it more or less all my life. I won't insult you by asking if I can rely on you. Naturally the family will be horrified. You can write and tell them that my wishes are not only spiritual in intention—I can't help it—but fundamentally Catholic. Burial as practised by the Catholics is indefensible from the Catholic point of view, because they honour the body which, in the eyes of Catholics, is nonexistent once the soul has left it. Kneeling in front of a soulless corpse, sprinkling holy water over a soulless corpse, is indefensible. The prohibition of cremation, on the grounds that God cannot resurrect a burnt body, is indefensible: if God can resurrect a skeleton, he can resurrect a heap of ashes and bone just as well. As for burial such as it is practised in churches, with coats of arms, heraldic coronets, decorations—and what decorations sometimes, sordid bits of tin—laid out on a cushion, it's an insult to Christianity. I'm reminding you of all this because, even if you share my views, perhaps you hold them with less profound conviction than I. And anyhow, you need to know what to say when you write to your aunt—you must tell her you simply obeyed my instructions."

"I imagine the Church would know how to answer you,

and I must admit your text is a bit much for my Catholic
atavism. But you're right in saying I would feel insulted if
you doubted my willingness to carry out your wishes."

Pascualita translated the text into French. Celestino
signed both the original and the translation. Then he put
them away in his files.

Seeing how calm Pascualita appeared, Celestino had said
to himself: "Since my death is a matter of indifference to
everyone, I don't know why it shouldn't be a matter of
indifference to me as well." This reflection took some of
the weight off his mind, and for the first time for many a
week the evening was a cheerful one.

One morning, a year or so before, the maid, while making Pascualita's bed, had found a black notebook which,
innocently or not, she placed in a prominent position on
her writing-table. It was a diary in which Pascualita had
been jotting down her secret thoughts in bed at night and
which she had tucked under her pillow and forgotten.
Celestino, without meaning any harm, had automatically
opened the diary and read: "I who am doomed to suffer . . ." He had closed it at once, and said to his daughter:
"See that you keep your diary locked up in your drawer."
She had said nothing.

Since then, hardly a week went by without her forgetting to lock the drawer. But it was so carefully locked on
other days that Celestino had no doubt that she still kept
her diary there. The day after he had written his last will
and testament, while she was out he noticed the key in the
drawer, opened it, and found the diary. "What can she
have written about yesterday? Nothing, perhaps. And what
about other days?" It did not even occur to him to open
the diary. He merely said to her once more: "Your drawer
was open again." And once more she said nothing.

If one had to start feeling pity, one's whole life would be eaten up with pity for the old, who are going to die soon, and know it, and moreover are never allowed to talk about it. Celestino had noticed that the French—among others—find it very tedious, and therefore impolite, for anyone to mention either illness or death to them: they immediately change the subject, or else rudely interrupt you, especially in good society. The same applies to domestic worries. No self-respecting Frenchman must ever discuss his anxieties about the departure of a maid or his anxieties about his own departure from this world. Celestino had even read in a French book that the obsession of the old with death is a disease, a disease called "necrophilia" or something of the sort. He himself considered that it was a disease for an old man not to think of death—a disease called "frivolousness." Celestino's fellow-countrymen were inclined to suffer from necrophilia. But, Pineda and Ruiz being no longer available, he had only Pascualita to talk to about his death. He was not interested in anything that might happen after it; but everything that might happen before it was the object of his zealous attention. In particular, Celestino decided to turn the boxroom into the "nurse's room."

"What's wrong? Aren't you feeling well?"

"I'm perfectly well. But I might fall ill any minute. We must be able to put up a nurse at a moment's notice."

One after the other, the plumber, the electrician, and the painter came to fit up "the nurse's room." Celestino complained: "The painter's going to block up the keyhole" and "the washers in the basin won't work." And, sure enough, the painter clogged up the keyhole, and the new washers made the taps leak. Pascualita said to him: "You're always pessimistic." Celestino had chosen one plumber who was slightly more expensive than the other, because he looked like an ex-foreman whereas the other one looked like a "gentleman." Pascualita prided herself on treating these arrangements with the utmost composure and tact. So everything went as well as could be, so to speak.

However, Celestino began to embroider on his malady. He would have a sudden stroke while alone in the flat. He would be incapable of reaching the telephone. Or else, at the same time as the stroke, he would have a perforation of the intestine. This time Pascualita would be there, and she would rush to the telephone to call a doctor, but it would be out of order. He bored into her like a vicious picador boring his *pic* into the back of the bull. She did not flinch, and she laughed a little as she teased him for his pessimism.

There was something strange about the "nurse's room," all spick-and-span, with its newly bought furniture and bed, the latter all made up with sheets and blankets as though it were to be slept in that very night. Pascualita said:

"Now all the other rooms are cluttered up because we had to clear this one. We mustn't touch it or put anything in it; it must always be immaculate, it's the nicest room in the flat . . . and nobody uses it! It's a holy of holies!"

"It's my fiancée's room. And you know who my fiancée is?"

"The nurse?"

"No, death."

"Ah, that's enough!"

But the room changed it's name. From being the "nurse's room," henceforth it came to be known as the "death chamber."

Thus did Senility and Virginity, those two so respectable estates, advance together hand in hand, with mixed feelings, when suddenly everything was transformed by a telegram from Madrid.

This telegram, which was from Celestino's brother-in-law, read as follows:

GRIEVED INFORM YOU DEAR ELISA DIED HEART ATTACK. ESSENTIAL YOU VISIT MADRID FOR SETTLEMENT ESTATE. AM COPING. LOVE TO PASCUALITA. VICENTE.

V

*Let us set out to die, with our feelings and our love. Let us
set out to die.*

Mariana in THE MASTER OF SANTIAGO, III, 5

CELESTINO READ the telegram to his daughter without
a word of conventional regret. Then, putting it down on
the table and covering it with the palm of his hand, he said:
"Just when I needed some money."

Celestino despised his sister and his brother-in-law, because they were political opportunists; he regretted that
they had got off so easily. Pascualita was therefore not
surprised by his lack of emotion. But she did not understand why he "needed money": this was very unexpected
from him! Suddenly her eyes shone: "It's for my dowry.
He's waking up at last." Then they shone even more: "He's
going to take me to Madrid." But she said nothing and
went out, for she had some shopping to do.

It suited Celestino to have a little time to himself, in order
to think.

First thought: "A visa. Ruiz told me that since 1955 they
had been given to political refugees without any difficulty
except in serious cases."

Second thought: "My safety. If they don't give me a
visa, well and good; I shall have to think what to do. But
what if they give me one, and later on start raking up the

past? It only needs some high-up person who doesn't like me . . ."

Third thought: "If I go, should I take Pascualita? Naturally she'll be longing to go. But isn't there a danger that she may adapt herself at once to the regime, that she may be homesick when she returns, thus causing more trouble between us, which may become serious? On the other hand, since Vicente is highly unreliable, she may be extremely useful to me in Madrid, not only in minor things but also in more important matters. She may be a buffer between me and a society which I shall certainly find obnoxious."

Fourth thought: "The settlement of the estate is bound to be complicated on account of my situation and my long absence. I've lost touch, more or less deliberately, with affairs of this sort, and I don't trust my brother-in-law. Will I be capable of defending my interests and those of my daughter, and how long will it take me?"

When Pascualita came home at seven o'clock he said to her:

"Moragas will deal with the visa." (All these exiles dreaded going to the Consulate, and invariably tried to send someone else in their place.) "If I get it, I shall wait until March the fifteenth before going to Madrid, because then the bullfight season will be on. I may be able to see one or two fights and that will make up for all the unpleasantnesses the trip is bound to involve.

"These unpleasantnesses are as follows:

"First, the settlement of the estate will drag on for a long time. My visa is sure to be for a limited period only, and I shall have to argue with my back to the wall, with the prospect of having to leave before it's all settled.

"Secondly, March is much colder in Madrid than in Paris—bitingly cold. I'll catch pneumonia, and will have to stay longer, which will mean complications. Besides, since you get irritated when I cough, you'll have a bad time.

"Thirdly, one or two of the *corridas* which I might be able to go to will be cancelled because of bad weather.

"Fourthly, I'm taking you with me but you're sure to acquire a taste for Spanish life, forgetting the condition in which people who want to be free live down there. This will alienate us from each other and cause a lot of trouble.

"All the misfortunes I've just described to you are *sure* to happen. The last, which I am about to tell you, is not sure but only a possibility. The political police will rake through my past, and I shall be arrested."

With the force and precision of arrows aimed by a consummate archer, his presentiments had hit their five targets in the irremediable worst: *lo peor es siempre cierto.*

Pascualita, as was only natural, went straight to what concerned her personally. She thanked her father for taking her, if he was able to go, then went on to the delicate question. No, she would not allow herself to be contaminated by the atmosphere down there. Had she ever given him the slightest cause to doubt the seriousness of the convictions she had acquired from him? Then she went on:

"What are you afraid of, if they give you a visa? What can happen to you in Madrid? Twenty years is a long time. Things are forgotten."

As we know, he had never told her anything concrete about his experiences during the civil war. However, irritated by the fact that she only knew his prosaic side (and how prosaic!), he occasionally tried to arouse her interest with vague remarks such as: "I who have been an adventurer . . ." or: "The number of enemies I've made . . ." It was a waste of time: Pascualita refused to rise; none of his shells exploded. This time he was really annoyed: "It's true

I've never spoken to her about my past. But why, when I show that I'm apprehensive, does she assume that there's no reason for it? Why does she assume that I'm being cowardly? Why doesn't she take my word for it? She ought to, if only out of respect. 'What can happen to you?' She's so cocksure about things she knows nothing about, and people who are cocksure about things they know nothing about are fools."

Next day Celestino went to see Moragas, who said to him:

"For a return visa you must apply to the Consulate (I'll do it for you if you wish) and ask your brother-in-law or a high-up friend in Madrid to hurry it up, otherwise it can take anything up to a month. But mind you, it's possible to give someone in Madrid power of attorney to represent you in everything to do with the estate. That would save you the journey, in case you feel it's tiresome or undesirable. But I would advise you to go, if you get a visa, which I'm sure you will. It's much better to be present for this sort of thing. Once you have the visa, there's no danger."

More sweeping statements! With Moragas, as with Ruiz and Pineda, he had maintained a discreet silence as to his conduct during the civil war. There are people who do not know why you are in danger, and who therefore make light of your situation. And there are people who do not want to know why, or if they do know, do not want to believe it, in order not to have to help you. Celestino Marcilla had known many of the second sort during the civil war. Now, with Moragas and Pascualita, he was becoming acquainted with the first.

Celestino asked Moragas to apply for the visa. If he obtained it, he would go to Madrid. Later he told his daugh-

ter, who commended him for overcoming his "emotion-
alism."

During the next few hours, the old gentleman seemed
rejuvenated. Three things had rejuvenated him: *la afición,**
his newfound cupidity, and apprehension. This moribund
old man—moribund in his own eyes at least—leaping out of
his tomb to snap up a golden doubloon, emulated the cupidity of the conquistadors for the wealth of the Indies, a cupidity which in their case too was no doubt mixed with
apprehension, although the chroniclers do not mention it,
speaking only of "the beard over the shoulder."** Apprehension of possible trouble with the police in Madrid. It
was this danger that attracted him above all: the attraction
of the abyss. He had braved the bull, for the first time
literally, at the age of fifteen. He had braved it a second
time when he had taken a gun in 1936. The third time, we
may remember, was when he had crossed the pigeon walk.
This time he was braving the bull by going into a Spain
that was fraught with danger without being forced to go.
There is good fear and bad fear. Fear in the face of the
bull was good fear. Fear of the police, or of Marie-France's
departure, was bad fear. Fear of shells was either good or
bad according to the day or the time of day. And indeed
that could be said of all fear: it depended on the day. At
that moment, surprisingly enough, fear of the police had
become good fear, and he needed it as he needed food. For
twenty years he had conducted his life with a view to not
being extradited—and now he was extraditing himself, as it
were, of his own free will. In a similar way, retired mata-

* Knowledge of and enthusiasm for bullfighting.
** A proverbial expression applied to the conquistadors. To have "the
beard over the shoulder": to look to right and left, to be on the alert.

dors suddenly come back to show everyone, themselves included, that they can still do it. Twenty years of waiting in vain day after day for something extraordinary to happen, but without ever doing anything to make it happen, and now it *had* happened. Twenty years of timorous caution obliterated by this sudden act of daring, which had given him back his youth and put death in the shade. And in this juxtaposition of caution and temerity there was an inconsistency which he did not find displeasing. "Since I'm going to die, why shouldn't I be brave once more, perhaps for the last time? What do I risk?" He was making what in the jargon of war is called a sortie; he was breaking the evil spell, the magic ring of hostile forces which had hemmed him in for months. With similar inconsistency, he also sought to dazzle Pascualita by his courage (just as, in his youth, he had dazzled the girls by his bravery with the young bulls), although he was fully aware that she was not in a position to know that there was any danger.

"Why did you say, when you received the telegram, that you 'needed money'?"

"Because I'm going to die soon, and I must have some decent furniture in my room because of the doctors who will come, and the nurse. Furniture like galleons. Deathbed furniture."

It was only recently that Celestino had taken it into his head to like money, which he had never cared about in his life, except when he was vegetating in the South of France after leaving the internment camp. It was through fear of being left in want in his declining years, a sure sign of senescence. The pleasure he experienced at the thought of his sister's inheritance was certainly connected, as he said, with the "deathbed furniture." That he knew. But what he did not realize was that this windfall also represented as

it were a pile of gold bars that he could stack up against
the door through which death was due to enter. There
was a little money for the furniture, and a lot of money to
keep death at bay. He might have wanted to *earn* money,
as many old men do because it gives them the feeling of
being still alive: they must be, since they are still capable
of extracting money from their fellow-men. But instead,
what he especially liked about his sister's money was that
it was money he had done nothing to earn. It was like the
money which might have come to him like manna from
heaven ever since, a year ago, he had started buying lottery
tickets. This money, indeed, gave him almost the same sort
of pleasure as money one has stolen.

Once the "death-bed furniture" had been bought, he had
no idea what he would do with the money, for he needed
nothing; and the fact that his daughter would eventually
come into it did not strike him one way or the other. But
he passionately wanted this money which he did not know
what to do with.

In the letter which he wrote to his brother-in-law, the
two most detailed paragraphs were the one in which he
went carefully into the financial aspect of his sister's death,
and the one in which he gave Vicente instructions about
the bullfights he wanted to go to. Vicente was to inquire
about the first bullfight of the season in Madrid or its vicin-
ity, and reserve two *barrera* seats as soon as the booking
opened: Celestino would not come to Madrid until he was
certain to be able to attend one or even two bullfights with
Pascualita. The estate could wait.

As a child, he already preferred the proletariat to his
own class, and used to go and mix with the urchins who
played at bullfighting in a suburb of old Madrid. When
they were in their teens, the lad who acted as the bull used

to hold two *navajas* in his hands which represented the horns, and one day he happened to kill one of his companions, whether accidentally or on purpose they never knew and hardly cared. Later, Celestino had fought in the bull-ring as an amateur, like most young Spaniards. When he came to France, he made a point of never going to a bull-fight in a French town, and his enthusiasm gradually waned. The trip to Madrid revived it, and, as he had pointed out to his daughter, it was also a defensive reflex against the anxieties of the trip. In France, his only gesture towards tauromachy was to perform a neat *estocada* with his knife on a fruit or a pat of butter during meals; and the expression on his face if he considered that he had miscued had to be seen to be believed. Now, at sixty-seven, he decided to take up the old Spanish custom of "car-fighting" again. He took his stand in the middle of the boulevard Saint-Martin, just opposite the theatre dedicated to the saint; Pascualita was the audience. He was no fool, and used a variety of tricks, like the matadors even before the war. In the first place he took up a position slightly in front of a pedestrian crossing, so that the cars reached him at a slackening speed; then he chose the smallest cars, *quatre-chevaux* or even *deux-chevaux*. But this was too easy: the drivers, approaching the crossing and seeing this grotesque figure standing in the middle of the road, slowed down so much that no skill was needed at all. So then, still keeping in the middle of the road, he boldly ventured away from the pedestrian crossing in the direction from which the bulls were coming, and the game became really dangerous. The cars swooped down on him in force. He flourished his gabardine at them. And the cars, according to speed, were more or less engulfed in it. Then he tried to "pass" them, standing stock still, with a graceful movement of the hips.

For the strange thing was that this old man, whose appearance was on the whole rather comical, had retained in these ritual gestures the same gracefulness that a good apprenticeship in the craft had taught him in his youth. At sixty-seven, executing passes at a *deux-chevaux* with his gabardine, there were moments when, if photographed in slow motion, he would have provided a spectacle not unworthy of those enchanting ballets sometimes performed by man and beast in the heart of the clamorous arena.

Eventually the driver of a *quatre-chevaux* braked hard after Celestino's pass, with the screech of a cat whose tail is being pulled. The car had passed so close to Celestino that its dusty coach-work had brushed against his black suit. "Bloody old fool!" shouted a young technician, poking his head through the window. But Celestino's blood was up and he was getting ready to challenge another, much more powerful beast. He was vaguely aware that people on the pavements had stopped and were looking at him, and vaguely aware that this audience was hostile. But the hostility of the crowd is part of the intoxication of bullfighting, and in any case Celestino needed nobody's approbation but his own. He was afraid, and not without reason, but his fear was itself an element in his enjoyment. The car did not have time to slow down and ran into Celestino, who stumbled. "Ha!" he said, his lower jaw sticking out like Charles the Fifth's. The car, which had carried the gabardine away on its bonnet, stopped, and another technician got out of it, older than the first, followed by an opulent and yapping lady-technician. The gabardine was torn from top to bottom.

"Do you think I'm going to pay for your raincoat because of a stupid accident like that?" said the technician calmly. "That sort of thing doesn't work with me."

"When you're nuts you go to the loony-bin," yapped the lady-technician, painted, bejewelled, plump and self-satisfied, very much the petty-bourgeois housewife on the run in 1940.

"I could have presented the *capote* when the head passed, as others do, but I wanted to do it honestly, because the bull was honest," Celestino explained (in Spanish).

Pascualita had joined her father and the technicians in the middle of the road. She begged him to come away, and he went back to the pavement without much persuasion. He had already done enough to prove, to himself and to others, that he still had it in him.

"You might have been killed."

"That's the whole point," replied Celestino, who at the same time was so afraid, and was going to be even more afraid, of going to Madrid.

On the pavement there were six or seven people eyeing him either with disapproval or stupefaction. A housewife inquired if he was suffering from concussion. A little old man in a *fin de siècle* boater which, like himself, was dark-grey with age, and gaiters of the same period and hue, seeing that Celestino did not speak French, addressed him in Italian, which he took to be more or less the same language as Castilian. Celestino could not understand a word but replied in Spanish: "The bulls didn't allow me to shine. You saw how the first one dipped his right horn." They exchanged several such remarks which were equally incomprehensible to both of them, and then the little old man kindly brushed the dust of the car from Celestino's jacket. "Hairs," said Celestino. (In passes made very close to the bull, it can happen that some of the bull's hairs are left on the matador's costume.) From the Italian's affability he guessed that he was a lunatic, and so shook hands with him. Then Pascualita and her father went back to the Café de Bondy, Celestino dried up inside but scintillating on the exterior, like a dead tree trunk covered with bright green moss. In the whole of this little scene, which had not lasted more than twenty minutes, he had touched the three limits of his genius: the Comic, for he had been ridiculous, the Tragic, for he had risked his life, and the Profound, because of the reasons which had led him to risk it.

Two days later there was a telephone call from Moragas: the visa had arrived.

Celestino was troubled rather than pleased. A fortnight, instead of the expected month or three weeks! This speed boded no good. The vetting must have been very superficial.

"We won't leave until we know that Vicente has booked seats for the first bullfight. I'm not going to Spain without seeing a bullfight."

A letter arrived from Vicente: all was well with the police. But no mention of bullfights.

"I told you that you were imagining things," Pascualita said. "But you never believe me."

Two years before, in the rue Réaumur, he had suddenly found himself face to face with a man who had tried to stab him for political reasons in the camp at Argelès. He was with his daughter in the rue Réaumur, and he had taken her by the arm and ducked into a doorway. "What's wrong?" "A man I don't want to see." She began to laugh. "How panicky you are! I don't like it when you panic like that. For one thing, it ages you, and nowadays one isn't old at sixty-six." Celestino thought: "She doesn't even know my age, and worse still she exaggerates it." Ever since, she had never recalled this little incident without laughing. And there was something as unforgettable about her laughter as about the yawn of the man he had asked to save his life when he was fleeing from the victorious Franco troops.

Now, once again, he heard this laugh. And once again he said to himself, as he had said the other day: "How stupid she is." Once again he hated this frivolity of hers for which he himself was responsible. "I think I'm naturally fairly brave," she had once said, artlessly enough. "It's easy to be brave when you're in no danger," her father had thought to himself. "Either she will not take my word for it when I tell her I'm in danger, in which case she has no respect for me, or she does believe me and doesn't care, in which case she doesn't love me." Meanwhile the atmosphere between them became increasingly conjugal in that he never spoke to his daughter about anything near to his heart. If he had received a letter saying, "We have been unable to print your articles for such and such a reason, but we were so impressed by their rare quality that we are prepared to publish them in book form at our expense," he would not have told her. On both sides there was a preconceived idea, a deadly alignment such as happens in revolutionary times: Pascualita was classified as someone who was "too stupid"; Celestino was classified as someone you did not take seriously. It was settled once and for all, and there was no way out.

After dinner, while the maid cleared the table, Pascualita would go into her father's room and give him exactly an extra quarter of an hour of her presence before they separated for the night. The old gentleman would look grimly at the clock every other minute, while Pascualita chatted away, always a mine of small talk. The boredom that emanated from her was so powerful that from time to time his head would droop and his eyes close, even though he was sitting right in front of her so that she could not help noticing. But she would carry on apparently without noticing, so delighted was she with her small talk. Two subjects were strictly taboo: no talk about political or social matters, for fear that she might start yawning straight away, and no questions, however anodyne, about what she did, about her life, about herself, for fear of meeting a stubborn silence— silence pure and simple: not a word. And then he would think to himself: "I'd prefer you to tease me, or even be disagreeable to me, than to say nothing. Please say some- thing to me . . . Anything you like, but not just nothing." If he lost his temper with her, she remained calm: it was the ultimate humiliation that even his anger did not move her.

Whenever he saw in the street a mother escorting her congenitally deformed, cretinous, theroid adolescent son, he was always struck by the grief and exhaustion indelibly imprinted on the face of this woman as a result of having lived for fifteen years with a monster; but he himself suf- fered from a similar grief as a result of having lived with a daughter whom he regarded as mentally deficient. He did not consider what a calvary it was for his daughter to live with a man who with all his deficiencies was nevertheless mentally far superior to herself.

He began to eat less. More and more often he indulged in his unconscious habit of moistening his lips when his mouth went dry in moments of anxiety or distress: a flick of the tongue to the right, a flick of the tongue to the left, just as the bull, when it is dejected, licks one nostril and then the other. The rings under his eyes grew darker. The rings under the eyes of bullfighters grow darker too, and they age rapidly, because of the fear and anxiety in which they live. He looked at these rings in the mirror and thought: "*She* doesn't notice them." In fact, Pascualita saw quite clearly that at the moment of decision he hesitated; let's face it: he was afraid. Blessed was the bullfight for giving him an excuse to put off their departure! But what if news of the bullfight arrived? Once she ventured to say: "How lugubrious you look!" to which he replied: "I shall look even more lugubrious when I'm put up against a wall."

If she asked him in the morning: "Do you need me today?" he would reply: "No, not today. But later, to lay out my corpse." She would turn her head away, exasperated beyond endurance.

At lunch one day she said to him: "You're eating nothing." It was on the tip of his tongue to answer: "I'm eating nothing because you're there." At the end of the meal, having inadvertently dropped some cigarette ash in his coffee, he deliberately drank the coffee, ash and all. As he rose from the table and passed by her chair, without saying a word he placed his index finger on the more fleshy of her cheeks. She lowered her eyelids, overcome with impatience and lassitude.

It was after this lunch that, his eyes having fallen on the pencil marks on a door which he had made when he used to measure his daughter's height month after month between the ages of fifteen and seventeen (she was too small, and was upset about it), he went to get a rubber and rubbed them out.

There had been a time when she used to ask him to help her with her Maths homework. He would have done so had he been capable of it, but he was not. So he said to her: "How do you expect to learn mathematics if someone helps you? You'll never learn unless you do it yourself."

But he would sit down beside her nevertheless and try to grasp her problems, and if he succeeded in doing so he would explain them to her. When she was too upset because neither of them understood, he would stroke her gently, as one strokes a machine gun, or he would simply put his arm over the back of her chair, wanting to put it across her shoulders and not daring to.

Later she was to tell him: "You were very patient with me," to which he replied: "I had no need to be patient with you because I loved you."

He had told her that she had two beauty spots on the nape of her neck. She was so lacking in vanity that she still had not noticed them by the age of fifteen. She was ashamed of these beauty spots and tried to cover them up with powder. He asked her why. She blushed. He gathered it was because she thought they made her look like a loose woman.

In those days they had a cat, and she liked it when the cat licked her hair.

Often he could not bear to see her go off to school without following her with his eyes from the balcony until she turned the corner of the street. She would look round and give him a little nod. That was all. But he would not have missed it for worlds.

The first sign of a change was when he noticed her arranging her hair at the back with a very feminine gesture. From that day forward, or thereabouts, she no longer paid any attention to what he said, no longer asked him: "Why?" From that day forward, or thereabouts, she no longer wore her little white ring, as slim as a thread. From that day forward, or thereabouts, something ceased to be, never to be again.

Often he tried to work out how much his share of his sister's estate would come to, without ever being able to make anything but the wildest guess. Nevertheless it shone as it were like a pale aurora borealis through the desolate twilight in which he lived. At first, as we have seen, he coveted the inheritance money fiercely, without knowing what he would do with it after buying the "death-bed furniture." Now he dreamed of buying beautiful new furniture for the whole flat. This attitude, so out of keeping with his ideology, might seem to suggest that the latter was losing some of its strength, giving way to a reaction that was seemingly aristocratic but perhaps more simple and elementary: perhaps the idea that his last glance would fall on beautiful things instead of the frightful things he was used to struck him as a solace which he had not needed when his strength was still intact.

Deprived of Ruiz, Pineda, Pascualita, and, to all intents and purposes, Moragas, his lot was a cruel one: he had no one to talk to, he whose ideal was to spend the whole of every afternoon talking in a café (easy to guess what about). He saw that there was a point beyond which a man cannot stand silence and solitude. Especially as regards his obsessions: an obsession needs to be aired. Even more than before, he talked to himself at home or in the street. He was like a pathetic King Lear as he wandered round the flat, from room to room, with Marie-France in the kitchen listening without understanding a word. His ghost-interlocutor was always Ruiz. Ruiz the traitor. As before, he confided in the traitor, volubly. More often now, too, he talked in his sleep, and his dreams alone showed the agitation of his soul. Nights full of presences, sometimes fearful presences, but at least he could talk to them! Often he dreamed of Pascualita as a child. The face was not quite hers; but it was she nonetheless; and he would wake and say: "But she's there, she's not a dream, she's not dead!" And then: "Oh yes, she *is* dead"—the true, the only Pascualita, whom he was so happy to love, and who was so worthy of his love. He, who was going to die, was living with a dead girl.

One night Pascualita, hearing him talk as she had heard him once before, went into his room and listened. He was saying:

"Yes, superintendent, I did all that. But also, at Marinas in April 1937, when some of our men were burning down the convent of San Pelayo, I turned a machine gun on them and kept them covered while six or seven nuns escaped. It's inexplicable, but it's true."

Silence. As he slept, his teeth opened and shut very gently with each breath.

"You could find out the names of the nuns who were in the convent. There must be one who would testify. I have a daughter, it's because of her. If it was only my-self . . ."

She was shattered. Akin to thousands and thousands of men throughout the world at that same moment, Celestino was preparing his defence. And he was doing it because of her! The girl's eyes opened wide.

The blaring of a police van rang out in the boulevard Saint-Martin. With a quiver of apprehension she wondered if the van was going to turn into the rue de Lancry. But the sound receded. Celestino, as he slept, had placed his hand on a moulding in the wall which ran alongside the bed, pressing it so hard in the passion of his sleep that a blister had formed on one of his fingers. It was a habit of his to cling to this moulding in his sleep, as though he were clinging to the bar of a prison window. Pascualita took her father's hand and placed it on the bed.

There must have been a sort of flashback in the old man's dream, as in certain films. The "man" must have said to him something like, "We want to know why you came here," for Celestino said: "You know quite well. I came about my sister's estate." Then the "man" must have said something like, "All right, that's enough, come along with us," for Celestino said in a loud voice: "I refuse." Immediately he sat up and opened his eyes. It was horrible, the wild expression on his face.

The moment he sat up, Pascualita had fled. In the corridor she waited, petrified with fear: one could have seen her thighs trembling through her thin nightdress. She expected him to come out in his long nightshirt (which she had such trouble trying to find in the shops) and shout at her: "You were listening!" But nothing happened. No doubt he had confused the moving figure with those of his dream.

Next morning, without mentioning, of course, what she had heard, she said to him:

"You told me you were afraid of something in Madrid. But I've no idea what it can possibly be. You've never spoken to me about the war. It's a very difficult situation for me . . ."

"It's not for the defeated to talk."

"Even here, where you've nothing to fear, you were a bit uneasy. Now, without being forced to, you're going to a place where you think you really have something to worry about. I don't understand. If only you'd explain . . ."

He made a vague gesture. For too long she had been someone to whom he no longer explained. Before, it was

she who took no interest in him. Now it was he who did
not want to interest her. Before, he was aware that she
never ceased to judge him, and he used to weigh carefully
everything he said in front of her. In this way he had developed a habit of being constantly on his guard which,
added to the longstanding circumspection induced by his
political proclivities, was extremely tiring. Now, what she
thought . . . He had had enough of fools. It was too late.

"Think again. If you're going to Madrid for my sake,
it's absurd. I can perfectly well do without it. Or you might
send me alone one day, to stay with Vicente. . . . No, don't
go, please!"

He made a gesture of dismissal, as though he were brushing away a fly: he could not bear entreaties. And once
more they returned to their silence, like a train going back
into a tunnel.

However, that evening he said to her, as though talking
to himself:

"To die in exile is fine. To die in prison is better. To be
murdered or executed, or to commit suicide, is better still.
I am going in order to fulfil a destiny which I had not fulfilled to the end. I am going in order to die like a true man
of my time."

Pascualita did not realize that there was a certain nobility in these remarks, but she was very upset by the incident
of the previous night. She went to see Moragas, whose
bank was situated near the Chaussée d'Antin.

She was fond of Moragas. She did not hold it against
him that he had not come to dinner with them; she would
have done the same herself. But Celestino had so often made
it clear how indispensable Moragas was to him, how much
he depended on him, that Pascualita felt with Moragas as
though she were in the presence of some terrifying Divin-

ity, who had to be placated at all costs: "Please don't desert us."

In Moragas's office there were files, a kind of machine gun that was in fact a telephone, bookcases full of directories, directories full of statistics, and statistics full of lies; a folksy pottery bowl on which the following maxim was inscribed: "Never speak ill of yourself. Your friends will do it for you"; and on the wall a vast nineteenth century painting representing a life-size or almost life-size sheep against a black background.

Above all, there was an unbelievably low, deep armchair for the use of visitors, who were generally regarded as enemies and were meant to feel crushed by Moragas as he sat at his desk. *Dominio* again.

"Do you mind if I don't sit in that armchair?" said Pascualita, taking an upright chair.

Moragas gave an unexpected smile, a smile that betrayed the childishness that lies hidden in every male, even when he is (as we shall see that Moragas was) recognized as an ace in his profession. The smile signified: "Of course, *dominio* is not for you."

Pascualita asked him if, having been concerned with her father's affairs for eighteen years, he considered it unwise to let him cross the frontier.

But first of all Moragas had to expound to her at length all the transactions, shady and otherwise, by means of which he had managed to keep Celestino in funds ever since he had been in exile. In this connection he did not fail to get his figures slightly wrong, because all important men of affairs must occasionally get their figures wrong. In his majestic way of dealing with things, the approximate was in any case the law. He never listened to what a client said to him, and if by any chance he did listen, he did not understand and moreover forgot it at once. He skipped every other line of the memorandums that were put in front of him; he gave two diametrically opposite opinions on the same point within ten minutes; he signed, without having read them, important papers in which his very French secretary had only omitted to type three paragraphs; he rewrote in gibberish a minute carefully drafted by one of his employees; and as for dates, the less said the better: under his pen they were nearly always wrong. This method of work had earned him such a splendid reputation, and such a solid position, that he looked after the affairs of almost all the Spanish émigrés in Paris. Nothing extraordinary here: the majority of great business men and lawyers and doctors and administrators work like this, all over the world. And the fact that they succeed while working like this is what makes them truly great.

Moragas's exposition took a long time, and he even drew a sketch-plan with arrows. Moragas, in fact, had lost himself in his dream of figures in the same way as Pineda had lost himself in his cultural dream when he described the châteaux of the Loire, and as the pigeons had lost themselves in their deglutitory dream when their one and only occupation was to gorge and guzzle. When he emerged from his trance, the man of Christ realized that Pascualita knew nothing of finance and was slightly annoyed that she should show it quite so shamelessly, with a candour he found rather provocative. At last they got to the point.

"My father makes no secret of the fact that his fears have aroused and rejuvenated him—at the beginning at least, because now they make him gloomy. He has presentiments . . ."

"Does he believe in presentiments?"

"He believes in them as long as they're sinister."

"But is there any foundation for his fears? That's the question. I can tell you there is none. In the first place, after all, they would have confiscated his capital. Your father, being an anarchist, has a totally unreal view of the world: anarchism is first and foremost an absurdity. His fears are also part of his unreal view of the world."

"The comparison is very striking."

"Another thing. Your father—God bless him!—gets very easily worked up about the dangers he's supposed to be faced with. Since he is unable to frighten others as he used to, he makes up for it by frightening himself. Children sometimes behave like this, and old men are often like children."

"How shrewd you are!" she exclaimed with admiration. "You're a psychoanalyst."

"One doesn't have to be a psychoanalyst to make psychological observations," said Moragas, galled. He had a horror of psychoanalysis, because he was right-wing. And he was right-wing because he was in business; if he had been in nothing, like Celestino, he might have been an anarchist, like Celestino.

He went on:

"Psychoanalysis is psychology pure and simple, when it's carried out by someone who isn't intelligent, or who's a bit corrupt. Three years ago I knocked my head against the door leading up from my cellar. Immediately I had brain trouble. So it was nothing to do with psychoanalysis. I was given the name of a famous neurologist, and I found myself—there was some misunderstanding—in the hands of a psychiatrist. The questions he asked me were so irrelevant (no connection whatsoever with my case) and so preposterous that I realized at once that I was dealing with a sick man. I felt sorry for him. I answered his questions in a way that I thought would soothe and console him. I hope I did him some good."

He then went on to tell the story of a man who had broken his thigh bone and was treated by psychoanalysis.

They reverted to the subject of Celestino. Pascualita said:

"My father is convinced that he won't be able to see a bullfight because of bad weather. He's also convinced that he'll catch pneumonia. One of his axioms is: 'Everything one dreads eventually happens, every obsession becomes a reality.' "

"If he's convinced that he'll catch pneumonia, he will catch it. He is putting himself into a state of receptivity. If anything does happen to him it will be his own fault . . . There's also a sort of snobbery about fear. For instance, matadors nowadays *have* to say they're afraid: the public expects it of them. If they are not afraid, and say so openly, the public says they're conceited."

How did the subject of Celestino's atheism crop up in the conversation (through Pascualita)? Moragas started to laugh.

"He's no more atheist than you or I. He thinks he's an atheist. His atheism isn't serious. Do you think I would have taken on his affairs, or had anything at all to do with him, if he was an atheist?"

She had read the "last will and testament," but she said nothing. In this family there always came a moment when they said nothing. But is this peculiar? In every family, and every person, there always comes a moment for saying nothing.

"Religion and civil war are problems that cannot be judged by elementary standards," said Moragas, infinitely profound.

Then Pascualita brought up the subject of her father's newfound taste for money.

"I had already noticed it," said the man of Christ with warmth. "It's a real sign of recovery. He has become completely normal on that score. It was high time."

On the few occasions when Moragas had met Pascualita alone, he had spoken to her with a mixture of severity and commiseration about her father's disdain for money. She had then taken the opportunity, very discreetly, of raising the question of her own future, and the advisability of her going out a bit and meeting people, even though by nature she was inclined to solitude, at least in a society as vile as that of present-day Paris. Moragas had approved, without going any further, although he had a large family who led a conventionally hectic life and among whom Pascualita might well have been "invited." And he lived, after all, on a fixed salary plus commission, whereas Celestino, after all, lived on the income from his land. But Moragas had some social standing, and Celestino had none. And Celestino had political views that were very very unfortunate.

Moragas must have remembered these conversations, for he sighed:

"Poor child, what a lot of trouble your father has brought you with his political ideas! Think of the pleasant life you could have led in Madrid if only he had kept quiet! Whereas now . . . And as for your future . . ."

"When I told him my future was a tragedy, he said it was nothing compared to the tragedy of Spain."

"He told you that! Spain! The real trouble comes from

the prejudices of an intellectual who thinks he is destined to do good to the working classes but in fact is not remotely interested in them."

Pascualita failed to react to this remark from the lips of a "friend," which insulted her father and treacherously sought to turn her against him. She remarked platitudinously:

"One cannot change people."

Thus Celestino came out of this conversation as a person who believes in God but pretends not to, and who does not believe in a cause but imagines that he does, in fact a complete fraud, whereas what was really unassailable about him was precisely his honesty and straightforwardness.

As long as it was a question of finance, Moragas, as we have seen, was a competent and intelligent man. Outside this field he was superficial in everything, and was soon out of his depth if he was required to be more than superficial. For example, if Celestino had said to him: "I shall be dead in three years' time. Why bother to get involved in all sorts of things for such a short time?" he would have laughed. Laughter is the reaction of the frivolous to everything that is serious. If Celestino had said to him: "Since I'm an absolute unbeliever, it would be absurd as well as cowardly to have a religious funeral," he would have been horrified. One might at a pinch be an "unbeliever," but one had to have a religious funeral. And so on. He was incapable of logic or reflection, which is the case with ninety-nine people out of a hundred; and he was a good technician, which is the case, let us say, with about seventy people out of a hundred.

"If there was any trouble in Madrid," Pascualita ventured timidly, "do you know anyone who . . ." She saw

Moragas's face darken. She was about to say: ". . . who might intervene"; but she merely said: "whose advice he might ask?"

"Er . . . let's see . . . er . . . yes . . . there's, for example, Ortega, the lawyer."

"Could you write to him?"

"Without mentioning anything, of course."

He tore off a sheet of paper from a writing pad and wrote on it: "Write Ortega."

"And . . . there's no one else you know?"

This time, Moragas's face hardened.

"I really don't see the need. . . . But if you insist, I'll warn Arias, who used to be on Pablo Guillen's staff. I'll send you the addresses. I haven't got them here."

He wrote down "Arias," and then, without hesitation, stood up.

"I don't know how to thank you," said Pascualita.

"Your father has always managed to survive," Moragas concluded, putting on his beaming look again.

He escorted her to the door. When she had left, he returned to his desk, crumpled up the sheet of paper from the writing pad, and threw it into the wastepaper basket.

Pascualita felt reassured; she could now go to Madrid. However, she wanted Pineda's advice, too, not because she felt there was any need for it but because she had decided that she ought to have it.

When she asked her father how he was, he would sometimes answer: "Not at all well."—"What's wrong?"—"Ideological deficiency." When she came home that day she asked him in the usual way, rather mechanically:

"How are you?"

"Worse than bad."

"Don't you feel well?"

"Yes, perfectly well."

"Well, then?"

"I am advancing step by step towards the fulfilment of my tragic destiny."

"In that case don't go to Madrid!" she exclaimed violently. But she was now determined that he should go, because she wanted to go herself.

"What I want," said Celestino with an air at once greedy and obstinate, his head down, like a mule that would rather die than move another step, "What I want is to get hold of my money."

She did not tell her father of her visit to Moragas. But she went to see Pineda. He lived in the rue Campagne-Première: how far everything was!

Pineda's studio was like every other studio, but there were no sheep. Unless a picture of some square circles represented a sheep.

Pascualita gently chided Pineda for having upset her father. Pineda exploded. Then they had it out, and soon realized that Celestino—whose good faith neither of them questioned—had gradually got it into his head that it was Pineda who had insulted *him*, and one day had complained of these insults to his daughter. "He has gone mad as a result of reading too many newspapers," Pineda concluded.

Pineda had no opinion to offer on the risks Celestino ran or did not run, and frankly admitted as much. Pascualita outlined to him everything Moragas thought and she thought herself. However, she did not mention Moragas by name, seeing that it is always a good idea to conceal something. But when she told him that her father was behaving like a hunted man, he pounced on this, since it gave him something to go on and saved him from looking a fool. In short, he was like most doctors, who like one to tell them what is wrong with one and how to treat it, and lawyers and business advisers in general, whose trick is to advise you to do precisely what you want to do anyway. In other words, in his artist's way he was exactly what Moragas was in his. Both were agreed that Celestino was in no danger, which was what Pascualita wanted to be told, because it meant that she could go to Madrid.

Whereupon Pineda changed his mind, because he was a decorator—which is to say that, like all artists, he was volatile. He forgot his original idea, without even noticing he had done so, and all the more easily because it was not his own. Also because he did not care, just as Celestino did not care about the châteaux of the Loire: tit for tat. He was Pineda-the-kind, Pineda-the-helpful, but even so he did not care. Worse still, he had it in for Celestino. Pineda had not forgiven Celestino, nor had Ruiz forgiven him, nor had Celestino forgiven Ruiz: in this little group, nobody forgave anybody anything.

Thus Pineda, who did not care, and worse still, now suggested without any transition that it might be a trap: perhaps the government was luring Celestino into Spain in order to lay hands on him. This idea would have terrified Pascualita, and perhaps persuaded her, if it had been put forward by Moragas the day before. Now it came too late. Pascualita was advancing like a tank, with a relentless determination to get to Madrid and out of the concrete box. She was sacrificing her father to her own whim, which was to go to Madrid, just as he had sacrificed her to his, which was to wrap himself up in politics. She had come to see Pineda in order to be confirmed in her resolve, not to be diverted from it . . .

"It's extremely unlikely," she said crossly. "Besides, five

minutes ago you were of the opinion that he was acting the part of a hunted man . . ."

"Well, if you're so keen to go to Spain . . ." Pineda murmured, annoyed at being put in the wrong by someone who had come to disturb him.

"I have no wish to go to Spain," she retorted, offended. Pineda, in order to irritate her, offered her a cigarette. He knew she hated women who smoked. He could visualize in advance her electric reaction, like a fish when you touch it in a bowl, or a Latin woman when a man brushes against her rather brazenly. She had the expected reaction. Pineda was amused.

She left him in a mood of impatience and scorn: impatience because he had annoyed her, scorn because he was not rich. She said to herself, whether sincerely or not: "My father treated him badly, so he revenges himself on me."

Another letter came from Vicente, in which he said, almost by way of an afterthought: "There is a bullfight at Puente del Progreso on March fifteenth. Should I book seats?" He hadn't understood a thing! But one knows what brothers-in-law are. Celestino thought of cabling: "Book two *barreras*." But it occurred to him that in the eyes of the police that could only mean: "Everything ready for attempt Franco's life." Moreover, he was afraid of importuning Vicente and antagonizing him at this juncture when it would be better to have him on his side. For some time now everything had gone against him so regularly that, faced with the slightest decision, he groped and fumbled. The horns of a fighting bull are to some extent like eyes and hands. When they are shaved, the bull is half in the dark (which was the intention). Celestino was like a bull whose horns have been shaved: he no longer saw things as they were, and could no longer aim straight.

Finally he made up his mind and cabled: "Book two *barreras*," like a bull charging half-blind.

And now, alas, there was nothing for it but to go. His genius for self-torment was going to be fully employed.

There was a Pullman which left Paris at 1:45 in the afternoon and arrived in Madrid the following morning at 9:30. Don Celestino decided to leave on Thursday, March twelfth. He would deal with his sister's estate on Friday and perhaps Saturday, go to the bullfight on Sunday, and leave on Tuesday or Wednesday, depending on the state of his affairs.

A letter from his brother-in-law had explained the mystery of Puente del Progreso, which they had searched for in vain on the map and which was supposed to be an hour's drive from Madrid: the first *corrida* in the capital was not till a week later. Puente del Progreso was the new name for Puente Real, a small township in the Sierra to the west of Madrid: a sop from Franco to the Left. One can imagine how Celestino sneered.

Packing seemed a mountainous task, even though the two women helped him. He made a list of all the things he had to take; the women fetched them; he himself put them in the suitcase, and then ticked them off on his list; and he was amazed how clumsy his hands were, those hands that had been wont to dispatch bulls and men so briskly. How slow and finicky he was! How different he had become! How much had been swallowed up in the gulf of the years, never to be revived!

There was long cogitation and long discussion with Pas-

cualita as to whether he should take clothes and underclothes for *average* cold weather or for *severe* cold weather
(what would the climate of Puente del Progreso—a bleak
place in the mountains—be like in March? He decided on
warm garments. "You're right to be cautious," Pascualita
told him. The remark gave him food for thought.

He was very taciturn, and ate less than usual. When he
had made up his mind to go, he had experienced something
that might be called the intoxication of tragedy. The continuous weight of bitterness and gloom, alleviated only in
moments of recklessness or concrete violence, had lifted a
little: he had returned to the land of courage, from which
he had been excluded for twenty years; at that moment, it
was the grimness of reality that had given him the will to
live, whereas before it was living that was grim. But now
everything that had sustained him had gone. Staring at the
tablecloth during a meal, he foresaw his arrest, his trial,
and all the rest, while Pascualita complained about the
French—how at the hairdresser's, although "service" was
included, you still had to give a tip as well; what a country!
Like the soldier on leave from Verdun who disappointed
his irrepressibly cheerful family because he remained rather
morose, and who told them: "I shall probably be killed
within a week, and you expect me to be cheerful"
(the family were shocked by this unheroic remark, and the
soldier, returning to Verdun, was killed within a few days),
so Celestino might have said to Pascualita: "I have an even
chance of being arrested within a fortnight, and you expect me to be cheerful." But natural sentiments have no
currency in France.

Besides, he was too much of a Spaniard to have spoken
in that way. "Are you a man, or aren't you? I'm a man.
Oh! so I'm not a man, am I?" The age-old Hispano-

Moresque gramophone record went round and round inside him, and always ended on the same phrase: "I am no longer a man." Still pitiless to others but now pitiful to himself, he had arrived at the cruel position of being a prey to risks he had taken when he was a strong man, and having to suffer the consequences of them when he had become a broken man.

The only time he again alluded to his presentiments, Pascualita said to him, repeating word for word what Moragas had said to her, like a child repeating what it has heard at home:

"If anything happens to you in Madrid, it will be your own fault."

When the bull collapses at the thrust of the matador's sword, but is still not dead, one of the *toreros*—sometimes unceremoniously perching on the back of the now inoffensive beast—severs its spinal cord with a dagger. Pascualita, sitting astride her father, was stabbing him to the heart. And yet she truly loved him. As for him, he no longer reacted, exhausted as he was by having continually to defend himself.

She did not feel for the spot before aiming her blow, as *toreros* do. She aimed it straight and true, like the sting of an insect.

At first, as we know, Celestino had paid little attention to Marie-France, because she did nothing wrong. Then he had lived in dread of her departure. It was Pascualita who gave a Racinian twist to the situation. One afternoon she curtly refused Marie-France permission to go out for a couple of hours "to see her fiancé," although she had no urgent work to do in the house. Celestino realized that it was the word "fiancé" which had bitten Pascualita, and that she was taking it out on Marie-France as well as on him.

It was then that he remembered, in relation to Marie-France, the sentiments of his party, which he forgot so easily when his fellow-countrymen were not involved. Marie-France was the proletariat. She obeyed, ceaselessly obeyed, morning, noon and night, with no right to complain, no right to answer back, even when she was in the right; and she would have found herself forbidden, out of pure spite, to go out for an hour or two to see the man she loved, had not Celestino overruled his daughter, at the cost of a row with her: "One must put oneself in the other person's place." "Marie-France is paid to do . . . and not to do . . ." This row also made it clear that Pascualita was jealous of Marie-France not only because of her engagement, whether true or false, but because Celestino supported her. How was it possible for Marie-France not to hate her "masters"? Yet she did not seem to hate them. It was incomprehensible. Centuries of servitude must have made it second nature to her. Sitting in his armchair, Celestino watched her on all fours looking for one of his trouser buttons that had come off, and he pondered. Quite irrespective of all ideology, he realized that it was unjust, and that he had acted rightly when, in peace and in war, he had worked to bring this injustice to an end. He had suffered in his pride when his daughter did the housework; he suffered in his better nature now that it was Marie-France who did it. And yet he had wanted his daughter to stop doing it, and he wanted—wanted passionately—Marie-France not to stop. He ought not to have to bend down to pick up trouser buttons, especially at his age.

Thus the relationship between the classes, which he had

experienced of old in the glowing companionship of war, no longer existed for him except in the relationship between "master" and "servant."

And still he told himself that Pascualita, too, was right: he ought to have "done something" about her future. And still the same obstacles loomed: he could not devote the last years of his life, so precious because so few, to finding a husband for his daughter—a ludicrous, unthinkable task—when he could spend them in the pursuit of his investigations into the social question (or rather in escape into his investigations into the social question); and then, he needed Pascualita for his dying days; he also needed her for his living ones (once Marie-France left, for he was sure she would leave). And still his guilt remained. But now he did nothing to eliminate the causes of this guilt, just as he did nothing to eliminate the causes of his guilt concerning the unjust situation of Marie-France.

When, two days early, his suitcase was packed and he had checked his list twice to see that everything was there, he was rather at a loss for something to do with these two empty days. So he settled down to tidying up his desk, with the thought at the back of his mind that once he had left the flat he would never return. Always that odour of death accompanying everything he did. . . .

He went through his unpublished articles and destroyed four of them. Every time he read in the newspapers that the French and Spanish governments had exchanged a smile, he would begin to worry about being searched and would destroy some of his manuscripts. He could have given them to Moragas or Pineda or Ruiz to look after, but he did not like to disturb these gentlemen. On this as on the other occasions it was appalling to see how blithely he annihilated the fruits of his thoughts and labours, by which, to judge from his bitterness at Pascualita's contempt for them, he set so much store, and which, though they remained unpublished, might be said to give some meaning to his life. But what meaning? These articles, which for the most part had encountered only silence from Pascualita and silence from the editors of reviews, about which Ruiz and Pineda had said a few words and never alluded to again, as though they had never existed, might well be destroyed with their author's blessing. As far as they were concerned, he was beyond sadness.

And moreover: "I don't know why I should bother to destroy four of my articles since my beloved daughter will destroy them all as soon as I'm dead."

He threw away Pineda's letters, not without a few pangs; but he had had to liquidate Pineda just as he had had to go to Madrid: these decisions were like kicking the bottom of the pool to get back to the surface. On the other hand, he reread Ruiz's letters to see if he could find anything compromising in them which he might be able to use against him one day. There was no shortage of "choice" phrases, thank God! An excellent crop. "I'll badger him to such an extent that I'll make him sh . . his guts out of his mouth," he said aloud, although he was alone in his room.

They were letters written during the holidays, when Ruiz was at his country place, and they were all of recent date: Celestino had thrown away the earlier ones. Our hero found in these letters a mixture of protestations of affection that were at once incongruous, superfluous, and almost outrageous, complaints about his silence (in order not to be distracted for an instant from his work, Celestino refused ever to write a letter), and passages of scarcely veiled malevolence, in particular those in which Ruiz carefully detailed all the most disobliging observations, whether true or invented, that other people had made about his friend. In short, every one of these letters, without a single exception, showed a clear determination to be unpleasant to him in one way or another. Celestino now saw how glaringly obvious it all was. His father had said to him on his deathbed: "Never a moment's inattention, either with a bull or a man, even if they seem to have been manageable up to then." How inattentive he had been over the past twenty years with the excellent Orselito! Nevertheless, when he had finished reading, Celestino realized that he missed Ruiz very much.

He slipped those of Ruiz's letters which were or seemed compromising into a spanking new folder. The wheel had come full circle: Ruiz now had his dossier.

At the bottom of the drawer in which he was stowing away Ruiz's letters, he found a small piece of black material. He had cut it out of the black and red anarchist scarf which he had been wearing when he crossed the frontier in 1939 and which he had had to get rid of. When he threw the scarf away he wanted to keep an unidentifiable fragment of it, and had hesitated as to whether he should cut it out of the red or the black. He had finally chosen black, because black represented nonhope, which was even more important to him than blood. In the weak state he was in at the moment, this little piece of cloth gave him a twinge of nostalgia: he pressed it to his heart before putting it back in the drawer. It was not only his party but his whole past that he was pressing to his heart. This gesture of Celestino's will seem flamboyant to a man of the north, but in his case it was absolutely natural, and therefore not flamboyant.

Later, bent over his map of Madrid, Celestino put a red

circle round a number of public buildings: the royal pal-
ace, the law courts, the stock exchange, police headquarters,
some churches (fifteen), ministries (nine) and skyscrapers
(three). When his daughter asked him what he was mark-
ing, he replied: "The monuments you must ask Vicente to
take you to see." In reality, emulating once more those
monks of old to whom Unamuno compared the anarchists,
Celestino was liberally plying the cleansing fire: he was
working out the ideal plan for the bombing of Madrid. Let
others be constructive, much good might it do them! *His*
job was to destroy. That was simple and uncomplicated,
just the thing for an ideological throwback.

Later still, he found something terrifying on his desk.
Carved in the wood of the table, which was a strip of lami-
nated oak, were the following words, inscribed as though
with a stiletto: *The State is always destructive, always
criminal. The State, the younger brother of the Church* . . .
He remembered having written this one afternoon on a
sheet of paper flat against the bare table, without a blotter,
and the hard ball-point pen had penetrated the wood. The
words were not dangerous, not the sort which he cut out
of his notebook after writing them and threw away. But
what if they *had* been dangerous? What if Marie-France
had had them there under her nose all the time he was in
Madrid? What if the police had searched the flat?

On the Sunday before their departure, they were lunching in the Café de Bondy when Pascualita suddenly noticed
her father's face harden to the point of violence. She followed his gaze and saw that the cause of this violence was
a group of people who had just come into the restaurant.

"They're fascists," he hissed at her.

They were in fact provincial bourgeois, who were no
doubt staying at the big hotel in the Placc de la République,

the men in old-fashioned suits heavily padded at the shoulders, the women elaborately behatted, and all of them as placid and inoffensive as could be. Not fascists, but conservatives, surely.

"Let's go," said Celestino, beside himself with animosity. "I can't eat any more. We'll have our coffee elsewhere."

"Do calm down. You get so upset about nothing at all . . ."

"I'm not upset. On the contrary, hatred of the Right has kept me going all my life. It was hatred that made me fling myself in the path of enemy bullets with the daring for which I used to be famous."

"If you think political hatred . . ."

"Political hatred? No such thing. There is only social hatred. But you never understand anything . . . Rich swine! Bursting with pesetas!"

"You yourself admit that you like money nowadays."

"I like having money, but I don't like others to have it."

In fact the "much-bejewelled country girls" did not worry him, because it meant that the people had at last acquired the money which it had always had a right to. What maddened him was money acquired long since, immemorial money in which people wallowed like sardines in oil.

They skipped dessert, regardless of Pascualita's infantile taste for sweetmeats. Before leaving, Celestino went to the lavatory and wrote in pencil on the door:

FRANCO LE SALOD

But as he was doing up his trousers it struck him that, being the only Spanish habitué of the café, he would immediately be identified as the author of the inscription, and this he wanted to avoid at all costs. So he licked his index finger and rubbed it out.

Outside, he was silent for a long time. They eventually settled down in a café in the boulevard de Bonne-Nouvelle, one which he never patronized because it did not have a quiet backroom where one could sit and think, and while they waited for the ritual drop of black juice, he once more repaired to the privy. There he wrote on the door:

FRANCO LE SALOD

then returned, his face relaxed at last, with the feeling of having done his duty. Scribbling on the walls of public lavatories is the futile revenge of minorities.

Back home, he lay down on the bed in the "death-chamber" with a book. Soon he put the book down. "This is where the nurse will be. She will let me go on ringing for her. She will get the prescriptions muddled up. As a matter of fact she'll probably leave, slamming the door behind her, at the very worst moment. Marie-France will also leave at the same time." He was playing with his death like a cat with its tail.

The day of departure came in an atmosphere of gloom. Having checked the contents of his suitcase for the third and last time to make sure that he had forgotten nothing, he took out a rather patched pair of underpants and replaced them with a new pair. He would at least be tidy if he was arrested.

He also cut his fingernails and toenails, because one cannot cut one's nails in prison.

More than ever wrapped up in his obsessions, he had recently been dreaming every night. Commonplace dreams, but above them hovered the avenging spirits—of whom? It would be better not to say. Slowly they glided past, lying horizontal with their long wings folded over their backs and their mouths open like fishes, silently and slowly. And the sound of their wings which did not beat was the slow and heavy sound of aeroplanes loaded with bombs. Above his dreams glided always this river of the air, interminably, interminably, against a background of severed heads.

As usual, Pascualita assumed that he was dreaming of the words he uttered in his sleep. But she no longer crept to the side of his bed to listen, because she wanted, whatever happened, to get to Madrid, and she was afraid of hearing him say things that might have weakened her resolve.

However, two nights before their departure, towards midnight, she heard him talking to himself in his room, and the way he talked was not the way he usually talked in his dreams. When he talked in his dreams his voice was jerky, broken by silences, indistinct. This time it was distinct and continuous, with short gaps for breathing. Pascualita was so intrigued that she went to listen at the door . . .

Don Celestino was reading one of his articles to himself, carefully observing the punctuation.

She did not realize that it was another article—the fifth—that he was going to destroy.

For several days after her visit to Moragas she had waited for the "addresses" which he was supposed to send her. When nothing came, she had had a mind to telephone him, but she was afraid of being importunate. Eventually she told herself that, if he had not written to the two notabilities in Madrid, it was because he had decided that her father was in no danger; and this silence of his, which had annoyed her at first, now reassured her, until finally she forgot all about it.

VI

THEY HAD CAUGHT the train at the Gare d'Austerlitz. For him it was the station of death, as the Gare du Nord and the Gare de l'Est were the stations of death for French soldiers returning to the front.

Pascualita was reading magazines, the nationalities of which could be recognized at once by their photographs: here, women showing their buttocks, there, idiots showing their teeth, there again, much-decorated gentlemen decorating other much-decorated gentlemen. Celestino, for his part, had taken out of his suitcase a translation of an Italian book called *The Collapse of the Catalan Front in 1939*, and now he was engrossed in it, hoping to find therein some discreditable observations about his Catalonian brethren. He was so indifferent to the outside world, which irritated him so much, filled him, in fact, with disgust, that anything would have done as an excuse for not having to look at it. But no, it had to be *The Catalan Front*. Completely engrossed in it. Anchored to the revolution as though to a blazing star. And then, after all, what was France? It was Europe, it was all those countries whose chancelleries, a week after the *pronunciamento*, knew that they were not going to support the Republicans, knew that the Republicans were already doomed, and regarded the war as a heaven-sent opportunity to judge, thanks to the corpses of six hundred thousand insignificant *caballeros*, the quality of the Italian and German forces who would be their enemies of tomorrow.

He had to close the book, because it was time for dinner —face to face with his daughter, which he did not like. In the dining-car, a quick glance at the menu, and in comes a ghost: if they come to blows, he plunges his knife into its neck and severs the carotid artery; to the police superintendent he explains: "I had to do it properly while I was at it." Pascualita begins to chatter about nothing, and after each nothing, a little laugh. That incurable, that uncontrollable laugh. Nothing to be done about her lumpish desire to be cheerful at any price. And all the more cheerful as they approached the land of fear. She was quite conscious of the fact that her father was not listening, but she continued just the same. In fact, she was talking to herself, as he did. His diagnosis was: ignorance, indifference (lack of love), stupidity. "You who are always laughing, stop, for your father is dying, your father who has never done you any harm except by being." These words were never spoken, but they were recorded in heaven, where an angel takes down all the words that are neither spoken nor heard.

The frontier: at 8:50. Another thirty-five minutes before the land of fear. It was his own country that was the land of fear. For the first time, or almost. But it was not he, Celestino, it was his old age that was afraid: pale fear, as sudden and brutal as a heart attack or an epileptic fit.

He, more sombre with every second that passed, scenting prison and death from afar, as the picador's horse scents the bull, and trembles. She, more and more carefree and gay. Each in his own world, utterly sealed off from the other.

His, the world of the civil war and its shattering memories. That she should be excluded from this world, remain exiled from it—that was only natural; though it was nonetheless one more reason for making her a stranger in his eyes.

But that she should remain totally insensitive to his fears! That he should have to conceal them from her, so as to avoid her sneers! She would say to herself: "What a bore he is with his fears! If his country frightens him, why is he going back there?" Or even: "What a bore he is with his death!" A man in danger is like a sick man: he is a bore to everyone. He knew that all too well.

As the frontier drew nearer, he saw what a mad situation he had got himself into by his courage, which he now called his stupidity.

Not only must he conceal his apprehension from his daughter, but he could not even say to her: "If I'm arrested at the frontier, either they'll send you back or let you go on to Madrid. If you go to Madrid, don't trust Vicente. Try and get in touch with Moragas . . ."

Not only that, but he could not get out at Hendaye and say to her: "I'm going back to Paris," as from time to time he felt tempted to do. He could not do this because he was afraid of what she might think.

In other words, although he was brave enough to return to Spain, he was not brave enough to face the contempt of his daughter, whom he himself despised. Thus it was his own daughter, whom he had brought along to look after him if he fell ill, and who in that event would certainly have proved utterly devoted, it was his own daughter who would be partly responsible for his death, since it was because of her that he refused to retrace his steps!

Finally, the only result of the trip which might have cheered him up and brought him back to life—bringing back his sister's inheritance—he had partly sabotaged by himself taking on the negotiations, in which he would inevitably be swindled, whereas an honest proxy with power of attorney would have conducted them in his best interests.

Such was the absurd situation which had gradually taken shape, or which he himself had shaped.

※

Another twelve minutes before the land of fear. In twenty minutes, in half an hour, where would he be? At Irun, sitting on a chair in a little room at the station, next door to the station superintendent's office. The assistant superintendent would have confiscated his passport. Sitting outside the door, smoking and chatting, would be three personages, all very different in appearance—a country bumpkin with a hangdog look, a young intellectual in hornrimmed spectacles, and an old gentleman with pince-nez and a silver-headed cane—but all, it was glaringly obvious, detectives or police informers. There would be fag-ends piled all round them, recalling the celebrated pigeon droppings of the Porte Saint-Martin. The room would be unbelievably dilapidated; there would be flies, in spite of the cold, and fly-dung on an out-of-date time-table on the wall. Two civic guards would be seated not far away. Celestino would say: "Look here, when will the superintendent be back?" and they would answer: "Don't know. He's having dinner. He's been informed." One of the civic guards seems to be eyeing the other in a rather nervous way; perhaps he has a bad political record, and is afraid. Celestino gets up, but the second civic guard says to him: "Sit down." "Look here," says Celestino, "I haven't been arrested yet. I asked the assistant superintendent to telephone Madrid."—"They can't telephone Madrid, be-

cause they're having dinner."—"Who's they?" No answer.
Celestino asks to go to the lavatory. The second civic guard
escorts him to the lavatory, which is dense with flies, and
stands behind him while he urinates. Celestino, in order to
annoy him, reads from beginning to end all the unbelievably obscene graffiti which adorn the urinal and which
confirm, if confirmation were needed, that he is back in
his native country.

They go back, and he sits down again. He must not look
arrogant, nor must he look obsequious: absolute naturalness
is the thing with the police. (Celestino no longer thinks
hermandad but "police": such fanciful conceits were all
very well in France, where there was no danger. Here,
things are more serious.) The civic guards play cards and
eat monkey-nuts. Five to ten. Celestino thinks to himself
that he will have to spend the whole night here, because
everyone is having dinner. Since his visit to the lavatory,
he has elicited only two sentences from the guards: "We
don't know" and "Wait."

Five past ten. An individual wearing a *képi* full of gold
braid, a cigarette dangling from his lips, comes out of the
superintendent's office. It is the assistant superintendent.
Celestino gets up. The two guards get up. The assistant
superintendent walks by, and, without turning his head,
says: "Wait. It takes three hours to telephone Madrid."
Celestino is grateful to the assistant superintendent for not
taking it upon himself to incarcerate him.

If he was arrested, what would he do? Nothing. There
again he had manoeuvred himself over the past twenty
years into such a condition of isolation that there was not
a single human being to whom he could turn for help. No

one to make a *quite*,* as usual! No one to make *quite*! His brother-in-law? Vicente would destroy him rather, if he thought it was in his interest to do so. Besides, might not his brother-in-law have set a trap for him? How prompt he had been to obtain the visa! Celestino sensed a trap, and irresistibly he was drawn towards it. His realization (of the danger of Vicente being so well in with the regime) was like the slow realization of the bull, slow and profitless for them both. He was reduced to this ridiculous solution: Moragas making a *quite*! Moragas, unique and indispensable! Pascualita sent back to beg for help from Moragas, Pascualita, his enemy, doing her utmost to help him! A ridiculous solution, shameful and odious. But the only possible one. And he could not breathe a word to her about it.

Eight forty-five: they were nearing the frontier, and the train was slowing down—slowing down as if it, too, was afraid, it, too, hesitated, on the borders of the land of death. How agonizing it had been when the train picked up speed after leaving the Gare d'Austerlitz: farewell to safety . . . But this slowing-down at the approach of danger was even more agonizing still. Hurry! Hurry! Let him but know the fate that awaited him!

The upper surface of his thighs felt cold, in spite of the overheated compartment. "That would be the last straw, to catch a cold from nerves."

"But be honest: if you were alone, would you go back?" Sometimes he answered yes, sometimes no. At one moment his fear kept him alive, at the next it made him die a little.

As in certain cinema advertisements in which the invitation to buy a certain product is repeated by a loudspeaker ever more loudly and ever more rapidly in order to create

---

* *Quite*—rescue action by a *torero* when another is in danger.

a psychosis, so the rhythm of the train repeated with in-
creasing strength and speed:

WHAT A BORE HE IS WITH HIS FEAR. WHAT A BORE HE IS
WITH HIS DEATH. WHAT A BORE HE IS WITH HIS FEAR. WHAT
A BORE HE IS WITH HIS DEATH.

In his eyes, waves of implacable determination alternated
with waves of implacable fear. And yet, the more he was
afraid the more he plunged towards danger, with the tenac-
ity of a man struggling forward against the wind, head
bent, eyes lowered.

He threw the book about Catalonia out of the window.

Five minutes late. Hendaye. The last chance of freedom
and life. Pascualita fluttery and overexcited. There was no
argument. He did not get off the train.

It was here that the French used to come in holiday
mood to watch through fieldglasses the Spanish forces killing one another, and to see Irun fall for lack of ammuni-
tion, while two trainloads of arms destined for the
Republicans were held up by the French government at
Hendaye.

He took down his suitcase, wielding it so clumsily that
it blocked the corridor, and he calmly left it there. Not
out of muscular weakness, but because he did not know
what he was doing.

The train set off again.

Through the window he could see his country in the
dark, under the night sky, milk-white like a frost-covered
meadow. It was as in the civil war, when he used to see,
beyond the opposing lines, the "enemy" country, which
was yet his own country. He saw the first black blobs and
a tangle of vertical lines, style 1900: Irun station. He saw
Franco's country, the enemy country, his country. "Abandon hope, all ye who enter here."

The train stopped at last, expired at last. It was Pascualita who hailed a porter; if he had been alone, he would have been unable to do so. Literally, he could not speak; he had suddenly developed a sore throat, that very instant: his throat was so raw he could hardly articulate a sound; his tongue rough as cat's; he had hardly enough saliva to lick an envelope. He wanted to go and moisten his throat in the W.C., in order to be able to speak, but the corridor was crowded with passengers. He saw a young man on the platform rush forward to carry a suitcase for a priest whom he obviously did not know. Claws gripped his heart, as though the Lion of Castille had placed a paw on his breast. When he gripped the handle of his suitcase, his hand trembled.

He saw the red and yellow flag, and his heart turned over.

He climbed down the high steps of the carriage as though in a dream. He nearly fell, but Pascualita held him up.

WHAT A BORE HE IS WITH HIS FEAR. WHAT A BORE HE IS WITH HIS DEATH. WHAT A BORE HE IS WITH HIS FEAR. WHAT A BORE HE IS WITH HIS DEATH.

Once on the platform, he set off in the wrong direction. He struggled on blindly, blundering into people and shouldering them violently aside—crash! bang!—like a man drunk or concussed.

Pascualita caught him up. When he was well and truly at the heels of the porter he pulled himself together and advanced stiffly but firmly, with a mechanical step.

A flick of the tongue to the right, a flick of the tongue to the left, at each corner of his dry lips.

A matador shuffling towards the bull is like a man walk-

ing on water. Celestino walking on the platform was like
a man walking on water. He was no longer trembling.

He plunged into the station building. In the main hall
he saw the faces of his race, like those of another planet.
He saw the three-cornered hats of the civic guards, and
his heart stood still. Hatred and fear, like twin serpents . . .

He looked at his watch, and saw that at the very moment
the train had stopped, his watch had stopped too.

Celestino had now been in his hotel room for twenty
minutes. Like an aviary filled with bird-song it resounded,
despite the closed windows, with the songs of the maids
washing in the courtyard. Everything had gone without
the slightest hitch at Irun; the threat of danger had vanished like smoke, leaving not a wrack behind. And Celestino, who had been so afraid of his country beforehand,
was no longer afraid once he had entered it. When he
woke up, the countryside through which the train was
passing was not one that he had known during the civil
war; it was unfamiliar, and said nothing to him. Celestino
was slightly worried, but no more than that.

Vicente was waiting for them on the platform at Madrid,
Vicente twenty years older, a sombre thought. Every illness, every excess, was reflected in some minute distortion
or oddity in his face: a perceptive man would have guessed
it all by looking at him, even the way he would die, and
the date (three or four years hence). Celestino had put on
a lugubrious air (by way of mourning), which he rectified
as soon as he saw that his brother-in-law welcomed him
with jovial expansiveness. Vicente was wearing in his buttonhole an enormous chunk of gilded metal, heavily

wrought, which was obviously intended to show that he was important, or patriotic, or perhaps both. Opulent, spruce and portly, a curvature of the spine gave him a slight list to the left. Had he been a government official, Celestino would have assumed that he was weighed down on one side by the weight of the decorations he had to wear at official ceremonies. But he belonged to the "private sector." That was still pretty suspect.

Vicente had booked a room for Celestino in a first-class hotel in the Avenue José Antonio in the heart of Madrid. Celestino refused to stay in a luxury hotel—not out of meanness, but because it offended his ideological susceptibilities, which preferred a "comfortable but modest" hotel. He also wanted—a less noble sentiment, this—to show Vicente, who had already seen the Pullman, that he had not betrayed his past: his whole life, and above all the failure of his life, would have no meaning if Vicente was allowed to judge by the Pullman. Finally, it would have been especially painful to him to live in the Avenue José Antonio, these being the Christian names of the founder of the Falange, after whom the city's principal artery had been named. Indeed, whenever he referred to the said avenue, he called it *la Gran Via*, its pre-civil-war name. Did this not "brand" him, from the very moment he arrived in Madrid? Very well then, let it brand him!

Vicente had to go and telephone from a booth in the station to book a room in the hotel Celestino had chosen, a little hotel, very nineteenth century, in the Calle Mayor, near the square of the same name (assuming this hotel still existed). There was a room free, and Celestino set off by himself, while his daughter and his brother-in-law drove to the latter's house. The old gentleman had agreed to his daughter lodging with the man he detested, so as to be rid of her.

And now he was washing his hands and face in his hotel room when there was a loud and peremptory knock at the door. He knew what it was at once: for eighteen years he had waited for this knock; everything was happening as he had foreseen. His foresight minimized the thing itself, made it almost gratifying.

"Who's there?"

"Police."

He pulled himself up to his full height, flung back his head so that his beard stuck out in front, and opened the door. Two men came in, both wearing blue nylon rain-coats, one built on police lines, with a beret, the other smaller and older, more seedy-looking, with a black felt hat. Both kept their headgear on.

"Your papers."

He handed them over.

"What have you come to Madrid for?"

"To settle my sister's estate; she died in February. Everything's in order with the Consulate. You can see for yourself."

"Oh, the Consulate!" said the man in the beret. Celestino was delighted to see that the traditional contempt between government departments remained intact.

He was calm—abnormally calm. All his fear had been drained out of him before the frontier and at Irun. There was no fear left in him.

The big man examined his identity card with scrupulous care.

"Someone has been trying to rub out your name at the edge here."

"You can see that it's just worn."

Good God! He had been ready for anything, but not that. Obviously it was worn.

Celestino tried to imagine the questions he would be asked, and to remember the fabric of lies which he had built up (unnecessarily) for the people at Irun, and which he had already almost forgotten—a fabric of lies similar to those which the man of Christ used to inculcate into him in case he was ever asked to explain the provenance of his funds. The inspector with the beret leafed through his passport. He had only to say one thing, "We'll keep this," and put it in his pocket, and Celestino was a prisoner. As his throat was a little dry in spite of his composure, Celestino put a peppermint in his mouth: he always had a supply of peppermints, which he sucked after smoking.

"What's that you're eating?" asked the inspector sharply.

"A peppermint. Look," said Celestino, thinking: "Well! If he thinks I'm already at the cyanide stage, I must be for it."

The smaller of the two still said nothing.

The big one took some papers out of his pocket and read them, apparently with some difficulty. As at the approach to Irun, Celestino was thinking: "If they ask me this or that question, I have my lies ready. But if they ask me *the obvious question:* 'What were you doing in Spain before going to France?' should I answer: 'I was a captain in the red army, as you know perfectly well'?" For weeks he had foreseen an interrogation of this sort, and yet he had not been able to decide what his answer would be to *the obvious question.* He also thought to himself: "If I had stayed at a grand hotel they probably wouldn't have come."

Suddenly, without warning, a ray of sunlight lit up a segment of the dark room. The shadow of an invisible bird,

flying outside, crossed this area of sunlight, streaking the
blue raincoat of the detective with the beret. O bird of
freedom, wandering as you please in the lawless skies! The
shadow of another invisible bird flitted across the sunlit
raincoat (the second detective was so out of favour that
he did not even have the right to a bird's shadow). The
sun vanished. The servants sang.

Suddenly the man in the beret handed Celestino back
his papers, with the little jerk of the hand which for Spaniards means "Thank you." Celestino was struggling to conceal his relief when he was disturbed by a remark from the
big man.

"Well, are you glad to be back in Spain?"

"I'm sorry it's for such a short time."

This kind of tendentious amiability reminded him of the
cigarettes traditionally offered by police interrogators.

The two men moved towards the door. Then the little
one said:

"The weather's not very nice for you. Usually it's
warmer at this time of year."

It was the first time he had opened his mouth.

Celestino wondered whether he ought to shake hands
with them. He would willingly have shaken hands with the
little one, because he felt that he was just as humiliated as
he was himself. He refrained. He would have given the
impression of thanking them for not arresting him.

The two men went away, carrying their mystery with
them, the mystery of those who could drown you with a
word, and who do not say this word.

For several minutes, emotion surging back like water
when the floodgates are opened, he waited for them to return. When they reached the pavement they might have
had second thoughts, and decided to apprehend him, if only

for further interrogation. But no, nothing happened. He said to himself: "They're humouring me. Is it a good or a bad sign?" It was a moot point, at least as far as he could remember from the days when it was he who arrested people.

🚩

Celestino was to lunch at half past two at his brother-in-law's, together with Pascualita, and then go and see the lawyer with Vicente. Until half past two he was free: he had asked Vicente to take his daughter for a walk, on the plea that he himself wanted to be alone with his memories in his native city.

While he was getting dressed, there was a rustle from the direction of the door: someone had just slipped an envelope under it. He did not like this. He looked for his key in order to open the door and see who had . . . By the time he had found it and opened up, there was no one on the landing. He opened the envelope in some agitation. It was a local hairdressing establishment offering its services.

There was no lift on the landing. His practised ear at once recognized the steps of a man coming up alone, then a woman's steps, then a man and a woman together, then two men together. At this he put his ear to the door. The two men overshot his landing, saying to each other: "Angelica would be quite wrong to go back to Oviedo . . ."

He was downstairs at a quarter past twelve. As he passed the reception desk on the first floor, he gave a sidelong glance to see if the manager looked askance at him after the visit of the police. But the manager was not there. There was only a waiter, who did not appear to have noticed him.

He stopped on the threshold of the hotel (how cold it was, really wintry!) and scanned the street from left to right: nothing suspicious, as far as he could see. He set off towards the Plaza Mayor, "his beard over his shoulder." Instinctively he had plunged both hands into his overcoat pockets, as he used to in times of *juerga*, when he always carried a gun in his right pocket, which never left him and which he even used to take out and slip into his jacket pocket when he visited anyone. In those days, at particularly dangerous moments or particularly dangerous spots, he would put both hands in his pockets because, if he had only pocketed his right hand, people would have twigged at once. One day a man had asked him why he always carried a revolver, and he had answered: "It's my soul." But he had another soul, whatever he might say.

At first, the lack of a revolver caused him acute uneasiness; what he needed was to feel in his palm the grip of a big Browning, thick as a male organ (like all his compatriots, Celestino was obsessed with virility). As he walked along the pavement there flashed through his mind the title of an old treatise on bullfighting he had once read: *Tauromachy, or the Art of Killing and not being Killed*. For him, the streets of Madrid were like that: a place for killing and not being killed.

Click! Both his arms were held in an iron grip: what he had always called "the crab's claws." The two inspectors. But no, not just yet.

He did not turn round to see if he was being followed, but crossed the street and, pretending to be looking out for traffic coming from his right, carefully scrutinized the crowd. How sharp his eyes were in this setting where, years before, he used to walk around during the bombing with his eyes wide open as though hallucinated. On reaching the opposite pavement, it seemed to him that a man was clinging to his heels. Adopting the wrong reflex, he hunched his back a little, as though the man were a shell. Then he said to himself: "The great thing is to shoot first." (Alas!) He stopped in front of the window of a tailor's shop, the dark background of which acted as a mirror: the man was behind him. Celestino turned round and retraced his steps; the man walked on. Celestino stopped: perhaps the man would stop and then come back towards him. But no, he still walked on and finally disappeared in the crowd. All these traditional tricks amused Celestino, rejuvenating him by twenty-three years without seriously exciting him.

He arrived at the Puerta del Sol. The square seemed surprisingly small, because as he remembered it last it was deserted, the iron shutters down on all the shops, which made it look bigger. Here Canalejas had been assassinated, here the Asturian miners had marched past, here Celestino had walked, sporting a red tie, after having eaten meat on Good Friday at one of the famous banquets of Niembro. Then there had been the drone of aeroplanes, cars covered in mattresses, snipers on the roof-tops, shelters and earthworks on the pavements, corpses covered with sheets, ignored by passers-by, and foodstuffs sent from Russia displayed on the pavements as though in a *souk* in Tetuan. Now there were double-decker trolley-buses. Splendid thing, a double-decker trolley-bus: easier to overturn when you want to shoot from behind it.

He was surrounded by chattering people, the men repeating the words *claro, coño,* and *vamos* in practically every sentence, the women *casar, corazon,* and *familia:* these six words, he now remembered, were the basis of the Castilian tongue. The people were in more of a hurry than those of old, because they worked. In the cafés people drank standing up: time is money. He flashed a penetrating glance at every passer-by, a glance pregnant with inquiry:

are you for the regime? do you accept it with resignation?
do you hate it, hoping and waiting, or are you perhaps
working secretly against it? He wanted each face to be an
avowal. He had envisaged Franco Spain with the camp at
Argelès in mind: a vast concentration camp. "Eighty per
cent of Spaniards are against Franco today," he had read
in a French book ("more or less the proportion of informers at Argelès," he had thought at the time). But what he
saw were either empty faces or happy faces, in other words
what one sees in every town, and gradually he ceased to
interrogate them. Almost all the young ones were laughing.
Moreover, they did not seem to feel the cold; some of
them were not even wearing waistcoats, the blackguards,
when *he* was freezing in his heavy overcoat. This loss of
bodily warmth must have coincided with his loss of courage: the years were to blame for that. Still, what a lot of
carefree people! In the old days in Madrid, when he was
suspect and threatened by unknown dangers, he had found
the insouciance of others wounding at times, and at other
times absurdly comforting as regards his own safety. Now
it only made him feel bitter. Of course, they could afford
to be insouciant, since their situation was different from
his. And then, happiness had always caused him an uncon-
querable aversion. All the more reason today. Happy when
Spain was what it was! Delighted with everything they
had not and were not! In Paris, although he did not mix
with them, he felt himself surrounded by a race of exiles,
for most of the Spaniards in Paris were exiles. Simply knowing they were there, without knowing who they were,
was heartwarming. In Madrid the rebels were lost in the
crowd; he was unaware of them; he was aware only of
himself, so that he had the feeling that he alone suffered
from the misery of Spain—that he alone was right, the only

just man. "For twenty years I have suffered because of the sufferings of my country, and perhaps these sufferings do not exist. I should no longer suffer, but now I suffer because my country did not have it in itself to undergo these sufferings. Once more I was mistaken." In these streets full of the pseudoblind, he thought he was the only genuine one.

Another thing. In Paris, he justified his unhappiness by telling himself that he was unhappy because his country was unhappy: that made it a noble unhappiness. But if his country was happy, his unhappiness in Paris was no more than the unhappiness of a failure.

"There are twenty-nine million of them, and they are well known to be a race who sacrifice their lives easily. But not one of them has risked his life to assassinate Franco."

Ruiz answered (he had often done so in reality):

"And what will come after him?"

"Nothing!" he struck back, in the tone of a bad-tempered child. Then, realizing that this was not, after all, enough, he added: "We shall see. But at least he will have gone."

A silent dialogue, for here there was no question of talking aloud to himself in the street, as in Paris, because here the remarks he made! . . . Civic guards brushed past him, and he muttered to himself: "Ah, if they only knew!" He looked away whenever he passed a priest or an officer, with a disgust bordering on nausea: hyena-priests, gorilla-colonels . . . In the same way, in Paris, crossing Saint-Germain-des-Prés in a taxi, Pascualita would bow her head and stare at the floor to avoid seeing the monstrosities one sees in that neighbourhood.

In the Calle de la Montera he came to life again. He had taken cover in that doorway over there; from behind this

column he had fired his revolver at the Falangists passing
by in cars. Navvies were digging a trench for some water
pipes: *that* would be a good place to shelter from the
bombs! Soon the sirens would begin to wail all together,
the end of one alert merging with the beginning of another. Soon the windows would start banging up and down
in the shattering blast. Suddenly his eyes widened: along
the edge of the pavement a trail of blood was flowing, thin
and diluted at first, but getting gradually thicker, reflect-
ing patches of light from the shop windows, as in the old
days the pavements used to reflect the fires. "The revolution proves everything, and proves it by blood": the phrase
of Trotsky's came back to him. Celestino realized that the
blood must come from a butcher's shop, and indeed he soon
came across it. Never mind, blood in the street was something . . . And yet, it had to be admitted, it wasn't much.

Many are those who are appalled, after a revolution, by
what they did during it: this is often said of the men of
'89, counts and peers under the Empire. Their idea is not
dead, but it has changed its appearance and lost its lustre,
like an aeroplane turning in the sun. Celestino had never
been appalled by what he had done during the civil war:
he had never ceased to believe that he had then realized the
best that was in him. But now, in the streets of Madrid,
what he had done, what he had experienced during the
war was as if it had never existed. He had expected to experience an overpowering emotion in Madrid, but he still
felt nothing. Not even fear, although he knew that he might
be arrested at any moment. If he were afraid, at least he
would feel that he was alive. But his fear had begun two
hours before arriving at Irun, and had evaporated as soon
as the train had left Irun; it had had a beginning and an
end, like an air raid. Just as one could no longer see the

pictures in the magic lantern of one's childhood if the focus of light faded, so his imagination, his sensitivity, and his memory had faded to such an extent that they no longer illuminated the pictures of the war. What a mockery! They shone more powerfully when he reconstructed the street-fighting in the rue de Nazareth and the rue Pissechiens. The flame-girt town, the deadly musical purr from the sky, the ambulance bells, the corpses like crushed bugs—all this had sunk without trace; as though nothing had happened. And nothing was now happening in his heart, and all this nothingness made the city baleful and lugubrious; he no longer felt at home in it, and wished he were out of it already. France was not his country—perish the thought! But neither was Spain.

When he had left the internment camp, a French inn-keeper of whom he had asked some favour had answered him: "Now you fellows have lost, so shut up and get out," and Celestino had thought: "How typically French." But over the past twenty years everything had hardened inside him. Was it because he had "seen too much," or because age had ossified him? The only oasis in this desert was the tenderness he had felt towards his daughter for three or four years. Nowadays, when he read in the papers the daily recitals of massacres, of just revolts crushed, of people being despoiled and innocents condemned, it must be admitted that he did not feel strongly about them; especially since his sudden decline, indignation and pity had dried up inside him. *He* was going to die soon; this being so, let others die too . . . And if they suffered, but still lived and would go on living, what more did they want? So that at moments—at moments only—terrible though it is to say, the men of his party who might be hidden in this

Madrid crowd inspired in him a fleeting: "You've lost, so . . ."

After Ruiz, who had betrayed him, after Pineda, who had betrayed him by not taking enough trouble about "resuming," after Pascualita, who had betrayed what she had been or seemed to be in her adolescence, he in his turn was betraying. But had he not begun to betray the working class on the day when he had begun to like money, the day when, not satisfied with wanting decent furniture for the room where the doctors would come to prepare him for death, he had wanted period furniture, "galleons"? So it was old age and the smell of death which had led him to covet money, just as it was old age and the smell of death which had dried up his feelings for these people among whom he had fought for two and a half years. He was undergoing the last change of life, similar to the crisis of puberty in adolescents, or the flowering of the virgin into the young woman.

As we know, he had never been a man of hope. Now less than ever had he the strength of mind to see that his country's civil war was but a chapter in the worldwide civil war that had long been in progress. To him, his war was something closed and dead, an extinct volcano. The active volcano, the drama of tomorrow, was the possibility of Marie-France's departure, among other terrible possibilities of the kind.

In his exhaustion he stumbled against the edges of pavements, and his vision grew clouded. He saw himself in a mirror, and turned his head away. His splendid face had grown ghastly pale, his nose pinched, the lines descending from the nose deeply hollowed, his lower jaw hanging loose like that of a man suffering from adenoids; his drooping eyelids hung down over the whites of his eyes, usually so clear and so wide-open. It seemed to him that there were people—especially children—who looked at his drawn face with fright.

He longed for it to be a quarter past two so that he could go to Vicente's. Why was he so tired after having walked for only an hour and a half? He was never as tired as this in Paris, when he went for walks along the *Grands Boulevards*. It was because here the tiredness of his legs was exacerbated by the effort needed to interrogate people's faces and to try in vain to tune his emotional system into the unfamiliar scene. In Paris he could walk as far as this without getting tired because he walked without thinking of anything.

On a sudden impulse he lifted the right-hand side of his overcoat, still thinking he had the heavy Browning in his pocket.

At about five o'clock Celestino emerged, drunk with money and at the same time very exhausted, from the double ordeal of lunch and the visit to the lawyer. Among the miradors and the gloriously uncomfortable green armchairs, Leonardo's *Last Supper*, the splendid silver in glass cases, the reproduction Chippendale and Queen Anne furniture, Pascualita had chattered and burbled with Vicente as though completely unaware of the grave misgivings this reunion was bound to cause her father, or rather as though unaware of his presence. Celestino, silent, invisible, transparent, had stuffed himself with beans and boiled potatoes, themselves rather transparent, greedily sprinkling them with oil. Supreme distinction: everyone drank water. The conversation between Pascualita and Vicente turned on life in Madrid. Politics were never touched upon, but simply from the tone of the questions and answers it emerged that all was normal and pleasant in Spain. As Celestino had expected, Pascualita saw Spain as her country—and then there was the journey, the novelty, the picturesqueness, and, of course, the culture! She did not go beyond all this, or so at least he thought. Whereas *he* was exclusively beyond it.

Before lunch, Vicente had shown him Pascualita's room. There was a crucifix above the bed. Celestino had muttered an obscene blasphemy between his teeth.

Since his departure from Spain, his family had almost completely dropped him; none of them had even written to him when his sister died. Nevertheless he expected to find a few invitations at Vicente's, which he looked forward to refusing gleefully. But there were none, and this annoyed him. So he was still the one who had backed the wrong horse! They were obviously irritated that he should have come back: there might be trouble, which would involve them, or force them to exert themselves on his behalf, which would be the last straw! For twenty years he had been in exile, and it seemed to him that they were disposed to welcome him with a "What! Already!" as soldiers on leave during the First World War were greeted when they reappeared after five or six months of hell (at least according to a joke of the time—not such a joke as all that).

The session at the lawyer's had been equally uncomfortable, but on a quite different plane. It had not been going five minutes before he was already out of his depth, just as he was soon out of his depth when the Communists started expounding party doctrine to him. All these people skipped around, thoroughly at home in a sphere in which he had failed from the start; and he resented it. Not only

did he fail to grasp the details of his sister's estate, complicated by his twenty years' absence and by the silence he
had had to observe as to his means of livelihood during his
exile, but he felt, and was persuaded that they were making
him feel, that he was a foreigner, a suspect, a black sheep,
who was only there through the good offices of his brother-
in-law and, what was more, of the Franco government.
He was no longer transparent as he had been during lunch;
he was there, solidly there, because he had to be swindled.
That, of course, Celestino had seen a mile away, but now
he was right in the middle of it, and his discomfiture was
increased by his awareness of his stupidity. His presence
in Madrid was unnecessary, and yet he had come, running
the risk of "trouble," running the risk of pushing Pascualita into the arms of the devil, more or less certain to be
outmanoeuvred in the negotiations over the estate. Why
had he come? Out of weakness and out of sadness: because
he wanted to free himself, by taking a risk, from his growing lack of self-esteem, his tendency to shrivel up more and
more. But, in coming, he had only confirmed these weak-
nesses.

After an hour and a half of palaver, to which Celestino's
main contribution was an occasional "Yes, yes," as when
confronted by the Communist dialecticians, and during
which his attention was concentrated not so much on the
financial figures as on the faces of these gentlemen, to see
whether or not they could tell that he was not following
(and he felt, terrifyingly, that his will was weaker than
theirs), the discussion was adjourned until the next morning. At which point he had pleaded an engagement and had
left first and alone, in order not to have to bear Vicente's
company any longer. And so at five o'clock he was once

more in the street, even more embittered and heavy-hearted than before.

Alone in this town where there was no one who wanted to see him, no one he wanted to see, and nothing he wanted to see. Silently he cried out: "What is the point of living!" Wander through these streets once more? He had nothing in common with this crowd, which bored him, jostled him, exhausted him. Go back to the hotel? Yes, to wait for the police to knock at the door. The best thing to do was to settle down in a quiet café with some newspapers. But Spanish newspapers were all very well when one could counterbalance their lies by reading the French papers. But here? Ugh! Well then, buy a book and go and read it in a café. That was the best solution.

As he was looking for a bookshop, a man of about his own age, likewise bearded, a sort of boarding-house Don Diego, nodded to him as he passed by and gave him a friendly smile. Celestino followed him with his eyes; the man did not turn round. Celestino did not know what to think; he was at once rather touched by this cordial gesture in a city where until then he had found nothing but indifference and hostility, and at the same time ill at ease. Either the man had mistaken him for someone else, or he had recognized him, after twenty years. Rather too good a memory! His life was full of ghosts. Which of them was about to loom up, in order to persecute him? For not all of them were dead, alas; there was an endless stream of them.

The bank buildings stretched eagerly towards the sky, crushing the church of San Gregorio. Well done, banks, that's the way: nearer and nearer to heaven! New sky-scrapers had arisen, vulgar and grotesque set-pieces, but the ancestor of them all was still there, the national telephone company's building, set right at the geographical centre of the peninsula, like a dagger in the heart of Spain. It had been built partly with the help of Yankee capital. Eleven floors in Yankee style, and two in Spanish baroque: a symbol. The ex-*Gran Via*, lined with buildings that were higher than of old, was a sort of funnel acting as an amplifier: the noise of the traffic swept through the narrow part, and a thunderous din emerged at the other end (Spanish cars are noisier than French ones). The traffic policemen controlled the rhythm, like the galley masters of yore. Among the splendid motorcars advertising the "Texas way of life,"* a man was pulling a handcart, holding the shafts high in the air, which gave him the look of being crucified. It was the eternal delinquent, the Accused.

Celestino had noticed in Paris that any innovation whatsoever, sooner or later, without fail—literally without fail —turned out to have been copied from the Americans. As a result he had come to the conclusion that the French had lost the art of invention and creation. But it was the same in Madrid. This servility went even further in that it was no longer simply a question of copying the Americans but of not offending them. In Spain, as in France, and no doubt elsewhere, things that were good in themselves, and long-established in the country, were abolished with a stroke of the pen, because they displeased American tourists—and heaven knows what tourists, heaven knows what specimens of superior humanity! Don Celestino was staggered by this international servility.

He looked for the college de la Flor, where he had been taught the love of God and of capitalism, his old college,

* In English in the original.

which he had had the honour to set fire to. But others had
later shared this honour: the nationalist airmen. The college had been razed to the ground and its site was now
occupied by a group of buildings shaped like filing cabinets. Celestino had an unexpected access of melancholy,
reprehensible and reprehended.

He came to a halt in front of a bookstall. Read a political book? Controlled publishing, after the controlled press?
Ah, a history book: *The Generation of '98.** A bitter story,
a story of defeat, an anti-Yankee story; yes, that was what
he needed.

He turned into a narrow side street—old Madrid lies
cheek by jowl with smart, modern Madrid—and stopped
after a few steps: through the window of a seedy tavern
he had seen a brazier alight. He stood looking at it; it was
a long time since he had seen an open fire—one never saw
them in Paris—and now he realized why it had arrested his
attention: because it was like the fire that would consume
him one day soon at the cemetery of Père-Lachaise. He
could not resist going in and ordering a cup of coffee, although he was nearly suffocated by the overpowering smell
of cheap wine and overcooked oil.

In the tiny, dark interior, men who looked as though
they did a dozen jobs or none at all, men with a six-day
growth of beard, were eating fried eggs and *calamares*, and
sucking their fingers as they ate: they were his *camaradas*
and *compañeros*** of yesterday. Half-filled glasses slid across
the zinc, as in Western films. Celestino drank his coffee

* The loss of Cuba and the Philippines, seized by the North Americans in 1898, had a profound effect in Spain, and the generation of
intellectuals which arose after this defeat, deeply imbued with melancholy, was known as "the generation of '98."

** *Camarada* was the term among communists, and between communists and socialists; *compañero* among anarchists.

standing up, staring at the brazier. The prospect of soon being consumed by a similar incandescent substance was not a disagreeable one. When, during the previous winter, he used to wonder what thought would strike him when he realized that this time it was really the end, he imagined it would be: "I'm not sorry to be rid of the French." Now he told himself that his last thought would be: "I'm going to have done with Spain and the Spaniards." It may be noted that this went no further than Lyautey's remark after his fall, when people started talking to him about Morocco: "I don't want to hear any more about Morocco."

It was for the people of old Madrid that he had fought, not for the people of the *Gran Via*. But now he did not want to see even them any more. All he wanted was to find a deserted café where he could be alone, alone with *The Generation of '98*. *Fuera todos!** He retraced his steps.

Splendid! Here was just the sort of café he was looking for. A café where one could sit down, where there was no noise, and where there was nothing to disturb you. Naturally, with such qualities as this, the café was empty. Empty and vast: two hundred and fifty square metres and three customers. Yet in the old days it used to be full: the opponents of every successive political regime used to meet there, inexhaustible ratiocinators and unquenchable drinkers of water. Had the Franco regime no opponents? The décor had remained the same as in 1938, indeed the same as in the nineteenth century, pretty well. The owners were different from those in 1938: the present ones were very old, a man and his wife, pale and depressed, silent, with

---

* *Fuera todos!* "Everyone out!" A quasiritual expression whereby the matador instructs his *peones*, or subordinates, not to help him in the *faena*, the series of solo passes before the kill.

lack-lustre eyes. What did they live on? What could be the turnover of this establishment? No doubt they realized that first and foremost they would have to alter the place from top to bottom, make it more up-to-date, or at least a little cleaner. But what a labour! "It will see us out as it is," one could imagine them saying to one another.

At the door of the café there was an old man—another one! Celestino only seemed to notice the old—selling odds and ends—laces, matches, cigarillos—from a tiny box hung round his neck, as in Arab markets. There were many such paupers on the pavements. The *familia* would stuff an assortment of junk into a box and send them off, to get them out of the house, where they were a nuisance to one and all. Celestino noticed that this old man *was none other than he*, Celestino: exactly the same face, like his reflection in a mirror. Further on, there was another old man, and this other old man *was also his double*.

Looking out of the window, Celestino noticed that the shop across the street—he could not make out what sort of shop it was—bore the sign PATRICIA.

Attracted at first by the bitter title of his book, then remembering that Cuba was an Indian not a Spanish territory, Don Celestino started taking notes with a view to the article he would write—in the Café de Bondy the following week—comparing and contrasting the "antediluvian" attitude of the Spaniards when they lost Cuba in 1898 with the pride which a European nation must feel on handing over one of its colonies today. Life became nonexistent once more behind the double screen of the dead past and the printed paper. This could not be called "life"—the two taciturn bachelors, as it were shadows of Celestino, who were drinking, at the opposite ends of the café, one a beer, the other a Coca-Cola, now obviously the national drinks. Nor even the canon who, unable to fit his fat stomach under the table, sat sideways on and drank with his right elbow on the table.

Celestino stopped taking notes because it struck him that in this country anyone who wrote in public must quickly appear suspect. Already one of the customers had looked at him two or three times, he thought. He glanced through some illustrated magazines. A full-page advertisement for facial massage. Beside it, an article entitled: "The Liturgy for Everyman." A full-page advertisement for a fashion house. Beside it, an article entitled: "Daily Rosary for the Family." Celestino growled, forgetting the Parisian papers which give the same amount of attention to the imminent outbreak of civil war and the latest imbecilities of some idiotic film star or some idiotic princess of the blood.

Opposite him was a staircase coming up from the basement, where the kitchen and the cloakrooms were no doubt situated. At one moment a servingwoman stopped halfway up the stairs, in such a way that her head, on a level with the floor, looked as though it had been detached from her body; and she stared intently at Celestino, without turning away. Don Celestino was not a specialist in decapitation; habitual during the Rif wars, decapitation was rare during the civil war. The head disturbed him. Yet he stared back at it, with his gimlet eyes. Finally it disappeared. Once more, Celestino had achieved *dominio*.

The canon appeared to make a series of rapid signs of the cross. Was he trying to exorcise Celestino? But no, he was brushing away the flies.

Celestino frequently looked at his watch to see how much time he had left before he could go home to bed.

Ah, yes! He would telephone the hotel to ask if anyone (the police) had called round to see him. It was more to pass the time than because he was afraid. . . . No one had called, but the trouble was elsewhere.

He talked to himself, Ruiz still his imaginary interlocutor. No sound came from his lips, but he went through all the motions, as in the silent cinema. Nobody seemed surprised. He had been adopted.

At half-past seven Celestino returned to the police trap. He was so exhausted at the end of the day that all he wanted was to sleep. He had drunk several cups of chocolate and eaten a number of *churros* and stuffed olives in the café, so he was no longer hungry. As he was getting ready for bed, the telephone rang and a harsh, peremptory voice said:

"Come down at once!"

("This is it," thought Celestino. "It's them.")

"What do you want?"

The voice wavered and then subsided.

"Aren't you the floor waiter?"

"No, I'm staying in the hotel, Room 9."

"Oh, I'm so sorry!"

He put the receiver down, still quite calm. He felt that he should have been afraid, but he had not been afraid, as a patient who is being hacked about in a part of his body which has been given a local anaesthetic *feels* that he is being hacked about and that he ought to feel pain, but does not feel it.

He fell asleep on top of his bed with all his clothes on. Waking up again, he washed and undressed, and quickly fell asleep again, and slept without any disturbing dreams, something that rarely happened to him in Paris, where he had nothing to fear. In fact he had a rather pleasant dream.

A figure (man? woman?) offered him some sweets and asked him: "Do you like them very acid?" Psychoanalysts, over to you!

𝕄

Saturday morning. The three of them are sitting round him in a semicircle, intent on outwitting him, confusing him, making a fool of him. Don Celestino, alone, apart, the victim and the accused, surrounded by his three judges, bound hand and foot but glaring furiously at them, like an eagle nailed alive to a palisade. The room is dark, with dark mahogany furniture. On the wall opposite him, exactly opposite, a crucifix. On the wall to the right, a portrait of General Franco.

Surprisingly, it is the clerk in particular who is after his blood. A little runt of a man, cadaverous, ill-shaven and pockmarked, he has for some reason or other (politics, presumably) taken against Celestino. It is he who keeps slyly springing the trap which is intended to trip him up.

All this, of course, was foreseen long ago. And it is odd that he should keep asking himself: "Why did I come here?" He knows quite well why he came. To save himself from death by risking his life.

The lawyer is wearing a black suit with a stiff collar and spectacles. He makes an error in his calculations. Everyone bustles round trying to find the error. It is Celestino, in spite of his stupidity, who finds it first. He is so used to Moragas's mistakes that he regards it as perfectly natural, and points it out without malice. From that moment he senses that the lawyer hates him even more. Moragas seemed to take it for granted that he would make mistakes; he did not even bother to apologize for them, and carried on perfectly calmly. This lawyer, on the other hand, is annoyed,

and turns insolent: "In matters of this sort one is bound
to make mistakes," (meaning: "When one's a refugee,
everything is in a muddle.") Celestino, who should have
every reason to feel triumphant, realizes that on the contrary he is even guiltier than before, because the lawyer
has made a mistake. At this moment, his fountain pen dis-
charges a copious stream of black ink into his hand (black
being Celestino's natural colour, he could not have used
anything but black ink). Now he looks ridiculous, and the
little assurance left to him is even further reduced, until it
is as pale and weak as the remains of the ink when he has
been to the cloakroom to scrub it off, passing through a
strange vestibule in which there are greenhouse plants,
wickerwork armchairs, and cement walls painted to imitate
wood panelling.

Now he is back in his stall. The lawyer, the brother-in-
law (not to mention the clerk) are simply arrangements
of pieces of calcareous substance, connected with one another by meat, and then a system of fibres known as nerves,
and an indefinable something that enables this mechanism
to be malevolent to the point of atrocity, although the
tiniest thing—a bullet—would be enough to render it inoffensive for evermore. It was appalling, and at the same
time it was not serious, or rather it was serious only because everyone accepted the convention whereby it was
forbidden to destroy the mechanism. The civil war had
brought some sense into all this: people destroyed what it
was so easy to destroy. And now they had reverted to the
rules of the game.

As on the previous day, all Celestino's exertions were
directed not so much at understanding as pretending to
understand; in fact he heard but did not listen. Not that
he needed either to understand or to listen: the swindle

that was being hatched under his nose was so patent that a child could have rumbled it. And suddenly, when he was in the trough of the wave, he had an idea, the idea that he should have had before: on Monday he would refuse to sign anything, he would leave Madrid, return to Paris, and if Moragas would not or could not come to Madrid with power of attorney from him, Moragas at least would surely know of an honest man here who would be capable of looking after his interests.

From that moment he emerged from the depths, and at once his natural violence reasserted itself.

"I have the impression, my dear Vicente, that the only reason you were so keen to facilitate my journey here was that you preferred to deal with me than with someone more experienced in these matters . . ."

His voice had a resonant, staccato, slightly mad vehemence which surprised him; he was no longer in control of it. It is somehow rather disturbing to be aware that one is no longer in control of oneself. He was at once feeble and aggressive, as he had been fearful and reckless when he had taken the decision to come to Madrid. A mixture of violence and blindness, characteristic of the fighting bull. He was surprised to hear Vicente and the lawyer answer in a much more amenable tone. They no longer stared at him arrogantly, but spoke to him with their eyes turned away—Vicente looking at a calendar on the desk with a picture of St. Pancras and a New Year message, *Health, Peace, Work*, the clerk looking at a bronze paperweight representing a bull, and the lawyer, a bronze group representing Don Quixote and Sancho Panza decorating an inkstand—presents to the lawyer from satisfied clients, no doubt, or wedding presents from legal colleagues. Celestino looked at the electric light bulb hanging from the ceiling: the same shadeless bulb as in his hotel room and in the station waiting room at Irun. Nobody looked at anybody. And suddenly, just as Celestino was about to charge, he stopped. Vicente obviously had his entrée to the government, since he had obtained the visa so quickly; and he, Celestino, had a dossier in the government's files. Moral: Vicente must be humoured. When you are on the losing side, that's how it is.

Having reached this conclusion, Celestino's sole aim was to bring the session to an end as quickly as possible, by postponing the signing of the agreements until the day after his departure. Now he was amiability itself. Like many simple and straightforward men, an occasional piece of trickery amused him. It was in a mood of high good humour that he took a taxi to the hotel, where Pascualita might be waiting for him: he had arranged to meet her at about this time.

In the taxi he had a sudden flash of inspiration: he remembered who the bearded man was who had smiled at him the day before near San Gregorio. It was his colleague Captain Ricardo Aguirre, who had been killed by a bomb on January 3, 1939 at Artesa, and whom he had buried with his own hands.

Celestino was fairly pleased with himself when he arrived at the hotel. He did not even think of inquiring if anyone (the police) had asked for him. His daughter arrived almost immediately. They embraced, Pascualita bringing in the freezing cold on her cheeks and the tip of her nose. He was about to announce his decision to her—

which would give her no cause for complaint, since he was going to allow her to stay for a few more days in Madrid —when her unwontedly sparkling expression froze the words in his mouth. She was like a plant which has just received its ration of dew.

She sat down in the armchair.

"Well, what news from the lawyer?"

"Nothing new. We'll go on with the talks on Monday and Tuesday."

He was so accustomed to telling her nothing of any importance that silence once again came naturally to him. But lying came naturally to him too.

"I see the air of Madrid suits you down to the ground."

"Vicente is much nicer than we thought. He's taken a lot of trouble to show me round. We went to the Prado this morning and the Armería this afternoon. He's sorry I'm not staying longer."

Where was the rather washed-out girl of the past few months? Naturally there was the excitement of seeing new things and new places. And the pleasure of being away from him for two days. But wasn't there a positive liking for the society she had found here? And the way she seemed to be hitting it off with that horrible brother-in-law!

"I've told you time and again that Vicente is not a nice man. I'm a little hurt that you should get on with him so well so quickly."

"Are you sure he's not a nice man? You knew him a long time ago, but do you know what he's like today? When one's been away for twenty years . . ."

Celestino thought: "She's never criticized me before for having to live in exile because of my beliefs. This is *the first time* she has criticized me."

He wanted to destroy her at once. He flung her the deadly bait.

"I can see that you'd like to live in Madrid."

"Oh, yes!" Then quickly she added: "With you, of course."

For five years he had filled her up with the right ideas and true facts. But in the past three years they had been draining away imperceptibly, as if from a cracked vase. Today she was at ease in the midst of shame and slavery, at ease with a swindler lacking both character and conviction. Everything was happening as he had foreseen.—But, since he had foreseen it all, might he not have brought her here simply in order to catch her out? Certainly he had undertaken the journey out of a desire for danger, but had there also been an unconscious desire to lose her? Why had he agreed to her staying with Vicente, and thus spending most of her time with him and under his influence? He belonged to the old civil war generation, always full of *agents provocateurs*.

In the lawyer's office, when he had begun to charge, he had had to stop short because his brother-in-law had the whip hand. With her it was different: he could charge with impunity. Each man is cowardly after his own fashion.

"In the train, as we were nearing Hendaye, how you fluttered and fidgeted and prattled! You sensed the approach of fascism, and that's what excited you . . . You've been a fascist for at least three years. At first you were receptive to what I told you—when you were small—then you were indifferent, then hostile. Here at last you've thrown off the mask."

This time the muzzle of the "machine gun" was really spitting fire.

"I'm not a fascist; you're talking nonsense. But it's true

that I'd had enough of living among guttersnipes and sluts.* A country that's being led deliberately towards communism!"

"How secretive you were! What books did you read on the sly that poisoned your mind?"

"Yours. I read your entire library."

"And the priests too, I suppose? Perhaps you've been going to church without telling me."

"Yes, sometimes, when I couldn't bear it any longer."

"When you couldn't bear what any longer? Me?"

One day when she was seventeen she had bought a pair of shoes with heels of a type that had been usual up to then. Celestino had been displeased, and had told her that she ought to have bought shoes with "stiletto" heels, in other words ridiculously pointed heels which were coming into fashion just then. He did not want her to appear "backward" to her schoolfriends because she was a Spaniard. This had so exasperated Pascualita that for a time she felt like killing him. Then the impulse died down. Now it had returned. In Paris, during their interminable silences, she avoided looking at him—partly because a sixty-seven-year-old is not beautiful to look at, partly (in the end) because of the exasperation he caused her; she had gradually been worn down by exasperation as a fortress is worn down by bombardment: nothing can withstand exasperation. Now she looked him straight in the eyes, as though in less than two days Madrid had turned her into another woman. And what he read in her eyes was this: "Why have I become a fascist? I've become a fascist in order to be the opposite of what you are." As they had the same pattern of hair-growth, the forest between his shoulderblades and the thick

* *Golfos y golfas.*

down she had in the same place had begun to bristle simultaneously, while his hatred and her contempt crossed like two swordblades.

"*You* have found what you were looking for here. In the past two days *I* have found new reasons for believing what I believe."

Another lie. For two days, alone in his native city which aroused in him nothing but emptiness and gloom, taking refuge in a café to read an old, out-of-date book, failing to reawaken the feelings which he felt evaporating like everything else, which were no more than a habit of mind, he had thought only of regaining the land of his exile. But his passion revived now that there was a chance of using it to condemn his daughter for having none. Family hatred rekindled social hatred and roused it from its torpor, like a torpid snake that one warms up between one's palms. He was rejecting her in the name of an ideal which he had ceased to feel in himself. Nonexistence had become reality.

The "big scene" failed to materialize. The "twentieth century debate" did not take place. There was no point in saying anything more, for everything had been said. Looking at her with a blank, expressionless face, he murmured—and the murmur was more vehemently expressive than a shout:

"You disgust me."

It was she who got up. Her handkerchief fell. She stared at her father without a word, struck dumb as he himself had been when Ruiz had insulted him in the Square Willette. He had certainly had his revenge now.

She walked quickly to the door, and went out without closing it. Celestino picked up the handkerchief, threw it on to the landing, and shut the door.

Celestino, eaten up with civil war. War against the

fascists, intermittent warfare against each and every sub-
section of his party, intermittent warfare against each and
every province of his country (except Castile), war
against his friends, inner warfare between his socialism and
his egotism, between his socialism and his pseudofascism.
And now open war, war to the knife, against his own flesh
and blood, against his daughter. Total war within the civil
war. And this time, with his daughter, the end of the chain
of executions.

Narvaez, a Spanish general of the nineteenth century,
asked on his deathbed if he forgave his enemies, replied:
"I have no enemies. I've had them all shot."

🖂

Celestino sat down again. As his violence subsided, his
strength subsided too. In front of him he saw not only the
three judges of the day before—Vicente, the lawyer, and
the clerk—but also Pineda, Ruiz, and Pascualita—all in a
semicircle around him, standing there looking at him, and
waiting. Waiting for what? Waiting for him to stumble,
to collapse, and to die? Extraordinary coalition.

And he himself, alone, at bay, before them, staring at
them with dull, lack-lustre eyes, unable to understand what
was happening. He had not even understood Pascualita.
He had believed that there was *nothing* inside her; but
there was not *nothing;* there was fascism. He arranged the
situation in such a way that he was conscious of having
been deceived by all of them. And thus was utterly alone.
"I have no friends left, no country, no faith, and no
daughter."

He had a fit of hiccups, and thought he was going to
vomit—a vomiting of bile, the bile of his race, the bile of

his twenty years of bile, about to overflow at last. He went to fetch a towel, held it under his beard, and waited. But the hiccups stopped. Once more, everything resolved itself in silence.

Fortunately there was the bullfight tomorrow: the only good thing in the whole business (he took the two tickets out of his wallet, and tore up Pascualita's; he could have given it to someone—a stranger—but he did not feel like giving pleasure to anyone). After that, he must return to Paris as soon as possible. And without either his daughter or Vicente knowing of his departure, in case of scenes. How would he explain it to them from Paris? Never mind, he would see about that when he got there. Probably he would put forward (with due caution) some political reason. Fleeing his country once more, as he had done twenty years before. And fleeing once more from Franco-ites: his brother-in-law and his daughter.

First he must act; he could think later. Panic brought back to life the man of decision who had been dormant for twenty years. In its first stage, panic gives wings; in the second, it cuts one's legs (and wings, of course) from under one; he was in the first stage. He must ask the hotel manager to send up a railway timetable, tell him that he felt unwell and was leaving tomorrow evening; get him to cope with everything.

He must put off packing until the last moment (tomorrow, on his return from the bullfight), in case Pascualita or Vicente forced his door.

Immediate action. The manager came up. There was a train at 10:20 in the evening, which arrived the following afternoon at 5 o'clock. The manager would get him the ticket.

If Pascualita or Vicente came round or telephoned that night, they were to be told he was asleep. If they called early next morning, they were to be told that he was still asleep, if late, that he had gone out. If they called after he had returned from the bullfight to pack, they were to be told that he was not yet back. He showed the manager his bullfight ticket, in a mood of feigned expansiveness, to prove that he was not a hunted man, that he was as free as air. If the manager thought he was on the run, he might call the police.

Celestino ordered two cups of chocolate and some *churros,* the same supper as the night before. All things considered, everything had gone very well. But in that case, why was it so terrible?

His supper was brought, but he was not hungry. He had made up his mind. Now, alas, was the time for reflection. Action had been coherent; reflection was less so.

Pascualita would stay in Madrid for good—would marry a brilliant officer. He would be alone in the rue de Lancry. Everything he had gone through was as nothing compared with what awaited him. It is not so much the ordeal itself that frightens one as the knowledge that one will not have the strength of mind to bear it: not so much an external object as one's own weakness. Whom would he talk to, he who so loved talking? And who would talk to him in return, who would save him from the slippery slope of despair down which he was beginning uncontrollably to slide, with that maelstrom of despair at the bottom in which he would be whirled away? And where would he fall ill? Where would he spend his last days? Where would he die? In hospital, no doubt. Now that monstrous plan to keep Pascualita near him to help him on his deathbed had been

undone. To be looked after by a right-wing girl! To be
touched by a right-wing girl! No, Moragas would take
care of everything. But how horrible it was to be dependent on a single person, and a person who had refused to
come to dinner with him because he considered him stupid,
boring, and socially unimportant! The man of Christ his
only sheet-anchor! Celestino remembered a remark of
Lazarillo de Tormes* in which he proposed to spend the
rest of his life "doing nothing but making friends." He
too now seriously thought of trying to make at least *one*
friend, in case Moragas died. A useful friend, like Pineda.

Suddenly—strange that he had not thought of it before,—
it struck him that all the money he was going to try to
recover through Moragas would go to her. His money go
to her! His money go to a little fascist couple, to a little
fascist captain of a son-in-law! He would rather throw his
money into the Seine. Or else . . . Or else . . . How did one
go about disinheriting a daughter? . . . But he turned his
head away, and retreated.

Celestino still could not eat. As when the train was approaching Irun, he felt his knees and the upper surface of
his thighs grow cold. It was his soul that was growing cold.

The telephone rang—God! It must be her!—The hotel
receptionist must have "eaten" his instructions. That, too,
was to have been expected.

"I'm sorry for what I said: you made me lose my temper.
Forgive me."

"All right."

"You're not cross with me?"

"I'll get over it."

---

* Hero of a famous novel by Hurtado de Mendoza (16th century).

"We're still lunching together tomorrow before going to the bullfight?"

(So that was her motive in telephoning. Prepared to do anything to get to the bullfight, just as she had been prepared to do anything to get to Madrid.)

"I tore up your ticket in a fit of temper."

"You did that!"

"You won't miss anything, it's a very ordinary bullfight. And I shall allow you to stay in Madrid until next Sunday's fight. You can go with Vicente. I shall go back alone on Monday or Tuesday."

"I'm glad you're letting me stay another week in Madrid. You don't need to worry about my sentiments."

(Alas, the truth had already been spoken.)

"Good. But don't go to the bullfight in Puente Real."

"No, now that I'm going to the one in Madrid. Will I see you tomorrow morning or after the bullfight?"

"I shall be going to the lawyer's office on Monday morning. We can lunch together on Monday."

(He would not have been out with her for three whole days. A flash of lucidity showed him that everything he was doing was extremely odd.)

"See you on Monday, then. *Je t'embrasse.*"

"*Moi aussi, je t'embrasse.*"

Deceiving one's daughter in a barefaced way is not a pleasant thing to do. But one has the right to deceive a fascist. Did not the Cid deceive the Jews?* Besides, hadn't Pascualita deceived him for years by keeping things from him?

His effort not to lose his temper had lasted only an in-

* The Cid—a model of "chivalry"!—owing money to some Jews leaves them a chest filled with stones instead of gold.

stant—the time to exchange half a dozen sentences—but the
strain had been such that when he put down the receiver
he felt a sort of dizziness, and his forehead throbbed with
neuralgia, which lasted the rest of the evening.

Sleep! Sleep! What else is there to do but sleep when one
is suffering? Tomorrow night he would be gone, and the
day after, France—that heartwarming country with its un-
emptied dustbins and cars on the pavements! But what if
he found on his arrival a note from Marie-France telling
him that she had found another job and would call round
in a week's time to collect her wages? Yes, that was what
awaited him: the worst is always certain. Who would find
him another servant? Moragas? But what if Moragas, out-
raged at his having "abandoned" his daughter, confined
himself strictly to money matters, refusing to have anything to do with anything else? For a moment Celestino
contemplated the ultimate humiliation: going to see Pineda,
apologizing for his nastiness and blaming it on Ruiz, beg-
ging him to renew his old friendship (meaning: Pineda-
the-helpful) . . . He dismissed the idea.

Whichever way he turned, he could see nothing but
cause for woe. Still, there was always the bullfight; he
clung to the bullfight. But would he still get any pleasure
from a bullfight? He did not know. Besides, would the
hired car turn up? No, it would not. He pounced on the
telephone to call the garage. The telephone was out of
order. If the car failed to turn up, how would he spend
the whole day? Remain in the hotel waiting for the police,
his brother-in-law, and his daughter? (It did not even occur
to him that in Madrid, as everywhere else, ordinary taxis
will do short out-of-town trips.) No, he would spend the
day in a café. But what to read? He had finished *The*

Generation of '98, and the newspaper kiosks would be closed on a Sunday. Panic-stricken in advance at the thought of solitude, he grabbed the telephone again with trembling hands. The garage answered: the car would be there on time. Celestino drank a whole cup of his chocolate, which had gone cold. He sent a waiter out to buy all the bullfight papers he could lay hands on, for him to read next morning in the café. Impatient as ever, like all desperate men, he lost his temper with the waiter. From the depths of his abyss, he was still in command.

Although he was usually so meticulous, the front of his black jacket and the knees of his black trousers were now grey with all the cigarette ash that had fallen on them while he meditated in his armchair. He brushed it off vaguely.

"Calm, my soul, calm! Enough of these ridiculous and sordid trifles. What do they amount to compared to the war? Yes, but in the war we had all our strength, the strength of our muscles and the strength of our faith, faith in a cause, if not hope in that cause; things still had some meaning; we were another Celestino Marcilla. Is it our fault if our entire life has become ridiculous and sordid, if there is now no more faith than there is hope?—Yes, it must be our fault."

The car would come, but the bullfight would be cancelled because of a snow storm; the only things left would be arrest—*at the last moment*—and an attack of pneumonia in an ill-heated prison, so that all that had been foreseen should come to pass. Celestino went to open the window, pulling up the Venetian blinds, to examine the sky. It was the same sky as during the daytime, but with the dark steel colour of night. The cold seemed even sharper. Below, the maids were still singing, chatting to one another in an argu-

mentative tone, then quarrelling outright, then bursting into
song again.

> *Quieréme, quieréme mucho,*
> *Como si fuera esta noche*
> *La última vez.**

If he opened the window wide and stood there with his
torso bare, he could be certain to catch pneumonia, and
that would simplify everything. There was only one way
out: to cease to exist. But no, he must not die in Madrid!
In Paris, yes, but not in Madrid! To be left without attention, on purpose, to be badly nursed, on purpose—murdered, perhaps, with injections—by fascist nurses, who
would have learnt who he was from his brother-in-law . . .
"Have I begun to rave a little, as a result of being so helpless and upset?" He clenched his fists. "I mustn't go mad.
The day after tomorrow, perhaps, in Paris, because Moragas will be there. But not here, not here!"

He went to open the other window. Over there, above
the wealthy districts, the sky glowed pink from the lights
of the city. Nearby, but clearly separated, above old
Madrid and the districts inhabited by those whom Tolstoy
calls "the obscure," the sky too was obscure. Two cities,
the Madrid that smells of petrol and the Madrid that smells
of Araby. And two skies, the sky of the bright ones and
the sky of the obscure ones, as they were yesterday and as
they would be tomorrow.

In the courtyard below, the obscure ones were still singing their heads off.

> * *Love me, love me again,*
> *As though tonight was*
> *The last time.*

Bésame, bésame mucho
Que tengo miedo perderte,
*Perderte otra vez.**

Suddenly, from the direction of the street, there was a
shattering noise (perhaps two cars colliding), and Celestino
threw himself back and retreated to the other end of the
room. In dangerous cities, one must keep away from
windows.

> * *Kiss me, kiss me again,*
> *For I fear to lose you,*
> *To lose you once more.*

VII

BULLFIGHT SUNDAY! Happy Sunday! And yet the morning started badly; he had scarcely opened his eyes before fear was upon him again. Fear! For the third time since his arrival in Spain the situation had changed focus: first under the cloud of fear, which had then disappeared, then formed again. The first thing he did was to look at his watch: in twenty-four hours he would have crossed the frontier. How terrifying twenty-four hours can be when they stand between you and safety! Last night, the scene with Pascualita had warmed him up and thus sustained him. But the night, a sinister night without dreams or nightmares—nightmares belonged to reality—had emptied him of everything. After nine hours of rest, he awoke feeling so weak that he coughed when he had to lift the armchair a little in order to move it. He had only one idea: to get out of the police trap as soon as possible, and only to come back to it after the bullfight to pack his suitcase. Ah, yes, the bullfight—he had forgotten about that. He lifted the blind. The sky was so white that a dove could have flown across it without being seen. The bullfight would be on.

In the courtyard, someone was whistling, uninterruptedly. If he went on like that on the same note, it must be the police. If there were several notes, it was someone whistling for fun. The whistling stopped.

Celestino went without breakfast, in order to get away more quickly. He settled the hotel bill: a good moment, which gave him the sensation of having already left Madrid.

And there he was once more in the street. The evil genius of his suffering led him back—this man who was no longer capable of anything except reading and writing—to the strange place where twice before he had gone to ground—to that café haunted with ghosts and debris which was now the only place where, buried once more in printed paper, he could recover some sort of peace and equilibrium. Even as he made his way there, he avoided looking at the crowd, avoided, almost, raising his eyes. For twenty years he had ceased to look; now he was no longer capable of looking. And then, tomorrow night, he would have finished with Spain forever—forever, do you understand? *Forever and ever!* So what was the point of looking at Spaniards? The fewer he saw the better.

He had not noticed that it was colder than the day before. But twice he saw people greeting one another with a "How cold it is!" And then he shivered. The icy wind from the mountains of Guadarrama.

He was so anxious to be gone that already his short stay had taken on the unreality of a dream. His imagination pushed it into the past, where it grew dimmer.

Fear of being arrested, fear not so much of death as of the preliminaries, the trappings of death, which would make it, as it were, a double death, disillusionment with his beliefs, the self-disgust he now felt for the first time at the monstrousness that characterized all his behaviour (especially with his daughter), the feeling of being already half-dead since he no longer had a grip on reality—all these convulsive knots which events and his own temperament had tied around him had brought him to such a pitch of anguish that his legs nearly gave way under him. However much he lowered his eyes, he could not help seeing the cinema signs and their comforting titles: *Death at the*

Crossroads; Provisional Liberty; A Man Must Die. And a hundred yards further on, yet another: *Ten Men Must Die.* They had multiplied: one for every ten yards. And once more the claws of the Lion of Castile gripped his heart. All was nightmare, and he stared at it with empty eyes.

He could not help seeing also—so strange the spectacle was (but was he not dreaming?)—a herd of animals pass by, the cars stopping in front of them: the billy-goat with his mauve beard, the heifers with their vernal udders; a tiny calf, with dark circles under its eyes, giving a paw to its mother and hopping along on three legs. This happened in the avenue of giant baobabs which the people of Madrid call la Rambla. What a country! And what an age!

In the café, he sat at the same table as the day before: only the second time he had been there, but already he had his little habits. But when he raised his eyes he could no longer see the sign PATRICIA. He spent a long time scrutinizing the shopfronts opposite, and had to admit that the sign could only have existed in his imagination.

He lowered his eyes, with a presentiment that he would also fail to find the stairway entrance where the severed head had appeared. And indeed he did not find it. He asked the waiter if there was a basement. The waiter said there was not, that the kitchens and the cloakrooms were across the backyard.

When he had breakfasted he felt better, and then realized that for one reason or another he had eaten very little since he had arrived in Madrid and in consequence was hungry. He decided to have lunch in a good restaurant (for tourists), a glorious Spanish lunch which he suddenly longed for. He had not eaten well for twenty years, regarding French cooking as over-rated and exorbitant.

He heard someone near him say "Snow . . ." He looked:

tiny flakes were falling. There would certainly be a snow-storm in the mountains, and the bullfight would be cancelled. The bullfight was no more than an anaesthetic which would drag him out of himself for two hours (four including the journey): something which for two hours or four hours would provide a relief from the tension and turmoil he had experienced with the lawyer, with Pascualita, and with himself. Strangely enough, though an anaesthetic was what he most needed at the moment, whether the bullfight happened or not meant nothing to him.

An excellent meal and a succulent cigar, conducive to a mood that was not a bad mood, but rather a bad frame of mind, and a frame of mind by no means disagreeable to the person concerned.

This frame of mind had to do with bullfighting in general, and with the particular bullfight he was about to witness. Celestino had spent the morning reading the bull-fighting press.

There is something frenzied about the literature of tauromachy—in the eulogizing of the maestros—which had exasperated him to a point which was scarcely rational. A man of Celestino's temperament has a horror of enthusiasm. No longer was he the accused (as he had been at the lawyer's office the day before). Now, even before getting out of the car and taking his *barrera* seat, he was the judge. And a judge whose verdict had already been reached before the case was opened. Only yesterday, in connection with his daughter, Celestino had revived the civil war, which had died in his heart two days ago. Now he had

revived it again. It was no longer a matter of killing such
and such a matador according to whether he was right-
wing or left-wing, which was the idea before and during
the war. It was a block verdict: to wit, that everything the
toreros did that afternoon would be bad.

Celestino arrived at Puente del Progreso at a quarter to
five, after a bumpy drive of an hour and a half during which,
four or five times, he thought he was being followed by
police cars, but each time the suspect car had turned off
down a side road. The whole village smelt of *retama*, a little
mountain flower. The bullring was a gasometer, blueish
against the grey-black sky flecked here and there with yellow, flanked by two iron chimneystacks which were not
smoking because it was Sunday. The gasometer style irritated Celestino, like the skyscrapers of Madrid: too obvious
sops to the Left. He would have been equally irritated had
he found a decrepit bullring crowned with a chapel.

There are all sorts of tricks in the world of tauromachy.
One of them consists in trying to penetrate the back-stage
area of a bullring before a *corrida*. These quarters are fairly
strictly prohibited except to those concerned. Among those
concerned are always a few ragged urchins and a stray dog.
Celestino slipped in on the heels of a civic guard: the height
of sadism.

Little courtyards thronged with attendants, urchins,
picadors who had arrived early to test their mounts, gentlemen enthusiasts. As these gentlemen were also smoking
cigars—this being a rite—the smell of Havana mixed with
the smell of horse-dung. On a white wall, all the drovers
who had ever accompanied a batch of bulls here had suc-
cessively inscribed their names and the crest of their herd.
The picadors walked like penguins. The bullring attend-

ants, old choir-boys of the taurine cult (except that their shirts were red instead of their skirts), were dressing ghost-horses, already injected with morphine, blocking their ears by tying them up with string to prevent them from being frightened by the noise, preparing the implements of the cult, *banderillas*, cascades of ribbon, rosettes for the mules, etc., which looked like souvenirs. The nags, all pitted and lacerated by the bulls' horns, covered with congealed blood, and wrapped in their patched quilts that might have covered the beds in some sordid hotel (shading from scarlet to the washed-out wine-lees of Moroccan fabrics) were dozing peacefully. The monumental mules, twice as tall as bulls, wagged their tails frantically with pride when rosettes in the national colours were tied to them. They too had scars, goodness knows from what, but one had to be in the swim. Their wounds, and their eyes, were surrounded with flies. For everywhere, as in Irun station, the flies were having a field day, in spite of the weather—infatuated by the dirt, which made them forget the cold.

Celestino was as apathetic as he had been in the streets of Madrid; he felt nothing, literally nothing. What he was waiting for was the matadors: the five-footed beasts before the four-footed ones. The *corrida* was to begin at five o'clock. The five-footed beasts make a point of arriving at the latest at eight or seven minutes to: ritual again. At eight minutes to five, there they were. The urchins gave them a tap on the shoulder: another bit of ritual. An aeroplane flew low, in order to increase the excitement, and the sleeping horses woke up and showed their yellow teeth.

The Romans called a handsome youth *pulchellus*. The French expression *beau gosse* is an exact translation of this (the appalling Clodius is nicknamed *pulchellus* by Cicero.)

By antiphrasis, the Italians called a deformed person *pulcinello*, whence the French *polichinelle*.* (This "discovery" is mine, and I am not a little proud of it.) The *cuadrillas* of the bullfight are composed of *pulchelli*—the matadors—and *pulcinelli*—their assistants. Disgustingly youthful the matadors were, and Celestino hated them at sight. He had always hated youth, and he himself had never been young. Where did they put their bowels, in order to be as slim as that? Yet they *had* bowels, because sometimes the bulls disembowelled them. And those light costumes, for the sake of comfort; in his day, they wore heavier costumes. And their mania for showing off their frontal assets! And the vulgarity of their bright pink stockings, gypsy pink! Like the detective in the beret, they were flanked by their *pulcinelli*, scruffy little old men, deformed by lack of exercise, heavy brown pockets under their eyes, little old men without either heads or legs; in fact, white-faced or rather blue-faced, with a week's growth of beard, they looked as if they had been raised from the dead. In short, dandies and dotards; only the picadors were normal men. And all of them, with their roses and gold braid and false hair** and bright-red ties and costumes both provocative and in some cases putrescent (on one of them, enormous patches of sweat that the cleaner had been unable to remove were outrageously visible), in the midst of people dressed like you and I, looked like clowns waiting to go on stage: there was something about them that degraded human dignity. Were they not ashamed of exhibiting themselves in this way? Ideologically, Celestino abhorred disguises—with the exception of Carnival disguises, of course. A resplendent

* And the English "Punch"—Translator's note.
** The *coleta*, an artificial chignon.

torero now seemed to him ridiculous: in his eyes, any costume meant a charlatan, or a presumptive charlatan.

But basically what Celestino wanted was to desecrate,
dishonour, destroy, trample underfoot everything he had
ever loved, sink under a sea of bile his old passion for bullfighting, just as he had already sunk Ruiz, Pineda, his
daughter, and, in the past few days, Spain, the revolution,
etc. . . . And doubtless his political activity—his political
philosophy, assuming him to have such a thing—had always
been directed towards destroying, as it were, the obverse
side of a medal, which is the important side, whilst what
he dreamed of constructing was simply the reverse side of
the same medal. But at the moment his urge to destroy had
another motive: since he himself was to disappear, everything else must disappear, there must be nothing left after
him, nothing for him to regret. . . .

Now comes the poignant moment when the *toreros* have
a pressing desire to go to the lavatory. A natural desire,
and one that is aggravated by funk. But they are due to
enter the ring in five minutes, and there can be no trifling
with punctuality when it comes to the start of a bullfight.
In any case, it would be equally impossible to go to the
lavatory if they had more time in front of them: the long
cummerbund that encircles a bullfighter's waist can only
be wrapped and unwrapped by an aide, and it is an interminable operation. So they are stuck. For an hour and a
half to two hours they will have to exercise *dominio* not
only over the bull, the audience, perhaps the elements, and
their own *virtu*, always precarious, but also over their
bowels. Quite a variety of bulls!

Now Celestino rushes posthaste to find his seat, his ticket
clutched tight in his hand. He would trample over his

mother's corpse rather than arrive after the *cuadrillas* have
marched out.

Now he is in his place at the *barrera*. The gasometer is
more than half-empty: spectators perched on the tubular
tiers at the back, black and isolated like swallows on tele-
graph wires or notes on a stave. A good number of eccle-
siastics, blacker still. Latecomers hurry along vertiginous
gangways almost without handrails. The bullring is domi-
nated by a *mirador* in which a man is standing. It is impossible to see whether he is armed, but he probably is, in
order to massacre either the spectators, or the bullfighters,
or the bulls, or all of them, as need arises (so Celestino
assumed). The higher tiers are surmounted with advertising
posters. In the ring, whose dark-grey sand looks as though
it had been borrowed from a cinder-track, a man in a
peaked cap is dragging round an old nag which in its turn
is dragging a cart bearing a placard reading: LITTLE
BRIGITTE BARDOT. This is an advertisement for a local
cinema. When the nag faints, the man gives it a jab with
a stiletto to restore it to health. Then the blood that flows
from it is seen to have traced in the sand a circular inscription: *SEXY Cigarettes—the Best—*Signed: B.B.

On the other side of the bullring, along the front row of
seats, the words ORDEN (administration), ARRASTRE
(the mules that drag away the dead bull) and BANDERIL-
LEROS are inscribed in enormous letters similar to the
advertisement hoardings. These hoardings indicate the po-
sitions where the three above-mentioned categories are
stationed during the bullfight until their participation, essential or hypothetical, is required. Yet, for two hundred
years every Spaniard without a single exception has done
without hoardings and knows perfectly well where the

administration, the *arrastre*, and the *banderilleros* are stationed during a bullfight, and in any case, even if they did not know, what would it matter? It was as though, in a circus, there was an enormous notice in letters three feet high marked CLOWNS' ENTRANCE above the door through which the clowns come on, and another marked ORCHESTRA above the platform where the band makes its noises. And all this was so unbelievably idiotic, so obviously conceived by imbeciles who treat everyone else as imbeciles, that Celestino immediately assumed that it must have been inspired by the Americans. We shall see later on why he was unable to verify this.

Above the *toril*, a loudspeaker strikes up one of the old traditional tunes: now Spain is trying to appear Spanish. The folding doors leading from the inner courtyards open. The matador in red makes a spectacular sign of the cross. The matador in green rearranges his flies. The matador in brown tightens his tie. The *peones* look as though they are trying to hide their spoilt priests' faces behind these young gentlemen. Then the *cuadrillas* march past. One of the *peones* is a dwarf. He is given an ovation, because he is a dwarf. He has to come out and take a bow all by himself.

First of all there was a whole cavalcade of deadbeat horses, excessively gay and playful and totally oblivious to the fate that awaited them. Then it was the turn of the bull, which had hardly entered the ring before it was giving a bravura exhibition, galloping to and fro in the same way as the horses and with the same regrettable frivolity. However, Celestino was solely preoccupied with the question of whether its horns had been shaved or not. He had learnt from the newspapers some years before that horn-shaving had been banned by the government. And he had grumbled at this because it was a good measure and it had been taken by Franco. But luckily he had discovered soon afterwards that horn-shaving had reappeared *sub rosa*. Whence he concluded that the horns of this particular bull had been shaved (which they had not).

Celestino soon realized that the gang of spoiled priests, in everything they did, were doing precisely the opposite of what they should have done. They should have been preparing, and preparing conscientiously, the bull for the matador. Far from it: out of professional incapacity they were doing all that was most fatal both for the bull and for the matador, inculcating the worst habits in the beast, the very habits which should have been eliminated or discouraged in the interests both of the matador and the art itself. Out of incapacity? It must nevertheless be noted that all their actions coincided as though by chance with the sole object of the *peones* in the ring, which boiled down to avoiding being killed.

"Brown" (the matador dressed in brown) then proceeded to execute a series of passes identical with those that used to be executed just before the civil war: standing on the tip of his toes with feet together, back arched, head bent—the self-same attitude as represented in hundreds and thousands of photographs published in the illustrated papers for twenty if not forty-seven years (Belmonte, 1912). It was the height of cliché, and cliché was what the public craved, applauded, and insisted upon.

Celestino affected not to know even the names of the three matadors, so insignificant did they seem. In fact he had identified them not only from their photographs but from the talk among his neighbours. But he referred to them in his mind as "Brown," "Green," and "Red," according to the colour of their costumes. He knew in advance that they were interchangeable and did not deserve to have names.

However, it was just about then that Celestino, being not entirely bereft of insight, realized that he was not altogether sure that he understood the psychology of this bull or the handling it required. There were also certain passes which he would have been incapable of naming, even though they were as old as the hills. Like an enormous body of water bursting through when the floodgates are opened, amnesia had broken loose and enveloped his mind. He was acutely aware of the need to keep his mouth shut or to reply circumspectly on certain matters, as with the Communists or at the lawyer's office, should an *aficionado* want to talk to him afterwards about the fight. He who had been not only a supreme connoisseur but a practitioner! And although the consciousness of his unfairness pleased him rather, the consciousness of the enfeeblement of his mind opened up a yawning gulf inside him. In spite of this, however, he continued to pass judgment on the activities of the *toreros*, which was not difficult since there was never any question but of running them down.

The president of the *corrida* fulfilled a sacred function, which was to direct and control the bullfight. As he was in the highest degree incompetent, he had somebody competent beside him, who surreptitiously directed it himself. The president brought to his lips a little spittoon perched on the end of a metal rod. It was an apparatus into which all the notabilities in the world (you can see it from here) vomited either nonsense or lies, which the spittoon amplified ad infinitum: no one was supposed to miss a syllable. The president spoke a few words into the spittoon, but as it was known to amplify a great deal, he said them in such a low voice, so as not to tire himself out, that the spittoon, amplify though it did, could not make them heard. Whereupon the president abandoned the spittoon, took out his pocket handkerchief, glanced at it to make sure it was clean, then waved it daintily, and everyone understood at once. They understood that he was ordering the cavalry to come on stage.

The first picador removed his bifocal spectacles in order to be able to see, and taking careful aim, drove some two-thirds of his pic into the hide of the bull. The pic nearly came out through the beast's chest, but he stopped it just in time. This excellent pic-thrust nevertheless displeased the purists among the spectators, not to mention the bull. This was to fail to recognize one of the basic rules of modern tauromachy, to wit, that the bull must be more or less killed by the picadors, who must leave him on his last legs in order to allow their bosses to shine. The other picadors did their best to emulate their colleague. The audience protested as a matter of form; the matador shouted to his picador: "Enough! Enough!"; the picador had another go; and thus chivalry was safe, the Cid remained inviolate, and the game was up. It sometimes happened that the horses, out of weakness and fear, collapsed before the bull even touched them. This made them laugh, for it was really screamingly funny, and curving their long and graceful necks in the air like snakes or swans, they died laughing.

The president once more waved his handkerchief, indicating that it was time for the placing of the *banderillas*. Celestino thought of the men who used to slink along the walls waving white handkerchiefs with both hands to stop one from shooting at them from the windows. "Ah! so you haven't taken sides? Well, we'll soon show you what good that does you." Bang!—Come to think of it, why not shoot the president?

Then, with "Brown" in action, a real circus act began: the placing of the *banderillas*, or rather the "artistic preparation" for this operation. He advanced by putting one foot immediately in front of the other; made graceful and inviting gestures to the bull with his arms; bent his head to right and to left; twisted his buttocks; flaunted, exposed, offered his codpiece ostentatiously to the horns—the whole thing meretricious and interminable and moreover identical, down to the smallest detail, with what used to be done thirty-five years before: in other words, stale.

This "artistic preparation" irresistibly reminded Celestino of the "artistic preparation" for the serving of a meal in smart Parisian restaurants (where he had twice taken Moragas). They present the dish for your inspection before cooking it (as though you were free to say: "It looks absolutely disgusting. Take it away at once"). They turn the splendid bottle of wine in the ice bucket. They pour you out a third of a glass (why a third?). The champagne bottle has to be wrapped in a napkin, etc., etc. The whole thing stinks of humbug, impresses only fools, and under the pretence of refinement is extremely vulgar, for simplicity is the only true refinement. Vulgar and insulting: "Who do you take me for, trying to impress me with petty tricks like that?"

If all this had served to get the bull lined up, it would still have been otiose, because five or six of these gestures would have sufficed instead of thirty; but it would have been merely otiose. In this case it was worse; it was odious as well as otiose: for it was all happening outside the bull's

angle of vision, in other words out of danger, as completely out of danger as if the *torero* had been separated
from the bull by an iron grill. It was not simply a fraud,
it was the quintessence of fraud. The dandy stopped at last,
and turning towards the audience, invited applause. Which
the audience provided, in abundance. For what the audience liked and wanted was precisely that: fraud. Here,
elsewhere, everywhere. Yesterday, today, tomorrow, always.

Seeing them in the bullring, Celestino despised the tricks
he had mimicked with the motorcars in the boulevard
Saint-Martin, even though, when all was said and done, he
had done so with the same sordid object as the *toreros*: to
reduce the risk.

Then "Brown," abandoning his fraudulent posturing,
finally did the decent thing. He approached to within a
reasonable distance of the animal, controlled its eye and
head with a few swift gestures, leapt forward as he should,
and placed a good pair. He was applauded once more, but
Celestino knew that what was being applauded was not the
good pair, but the charm act. The boy was perfectly capable
of doing the right thing if he wanted to, but was prostitut-
ing himself out of a desire to please. The bull, which was
of an affable nature, also patently wanted to please.

A *banderillero*, who as a subordinate was not entitled to
indulge in "artistic" affectations, cited the bull rapidly and,
without any fuss, placed a very successful pair, far superior
to that of his boss. A score of spectators applauded. Seriousness doesn't pay.

When it came to the *muleta*, "Brown" made three aesthetic passes, then stopped, and looking up at the crowd,
solicited more applause, which was immediately forthcom-

ing. Then another three aesthetic passes and another pause for applause. Then a third time. The crowd, as stupid as the bull, obliged each time.

At each successive outburst, tilting above the arena, anonymous birds streaked across the sky like tracer bullets.

Then "Brown" made some beautiful and extremely daring passes, which drew shouts of excitement from the spectators. But Celestino, who was brave (which did not prevent him from being afraid, as we know), was not a man who was much impressed by bravery, or who was satisfied by it. And he had decided that with "Brown" temerity was a substitute for competence, a phenomenon which he recognized from having observed it during the war both in himself and others. So that each suicidal pass the young man made was placed not on the credit side but on the debit side. Even if "Brown" had said, like Briand: "Does one have to get oneself killed in order to prove one's sincerity?" and got himself killed out of sheer bravery, the old man would still have maintained, over his very corpse, these superior airs which rather resembled those which his daughter adopted towards him.

Moreover, although he considered it respectable for men to risk their lives for political motives, the fact that others might risk theirs in order to earn money and because they enjoyed it, like matadors and trapezists, or simply because they enjoyed it, like mountaineers, did not seem to him, and had never seemed to him, worthy of respect. He had never felt particularly proud of himself when, as a young man, like thousands of other young Spaniards, he risked his life in little amateur *corridas*.

Denigration is a self-sufficient passion. But in Celestino it had the profound roots which we have described. Moreover, Celestino had no feelings about this *corrida*, and the

dramatic universe from which he was excluded provided
him with additional proof of his old age and imminent
death; unjust and vicious by virtue of the decision he had
made before even arriving at the bullring, he was also unjust and vicious in the way that a frigid woman is when
she bites and scratches a man who does not satisfy her. And
yet, though his insensibility was painful to him, the injustice it engendered caused him pleasure rather, just as it had
when he had unjustly liquidated Pineda. His injustice
sustained him, he used it as a prop; it was part of his energy.

Besides, where was the justice here? Not in the ring,
which was called, presumably as a joke, "the terrain of
truth," for, though everything there seemed honest, everything was in fact *dis*honest. Not on the terraces, where the
general public was incompetent and ignorant and the press
—from time immemorial—was in the pay of the matadors'
impresarios. He, Celestino, was unjust out of genuine passion. But they were unjust out of ignorance or out of
cupidity.

In addition to all this, a little incident that had happened
that very morning had stirred up his bile. The waiter in
the café, seeing him rather at a loss having finished reading
the bullfighting papers, had lent him, with amiable Spanish
egalitarianism, a book of his which was a rave biography
of the man whom the Spaniards considered to be the greatest matador of the twentieth century. And Celestino had
noticed that one out of every three photographs of the
hero in action, intended to show the sublime quality of his
style, was a *montage*—a montage so crude that anyone
without too dull an eye or obtuse a brain could have
spotted it at once: the picture of the bull was artificially
joined to the picture of the man, in order to give the impression that the pass was "closer," and the man in greater

danger, than they were in reality. Certainly the man did risk his life, since he had died in the bullring. Nevertheless, the imposture was flagrantly there, and it had filled Celestino with disgust.

"Brown" executed four so-called "statuary" passes. This very term "statuary" indicated very clearly that it was not so much a question of fighting a bull as of embodying a jejune and simpleminded view of aesthetics: so, at any rate, thought Celestino, who, having always hated art, and hated youth, could not but be sickened by "statuary" passes.

Still, whatever the merits or demerits of "statuary" passes, "Brown" spoilt everything by his conclusion. Having finished his series of passes, he knelt on one knee, called for his *montera* (hat) and hung it on one of the horns: back to the circus. The bull, with a headdress dangling from its horn, looked a proper mug, like a performing dog wearing a pink hat. But the matador, beaming with self-satisfaction and turning once more to the crowd to beg for applause, was intolerable.

Furthermore, "Brown"—as his colleagues were to do after him—had executed all his *muleta* passes while holding in his hand a *wooden* sword! He exchanged it for a real sword when the time came for the kill. These young gentlemen mustn't overstrain themselves! A killer with a wooden sword—what was one to think of the frame of mind that tolerated such degeneracy?

A terrified *peon* dropped his cape under the bull's feet. The bull became tangled in it, dragging it round the ring. Thus everyone was ridiculous, and this was as it should be.

"Brown" showed himself brief and efficient at the kill. While he was making his tour of the ring, lifting up his triumphant little mug to acknowledge the cheers, with his hand on his heart like a provincial tenor, Celestino sat pro-

testing, frozen in the silence and immobility of stone. The
black masses of party justice are familiar with these faces
locked by holy insincerity.

Disappointing the almost unanimous expectations of the
crowd, the dead bull failed to rise up to receive its share
of the applause.

The trumpets sounded the arrival of the second bull, and
the gate of the *toril* opened. But there was nothing to be
seen except the black depths of the *toril*, gaping and empty.

This lasted for some time, and the spectators and ring
attendants began to beat a tattoo on the roof of the *toril*.
But still nothing appeared in the gateway, and the terraces
began to grow restless.

Then something pale could be seen taking shape in the
entrance to the *toril*. Gradually it became clearer, and
finally revealed itself as a backside: the bull's backside, a
backside as pale as a piece of soap. Gradually the bull
squeezed its backside into the narrow gateway of the *toril*,
where it stuck. And from the terraces there rose a great
clamour, like the clamour of the peoples of the ancient
East at the rise of the full moon.

The drumming on the roof of the *toril* intensified, and
one or two spectators whacked the pale backside. The
latter emerged a little bit more from the *toril*, then stuck
again.

The president gave a signal, and the band struck up
a *paso doble* in the hope of rousing and encouraging this
recalcitrant infant and hastening its birth. But the only
effect was to make the bull wag its tail in time to the music,
without moving anything else.

The dwarf unfurled his cape, and bursting with pride,

challenged the bull's backside. The bull did not budge. The dwarf was given an ovation. The music was still blaring.

Then the dwarf, drunk with self-approbation, gave the bull's tail a violent tug, and instantly leapt over the barrier. The bull backed out, and suddenly the whole of its body appeared. Straightway it wheeled round, dazzled by the light, and was about to gallop off when it slipped and fell flat. Instead of taking advantage of this godsend to kill it then and there, they patiently gave it time to pick itself up. It was a shaggy little bull, like a small boy who is always sleeping in haystacks.

When it was back on its feet, the matador in green went towards it. Seeing this slim young man approach, the bull was taken aback. If it had been able to blush, it would have gone purple; but there was no question of this.

It pawed the ground, then retreated as the matador advanced. Quite obviously the poor beast was terrified. When it could not bear it any longer, it turned round and trotted off towards the barrier, pursued by the horde of *toreros*. The *corrida* had turned into a hunt.

Celestino, like everyone else, had come to see the bull-fighters being frightened, being wounded, and, for better or worse, to see at least one of them being killed. Not for a moment had he expected to see fear—to see *his* fear—in the bull.

Four of the *toreros* cornered the bull against the barrier in such a way that, in order to extricate itself, the bull was obliged to charge—which it did, though not without giving itself a certain amount of time for reflection: the need to make decisions was a disagreeable one for this bull, whom God had created irresolute. Then the matador in green, standing on the tips of his toes, feet together, back arched, head bent, made exactly the same pass as the matador in brown had made at the first bull. This sent the public into raptures.

This pass had also been made in a position of safety. The matador was pressed so close to the bull that the curve of its charge could not reach him with the horns: he was inside it. In the same way, when a woman has bad breath, if a man presses his mouth against hers he can no longer smell it. And one imagines it must be the same in ballistics, little of a gunner though one is.

Suddenly, from nowhere, there appeared forty matadors together in the ring, all making the same safe and stereotyped pass, forty young dandies all in the same plastic pose, like forty lead statuettes (lead soldiers) all cast in the same mould, or forty puppets controlled by the same string. Forty dandies meaning eighty buttocks and forty frontal assets. And forty miniature bulls wrapping themselves round these dandies, meaning eighty filed horns, or let's say seventy-eight. The picadors were sitting astride very old chairs, the backs of which were horses' necks. Each chair, disembowelled, had its springs dangling from it like intestines. And the chairs advanced on the coils of these springs. Then the forty dandies triumphed, and held up high forty ears and thirty-nine tails, for one of the bulls had lost its tail, God knows how. And so it went on, always the same *ad nauseam*, always the same, the quintessence of vulgarity.

And Celestino was dreaming of what it would be like to be the man on the *mirador*, clearing the bullring of all this riff-raff with a machine gun, when he received a violent blow in the stomach, as though a bullet from his machine gun had ricocheted.

"*Hombre!* Look out, it's burning."

He realized that he had dozed off, and that his cigar had

fallen into the folds of his muffler. It was his neighbour
who had woken him up.

He looked at the ring. Quite close to him, the matador
in green was executing a pass. But the bull did not react.
Motionless, it simply bellowed, and its bellowing seemed
to say: "Why are you tormenting me like this? What have
I done to you?" It was standing in front of the second L of
CHOCOLATES GONZALEZ (the advertising poster).

Celestino was so certain that there was a note of interrogation in this bellowing, and that the question was that and
none other, that he was moved. For the first time, he realized that it was not the bull that hated the man, but the
man who hated the bull. And he had pity on the bull. And
if he had read St. Francis of Assisi he might have said:
"Brother bull . . ." And at the same time he had pity on
himself. This pity showed that he was very old.

And because of his pity, the meaning of everything that
was happening around him slowly began to change.

At first the *corrida* had struck him as a sort of fandango
danced by a trio consisting of the Sinister, the Grotesque,
and the Odious. Then a ballet solo performed by Boredom,
which plunged you into a magic sleep. Now it was something else.

When he was young he used to say that life was a fighting bull. Now he thought it was man who was a fighting
bull. What was being fought in this bullring, in hundreds
of bull-rings every Sunday, was man. A beast was killed
instead of a man. It would of course have been better to
kill men, and this had been done on both sides during the
civil war, when political adversaries were done to death in
accordance with the rules of the bullring in many a city
street or village square. Unfortunately this was out of the
question in peacetime. So the bull took upon itself, com-

pressed into quarter of an hour of conflict, the whole of human destiny. And men came to see, in safety and respectability, what they would have liked to do to other men. Spain acted out the passion of man under cover of the passion of the beast, as the Church claimed to act out the passion of a god under cover of the passion of a man.

Celestino's thoughts had reached this point when the boy in green thrust the sword home, too low. But the bull fell. There were cheers and boos. Celestino was engrossed in his new idea, and this finale did not interest him. With traditionally artificial excitement, the mules dragged away the dead bull. Around the ring the equine sea-serpent unwound its coils with wild and quivering hoofs.

The third bull entered the ring, or rather *man* entered the ring, and his fate was already sealed: whatever he did, whether he was brave or cowardly, he would perish in the end; there too, a special court had passed sentence. (A few exceptionally brave bulls had been reprieved by the president of a *corrida* at the request of the public. But how many? One in a thousand?)

He was alone against the world, in the holy solitude of the condemned. Only the horses were not against him, those morphiomaniac sea-serpents who did not understand either, and whom nonetheless he was going to impale: "Why are you killing me?"

When he had been sufficiently teased and baffled, he stopped, and turning towards his persecutors, bellowed his first "Why?" Then he had tried to escape, trotting along the *barrera*, but the infernal circle hemmed him in. Then he had taken to finishing each pass by extricating himself from the cape and galloping off at random, pursued from one side of the ring to the other by the bewildered *toreros*. Now he had grown suspicious. He sensed traps everywhere, and indeed they were there. He sensed them and yet, in the end, he walked right into them head first. He never achieved more than a sort of semi-intelligence, because he was simple and straightforward. He panted after each pass, cheated every time, and Celestino, each time, panted with him.

Celestino never saw things as they were in reality: neither society (*vide* his utopianism), nor people (*vide* his mistakes about Ruiz, Pineda, and Pascualita), nor objects (*vide* his distortions and mirages). In the same way the bull cannot see things as they are: he mistakes the bait (the cape or the *muleta*) for the man, he thinks that by jumping over the *barrera* he will find freedom, he thinks the *querencia** will protect him, etc. . . . And this is to speak only of normal bulls; a bull whose horns have been shaved has, as we know, a defective vision. The capacity to make mistakes is so inherent a part of what is expected of the bull, that a bull who does not make a mistake is described as "criminal"—criminal because clear-headed: quite a thought. In the role which is allotted to him, playing the game consists in being duped, no more and no less.

While the third bull was being prepared for the picadors, a few flakes of snow began to fall, which soon grew thicker and more numerous. The spectators, grimacing against the snow, pulled their berets and caps and hats over their foreheads and covered their chins with their scarves and mufflers. Their black silhouettes grew blacker still. Celestino pulled his muffler up to his nostrils and held it there with a trembling hand.

---

* A section of the bullring, usually near the *barrera*, to which the bull constantly returns and where it takes its stand when the end is near.

The bull gored a horse, and seemed to have had enough; the *toreros* tried to cut the episode short; everyone seemed to want to get it over with as quickly as possible. Alas, one cannot finish a *corrida* in a hurry.

Within minutes the sand was completely white, and the terraces too were white, not only from the snow but because the spectators had huddled together as though to warm themselves by contact with one another, or perhaps simply to move to dearer seats. Almost everything was white, against the dark, lurid sky. The bull slipped on the snow. The *toreros* wiped their faces with towels or with their capes, now stained with sand and blood. The snow stuck to their eyelashes, and also to those of the bull, who blinked like a man.

Some of the spectators looked towards the president, expecting him—rather than expressly asking him, for they had paid—to stop the fight.* The matador in particular interrogated the president's box with a furiously impatient eye, and the *peones* looked daggers at him; the picadors themselves yelled at one another, opening their black mouths. But the president, either because he was stubborn and enjoyed holding out against the majority, or because he was curious to know how it would all end, or simply because he liked snow, did not give the signal. And in any case the snow had eased off, and then stopped altogether.

The *peones* went to fetch dry capes, which were full of stale blood like women's underclothes thrown into the dustbin. One of them sharpened the *banderillas*.

The "Red" matador challenged the beast with the

---

* The president is not obliged to stop a *corrida* in the event of rain. He *is* obliged to do so in the event of a snow storm, because the snowflakes blur the distances between the men and the bull, and upset the fight.

banderillas, but as soon as it charged, he turned tail and ran. Celestino muttered insults into his muffler, oblivious of the fact that this mixture of defiance and fear was precisely his when he had decided to come to Madrid.

The matador, enraged, sketched rather than executed a few muddled passes, and then flung himself at the bull. The sword went in and stayed there. The *peones* made the bull go round and round, jostled it, dazed it, struck it savagely in the legs and back with their capes, as policemen, it appears, are wont to do with demonstrators. This systematic bullying had something in common with what the lawyer, the clerk, and Vicente had inflicted on Celestino. The more helpless the beast, the more they harried it and ridiculed it —having run away from it five minutes before.

More and more wary and more and more duped, more and more vicious and more and more mocked, more and more both impotent and dangerous, ineluctably doomed to die and yet still capable of killing: such was the bull at the end of its life, and such is man.

The snow began again, and once more people looked at the president's box. But the president did not budge; he was obviously a president who liked snow. The bull came to a halt by the *barrera,* opposite the A in ANIS DEL MONO, near the prostrate horse which was slowly dying: very much a retreat-from-Moscow horse, for, as it was the only stationary object in the ring, the snow had piled up on top of it, whereas from everything else it had gradually been shaken off. The belly of the horse, pushed up on one side by the ground, appeared enormously fat. Awkwardly it scraped the sand with its legs, and its hoofs kept colliding with one another. It sighed, poor creature—gentle little sighs and lewd little moans; if one had shut one's eyes one might have taken it for a woman in the act of love. The beast seemed almost to be enjoying its death; perhaps, sometimes, there can be pleasure in dying. Celestino thought he recognized the horse as the one which had pulled the cart with the Brigitte Bardot poster: it was like one of those actors in provincial touring companies who play several different parts in the same play.

The trampled snow had made a mess below the expensive seats, for most of the fight took place in front of these, which is as it should be. Just as the population of Madrid had invented the idea that there was one part of the town (known as the Salamanca district) which would be spared by the Franco planes, and all tried to squash into it, so the bull was persuaded that there were four square feet of the ring where he would be free from torment—the *querencia* —and persistently returned there, although they came to persecute him there as well as everywhere else. Now he was back there again, placing his muzzle on the *barrera*, as though to say: "I wish I could go away," leaving a trail of slaver on the wood. Blood flowed down one of his front legs. From the corridor behind the *barrera*, gate-crashers spattered him with the dried melon pips which people suck and spit (another ritual) at every self-respecting bullfight. The matador lured him away with a *muleta* weighed down with melted snow, and plunged his sword in a second time. It hit a bone and bounced in the air, and the men in the front row raised their sticks to ward it off if it threatened to land on them (ritual again). Celestino shuddered; this blow had hurt him; he was shivering with cold, his muffler round his ears, his hands deep in his pockets. His cigar, which had gone out, no longer kept him warm, but he kept the butt in his mouth to chew on savagely, as though he were chewing the tender flesh of a young matador. The *peones*, all shame gone, kicked the bull's legs to make him fall, but he responded by lashing out, making the crowd laugh. A *peon* unbuttoned the matador's collar; this was not a pose, whatever Celestino may have thought.

The crowd booed the matador. They also booed the dying bull, who was not dying with sufficient dash: panache, damn you, panache! His back had been broken, he had been kicked and beaten, drilled with a pic, stabbed with a sword, and enticed on to the horses' trappings, which hurt his horns (the point of a bull's horn is very sensitive). Yet the crowd did not know or did not wish to know the real reason why, if one may venture to say so, he was not at his best, and they insulted him for a weakness which was not his fault; they insulted him not so much for what he was but for the treacherous wrong that had been done to him. The victim had given his vigour and fire, at the start. He had given his blood. He was about to give his life. Now he was giving his humiliation. Truly, he gave everything up to the show. Bullied, tortured, flowing with blood, insulted to the point of being smacked on the muzzle by a young whippersnapper of a matador—and all this against a background of hypocrisy which insisted that *he* was the guilty one, when he was not. It must be said that when "Red" took the liberty of slapping the dying creature, there were protests from the terraces.

Then Celestino saw that the *mirador* had turned into the statue of a human being. It grew bigger and bigger, as big as the Statue of Liberty in New York harbour, even bigger still. Its face wore the self-same expression as he himself had worn throughout the *corrida*. Its pedestal bore the inscription: BAD FAITH. This goddess reigned over the bullring, but he had now realized that the bullring was the microcosm of the whole world. . . . So it was not Liberty but Bad Faith that reigned over the world, holding in its hand, like a funerary Eros, a torch upside down, dashing to the ground the flame of Truth and Justice.

To everyone's surprise, the bull jerked its head upwards, scattering the snow which had gathered on its horns while its head had been hanging low. It was like a dying flame that every now and then still raises a fitful gleam. The matador tried the *descabello*,* without success. Barracked, he showed his right wrist to indicate—whether rightly or wrongly—that it was the fault of his wrist. A *peon* put a crape bandage round his wrist.

The bull made water and excreted simultaneously. Once more, people laughed: once more suffering and death were amusing, hovering above this submerged courage. "Red" flung himself at its withers. The sword must have pierced the lungs, for the bull vomited blood and prostrated itself. And, whereas he had drooped sadly when he was on his feet, now that he had lain down to die he raised his head and held it high in pride.

A *peon* dispatched him with a dagger. Within a second, the proud fighter had become meat.

While, to add a final grotesque touch of insult to injury, it was being dragged out of the ring by fat half-donkeys, "Red," in spite of the cold, soothed his parched lips in the paradisal bliss of water and then, with an air at once furious and contrite, went to salute the president's box, disgustedly dragging his *muleta* behind him in the dirt, as if *it* was the guilty one and not he. People turned their heads away in contempt.

Don Celestino got up to go. Physically, he was at the

* A stab with the sword between the first and second cervical verte-brae, which severs the spinal cord and instantly fells the bull. This blow is allowed when the bull has received several *estocadas* without collapsing.

end of his tether. He felt sick. The bullring swung completely over to one side, then righted itself, quivering. Don Celestino slid along the row, knocking against people's legs, leaning on shoulder after shoulder with the unanswerable effrontery of children, the old, and the sick: a sleepwalker, but an imperious sleepwalker. Some of the people in the row turned sideways in order to let him pass without having to get up; others took up even more room so that he would have to jostle them and so they could swear at him. His only thought was: "I won't find my car."

Outside, he wandered round vaguely. People who had not been to the bullfight stared at him with surprise and sometimes malevolence; they had not been to the fight (though they could have: half the seats were empty), but they were indignant that one of the spectators should leave after the third bull. He would have liked to explain to them: "I'm leaving because I'm going to die, like the bulls." The snow creaked under his feet with the noise of a saddle under a horseman, but in a very different rhythm. A man got out of a car and signalled to him: the chauffeur. "But will the car be able to start?" His anguish was part of him like a burning tunic mingling with his flesh.

VIII

. . . and the confusion of the world, detached from us and falling behind, will be no more than a nebula of lies revolving in the depths of the past.

Henry de Montherlant: *Service Inutile* (1935); p. 336.

IN THE CAR on the way back:

"What I must do, in the state I am in, is to gather enough strength to pack, to find my way to the train, etc. . . . What an ordeal! But the main thing is to cross the frontier. Better to be in hospital in Paris than here, in the hands of Pascualita and Vicente, perhaps even the police.

"It's pneumonia. How guilty Pascualita will feel! She made fun of me when I told her it might happen." The consciousness of being right, and the thought of Pascualita's remorse, revived him a little. The car raced down the mountain, "sniffing the stable." Celestino had pulled his hat down over his eyes. He did not want to look at the landscape, he did not want to look at Spain, which in a few hours he would never see again. All was disillusionment: the revolution, the war, his youth, the people, the bulls. . . . At least France did not mean disillusionment, because France had never meant anything to him. Besides, what did France matter, or Spain? Already his country was elsewhere.

There had been no *mirador* in the bullring, no dwarf among the *peones*, no herd in the streets of Madrid the previous day. He realized this now. And at the same time he was suddenly ashamed of his unfairness towards the *toreros* and towards bullfighting in general. And this sudden volte-face frightened him. Why was he now ashamed of his unfairness when it had given him pleasure only a few minutes before?

From time to time he raised his eyes, and was struck by certain sights, which he recognized, on the opposite side from the one he had seen them on coming the other way. This waterfall was the same waterfall, and yet, from this side, it looked quite different. This inn, which had a poster on one of its walls advertising such and such a brand, which he had seen when coming, had a poster advertising another brand, on the opposite wall, which was visible on the way back. Everything he saw was the same and yet different. And it seemed to Celestino that there was a symbol here of something or other, but he could not grasp what.

His body was burning and throbbing with fever. He tried to feel his pulse, but was unable to. He had never been ill in his life.

"I couldn't understand the *corrida*, because I know nothing about the new techniques, and I've forgotten the techniques of the past. But perhaps I never understood anything about the revolution either, or about politics. A bogus man of the left . . . a bogus *aficionado* . . . a bogus intellectual . . ." Everyone had told him he was an imbecile: Ruiz in so many words; the editors of reviews by rejecting his articles; Pascualita, the Communists, the lawyer, Vicente, by their behaviour towards him. Driven back, like the bull, against a barrier through which there was no escape, he too dully surveyed the incomprehensible scene. He too had given his blood, or at least done everything he could to give it. "Blood is the proof of revolution." But man did not prove himself by blood. There was, of course, another kind of blood, the blood from the other kinds of wounds that had been inflicted on him, and through which his life was ebbing away. But that blood proved nothing either.

When he looked for his wallet to pay the driver, he could not find it at first, and thought it must have been stolen. He found it almost at once. But during the short time his error lasted, he had become aware that the loss of a certain sum of money meant nothing to him, and the fact that he no longer cared for money had seemed to him a sinister portent, as had his unfairness towards the *toreros*. Something very grave must be happening to him for everything to swing round like this.

"What will become of me if I no longer care for money?" All through his life he had despised money, but now that everything was being taken away from him, the removal also of his love of money, so recently acquired, was like removing a stick from a blind man.

If he lived, he would convert the money from his sister's estate into notes, and while Marie-France and Pascualita were out of the house, he would put it in a bucket with some petrol, and burn it.

Celestino climbed the hotel staircase with difficulty, clinging on to the banisters. When he arrived in his room, he saw all his belongings scattered around, and realized that he would never have the strength to collect them all and fit them into his suitcase. How, indeed, had they fitted before? It was incomprehensible. But there were so many things in the world that were incomprehensible. . . .

He telephoned the reception desk to ask someone to come up and pack for him. Nobody answered: it was Sunday.

A thought had come to him on the way back from the bullfight, which he had been unable to make a note of—for one of his articles—because the car was shaking so much. Obsessed as he was by death, he felt he had to make a note of his thought, which perhaps was not a thought at all. He found a blank sheet of paper on the table and wrote: "In France, the aim of the Right is, basically, to steal the Left's thunder, and, secondarily, to seek to compromise independents. We Spaniards must . . ." He did not finish it: what the Spaniards were to do had gone right out of his head.

Exhausted, he lay down on the bed in his shirt-sleeves. The suitcase? the train? Already the suitcase and the train belonged to another world, the world of the impossible. He became aware of having crossed his hands over his breast in an attitude of prayer. If he were to die suddenly, what a tissue of lies would be built up round this final crossing of hands! He uncrossed them and placed them on the bed. It was a gesture not so much of anti-Christianism as of honesty.

Suddenly a noise that was by way of being musical erupted outside: somebody's radio was belching forth a North-American popular song, based on a hysterical rhythm, a hideous twitching and shaking of male and female monkeys. Nothing that Celestino, even in his worst nightmares, had imagined happening at such a time was comparable to this. He had been ready to face death in a spirit of conciliation. And now this noise was forcing him to die in a mood of just revolt and just hatred. The nation that had corrupted the world—that had corrupted Spain and Russia even, the only two countries worthy of his interest and his love—had risen up to corrupt his dying breath. It had arrived just in time to destroy the solemnity of his final hour, to snatch his soul from him or make a mockery of it, at the moment when it was his most sacred right to be in possession of his soul, his own soul as he wanted it to be.

The tragedy of it all was such that, as on the day when Ruiz had insulted him in the Square Willette, the sweat broke out over his body and drenched his Aertex vest. The ear-splitting squawks and hiccoughs went on, depriving him of all consciousness of being a human being, for the dehumanization they implied was such in his eyes that any-one who listened to them became dehumanized. And yet, almost throughout the entire planet, millions of people were listening to it with enjoyment! Yankee baseness, with demoniacal cunning, had probed men's baser instincts, exacerbating them and sometimes bringing them to the sur-face. He remembered the final sentence of his "famous" article on the United States, the one he had intended to read to Ruiz the day they had quarrelled, and which in the end he had not even tried to place: "A single nation that has succeeded in lowering the intelligence, the morality, the quality of the human race almost throughout the globe is a phenomenon never before experienced since the begin-ning of the world. I accuse the United States of being in a constant state of crime against humanity."

The strange thing was that if only Celestino had taken the trouble to provide himself with ear-plugs, he would have heard nothing and the tragedy would not have ex-isted. Man makes tragedy, and man dispels it.

The noise stopped, but how could he breathe in his anxiety that it might start again? What came next was some church music. It seemed to have welled up from his most distant past: the ectoplasm, as it were, of a right-wing

adolescent, one of those inexorcisable ghosts he had con-
jured up when the bearded man had smiled at him in the
street; but this time the ghost was himself. Celestino did
not remember the apparently rather ludicrous remark he
had made to Ruiz the previous summer in the rue d'Orsel:
"I prefer the Pope to the United States," but he acknowledged to himself that he did not mind religious music.
"Catholicism has made man stupid, but it has not degraded
him; it has introduced as many good and beautiful things
as bad things. The United States has simply degraded
humanity. Catholicism has done less harm in two thousand
years than the United States in two hundred."

Celestino's neck was bathed in sweat, so much so that,
loosening his collar, he mopped it with his handkerchief;
if he had been sure of being able to stand on his legs, he
would have gone to fetch a towel. Around him were the
antiquated bed, very high, with brass knobs, the dark-red
quilt, the print on the wall of a girl carrying flowers. All
this, at least, was acceptable as a sight for the eyes of a
dying man; but what was not acceptable was the anguished
waiting for the hand of Evil to grip his soul.

Lying there in silence, he felt a terrible shooting pain
between his shoulder blades. Was it his lungs? Was he
going to vomit blood, like the bull? The pain was even
sharper when he moved. He turned on his side and put his
hand down inside the back of his shirt as though to feel
the wound; then he lay back again, with his mouth open.

Here was a man who had dedicated his life to the community, within the circumscribed limits of his mind and
heart; but at the moment of death only he himself was left:
the individual had the last word. Celestino had said one day
to Pineda: "The advent of socialism is more important than
the conquest of the moon." Now he might have added:

"But my death is more important than socialism." And yet it was he who had so often repeated ("repeated" is hardly the word for something that was literally part of his flesh and blood) Trotsky's words: "If human life is sacred, we must abandon the revolution." The fall of Franco, the conquest of the world by communism, the outbreak of world war, the blowing up of the planet by the hydrogen bomb— all these were as nothing compared to this single fact: that he was going to die, that there was no hope, and that it was imminent. There it was, the thing that people talked about so much, that he himself had talked about so much all of his life, that he had dealt out indiscriminately, without a scruple, that he had risked indiscriminately, without a qualm. To cease to be: the most banal, the most improbable, the most unbelievable thing. And in importance it outstripped everything that existed whether in reality or in the imagination, it was utterly incommensurable with anything that was or that could be conceived of: a unique, unprecedented disaster. Something that in his youth and middle age had seemed of little consequence had now taken on a terrifying importance, was indeed *the only* thing that mattered.

He picked up the telephone again: still no reply. That, too, he had foreseen (with a slight variation: an electricity failure just when he had an attack of peritonitis). But what he had not foreseen was the music he heard on the telephone instead of the manager's voice: an exquisite *sevillana*, wild and gay. The manager had gone off to another part of the hotel leaving his radio on. Celestino listened for a while: to be able to talk to the manager might save his life. And then there came a moment when he could no longer bear all the carefree gaiety, all the essence of Spain pouring out of these machines telling him it was the last he would hear of them. Very well, let it be the last! He hung up. He did not appreciate Spanish music, because of his hatred of art, and he did not like the Andalusians, because they were nonpolitical. But in the hour of death he had adored the *sevillana*, because he could suffer from hearing it for the last time.

Besides, it was better this way. There was no need for the hotel manager, no need for a doctor, and as for Pascualita, even if he had not turned against her, even if he was back in the period when he could visualize himself placing his daughter's fingers on his eyelids so that she should close them, even then—and even though he had brought her to Madrid partly in order to help him if anything went wrong—even then he would have been glad not to have her there. She would have disturbed him, just as the manager and the doctor would have done. And if—God forbid!—a priest had appeared, he would have found the strength to sit up and tell him, quite calmly but with the utmost firmness: "There are worse things than you, but do not come in here. Pray for me if you wish, but do not come in here. You too, like that ignoble music, must be prevented from taking possession of what I am."

"Hide your life," said the sage. He should also have said: "Hide your death." Our bearing, or our lack of bearing, at that supreme moment, could do with being hidden. *Fuera todos!* "Everyone out!" Ruiz brushed aside. Pineda brushed aside. Vicente brushed aside. Pascualita brushed aside. The hotel manager, the doctor, the priest brushed aside. Like iron shutters closing one after another along a street when the rioting begins. Alone for the final confrontation with death, alone to do with it whatever had to be done, correctly. And his *fuera todos!* was nothing more than his old passion for creating a vacuum around himself brought to its ultimate logical conclusion. It was also the attitude of the anarchists during the civil war—rejecting everything, the conquest of power, intervention, isolation, Franco, Negrin, Stalin. But most of all it coincided with the battle-cry of medieval Spain, the slogan that expressed the deepest heart of Spain: *Santiago, y cierra España!* "Saint James, and close Spain!" Let Spain be closed, apart, alone, aloof and shielded from all the rest. *Fuera todos!* Let this old gentleman who was dying be closed, apart, alone. Aloof and shielded from all the rest.

He felt another sharp pain in his back, this time lower than the other. Suddenly he knew that he was going to die, perhaps that very instant, and he was content. Death was the only thing that mattered, and yet it, too, was a matter of indifference. *¿Y que?* "What then?" he said to himself: "This is what I expected all along," but it was untrue: during the war he never expected to die, he never thought of it; he had only begun to die when he had collapsed into his armchair because the charwoman failed to turn up; and begun for the second time when he had seen the bull being killed with those four sword-thrusts.—Yes, he was content. Or rather his anguish was transfigured by the boundless release which it opened up before him. How nice it was to be giving them all the slip! No longer would he have to worry about the death-bed furniture; no longer concern himself with ways and means of disinheriting Pascualita; no longer be terrified by the thought of Marie-France leaving; no longer have to bother to disentangle his sister's estate. He would not even—and this was the ultimate pleasure—have to put up with all the trouble his death would cause: that was a task for the living, it was made for them; "What a nuisance he is with his death": yes, he *would* be a nuisance to them, especially his brother-in-law, whom he had left alone for twenty years. He was going to die, and he would not have been arrested. His fear was at an end. And he had finished with always being wrong; finished with the ignorance and inconsistency and superficial judgements which had been the very fabric of his life, as of all lives; finished with futile enthusiasms and futile hatreds and futile words; finished with foolish nonsense. And by these few moments of belated indifference he would in the end have achieved his tiny foretaste of paradise, if truth is paradise.

During the civil war, loudspeakers on both sides used to hail the opposing lines inviting men to desert. Now, from left and right, boomed the loudspeakers of death.

From the left:

"Comrades! In a few moments, beyond hope and beyond appeal, you will have no more power over what you have spent your whole life trying to build, and you will no longer even know what it was. Nothing exists, since everything will cease to exist when you yourself cease to exist."

From the right:

"Nothing that you do makes sense unless you regard it as a game; otherwise you're dupes. Desert! Desert! What is the point of toiling on earth?"

One of the loudspeakers was on the left and the other on the right, but they boomed out the same "message." And for once—this was the extraordinary, the almost inconceivable thing—it was a "message" that was neither lies nor nonsense.

From the left, once more:

"Comrades! How foolish you have been to suffer—to suffer for the sake of chaos, which will dissolve into night."

From the right:

"There is no such thing as 'human progress'; it is simply

a question of passing the time. You can pretend if you like, you can behave 'as if' . . . But deep down inside you, desert. Desert! Desert! For there is nothing serious on earth."

"There is nothing serious, but there is tragedy," thought Celestino.

Voices rose from somewhere, saying: "We are on the side of life. What do we care about death?" Celestino turned his face to the wall. To hell with life!

"From his talk one could tell he was a madman, full of zeal for the affairs of government." He had always remembered this sentence from *Don Quixote*. But why did he need the loudspeakers of death to bring home to him how true it was? And why did he need the loudspeakers of death to remind him of the rather odd remark Ruiz had once made: "When you are finally liberated from your socialism and your patriotism . . ." Now he no longer grieved over the condition of his country (that is to say, the social problem considered in relation to his country). Spain wanted to be Franco-ist? Well then, let her be. The selfsame iron curtain that had fallen between him and Pascualita the previous day had now fallen between him and his country. Since his own death—his *own death*—meant nothing to him, wasn't it only natural that his country should cease to mean anything to him? "If I am capable of losing everything and not taking it too badly, I've got to admit that my country can lose everything without my taking it too badly." A vision of Franco, head and shoulders, swam in front of his eyes. Gradually the Caudillo's moustache grew longer, his hair stood up, the ribbons faded from his uniform, which turned into a smock: then he saw that Franco was Stalin. Contrary to what he had always imagined, there was no "yes" and "no"; everything was "yes" and "no" at the same time. And it was this mixture of "yes" and "no" that was the promised land he had always failed to recognize. In discovering that Franco was Stalin, he had discovered the promised land, he had discovered everything. A hallowed but godless atmosphere now surrounded him.

Through the gathering mental fog that enveloped him, would he have recognized the waiter if he came into the room? Would he not have mistaken him for his brother-in-law? Like Franco and Stalin, waiter and brother-in-law were identical.

And the men of the civil war were also identical, his comrades and the people on the other side. Interchangeable. All swarming like worms in a corpse, indistinguishable from one another and interchangeable, except that some worms are bigger and others smaller—the only difference. Prieto and Mola* were interchangeable, except that one was fat and the other thin. And the only gesture of the worms was to raise their heads from time to time with pride and exaltation: the worms were enthusiasts; they believed in causes. In fact these worms were men: restless, enthusiastic, indistinguishable and interchangeable.

He looked back at his life. And he saw that what he had done and what he had not done were one and the same thing. Identical. All his actions were indistinguishable and interchangeable.

"As soon as I begin to die, everything turns out to be the same thing. But I've always been condemned to die; it was a question of time. Therefore everything has always been the same. I should have looked at the world, enjoyed it,

---

* Mola, a Nationalist general (thin). Prieto, the socialist leader (fat).

and shielded myself from it; but never taken part in it."
And what of his last wishes—unfulfilled? Bah! What did
it matter? That too was absurd and meaningless.

His eyes were fixed, with the unblinking stare of a man
already dead, on the single electric light bulb hanging on a
long string from the ceiling, covered with the national
fly-dung, which had formed into a dense crust over the
years.

From above him there came a noise of plumbing being
put into operation. Someone was washing, tidying himself
up. Life and death were contiguous, but unaware of each
other. And if they met they would ridicule each other.

In an angle between wall and ceiling a large wet stain
appeared. Celestino took his eyes from the electric light
bulb to look at the stain, the lines of which, it seemed to
him, represented a suspension bridge, the profile of a laughing man, and a pug dog with a ribbon round its neck, all
mixed up together.

A round face drew close to his. He recognized it as
Ruiz from the spectacles. Ruiz said to him: "I was unfair
to you. Will you forgive me?" Celestino smelt his bad
breath. He shook his head. Ruiz persisted: "I've been unfair. Forgive me." Celestino clicked his tongue against his
teeth, which in the language of the Mediterranean and of
Castile means "no."

Perhaps, as death drew near, most men saw the truth in
a new light. Either the things of this world, to which they
had always passionately devoted themselves, now seemed
to them futile, and only indifference made sense—which
was what the loudspeakers had preached. Or else these
things seemed futile, and only religion made sense, even
though they had ignored it since childhood. But this was

merely the last of a series of metamorphoses: their vision of the world had changed with each new period of their lives.

But if there was a truth for the age of twenty, a truth for the age of forty, a truth for the age of sixty, a truth for the hour of death—if there were so many truths there was no such thing as *the* truth. The "problems" of the world vanished, as clouds vanish from a sky that is clearing. And to think that he had lived ever since childhood by the notion that there is truth on one side and falsehood on the other, with no halftones between! There was life, which was confused, incoherent and unstable, and then whatever exists before a man's life and after it, which was fixed and absolute. The loudspeaker had spoken truly: there was Chaos, which was life, and Night, which was whatever exists before life and after life (Chaos and Night, two characters in the divine comedy of Hesiod, whom Celestino had never read). There was non-sense, which was life, and non-being, which was what exists before life and after it.* Or rather, wasn't there only non-being and an appearance of being? *"Nothing exists, since everything ceases to exist when I cease to exist. That's what I ought to have understood sooner: nothing exists."* But he understood it now, and this sudden illumination was so strange and awe-inspiring that only his death could call it into being. It was a sure warning of his death, if he still had any doubt on this score. One quarter of an hour of insight in an entire lifetime, and that at the moment when it was coming to an end!

He could no longer make out the pug dog in the damp stain.—Ah, there it was!

* If the entities of Chaos and Night conceived by the dying Celestino are—without his knowing it—in Hesiod, the identities he gives them are neither in Hesiod nor in any of the other Greek cosmogonies.

His legs, stretched out on the bed, were flaccid, and the expanse of empty trouser-leg lying on each side of them emphasized the thinness of his thighs. The legs of a puppet sprawled on the floor.

He imagined that Pascualita was beside his bed and he was saying to her:

"Do you know what the greatest power in the world is? Indifference."

"More powerful than hatred?" she asked.

"Yes, more powerful than hatred."

"Indifference! So you're a sceptic, too, and if you're a sceptic you're a fascist."

"Fiddlesticks!" said Celestino. "Fascist or not, the game is up. But armed with indifference I shall not die defeated."

Pascualita? Back again? But of course! Wasn't he a slave to habit? Pascualita and her little dry voice. And yet the steel blind that had come down between the two of them remained—outliving some of the reasons that had caused it. Pascualita could be as Franco-ist as she liked, but she could not have despised him with impunity, and he could not, with impunity for her, have loved her in vain. Even more than her contempt, it was the fact that he had loved her that had brought him to condemn her, and he had condemned nobody more than her because there was nobody he loved more than her. In one case only was hatred stronger than indifference: when it was inverted love.

Pascualita was leaning over him. She again said something about fascism, and he replied—for the first time aloud: "I don't care. I don't care. The game is up."

It was then that he felt a third blow, at the back of his neck, and suddenly everything inside him was swept away, like a cloud swept away by a hurricane. It was so horrible that everything, thought, memory, his newfound indifference, was swept away in a flash; chaos and night themselves were swept away; only horror remained. He slid off the bed with the intention of going to the door and calling for help, but he was seized with dizziness and fell forward; he put out his arms to break his fall, and found himself on all fours. He advanced on all fours, hugging the wall all round the room, trying to get away from the world of death, from the world of horror, trying to reach the door and open it before crying out. A ray of consciousness flashed across his rapidly darkening mind: "Is it me, is it really me this is happening to? Isn't it a dream? Is it really me it's happening to? No, it isn't possible."

When he got to the door, he tried to lift his arm to reach the handle, but could not: leaning on the floor with one arm, he lost his balance. He heard a noise on the staircase; the panels of the door were thin; somebody passed by along the landing, and he had only to shout, or simply knock; but he could not bring himself to do so, because of the humiliation of calling for help. The steps receded down the staircase.

There was still that lingering ray of consciousness. "Oh my God," he thought, "not yet! Later, even if I have to suffer, but not yet!" Again he felt ashamed: "Oh, how cowardly!" Then he thought: "Since God doesn't exist, there's nothing wrong in my invoking him. In any case, even if it was cowardice, in the state I'm in now, what does it matter!" Then he thought: "To invoke God, who does not exist, is nonsensical. But since everything is nonsensical . . ."

A fourth blow in the back—this time so savage that his arms gave way and his chest touched the floor, while his legs still held him in the same position. He groaned, and blood dribbled from his mouth, at the same time he felt a warm, soft substance flowing gently along his thighs, accompanied by an unspeakably foul smell. This substance was halted by the bends of his knees, where it accumulated. In this nadir of abasement, he lifted his head so that his beard became almost horizontal, in an attitude of defiance, and a gleam of ferocity appeared in his eyes. Then his legs gave way, and he rolled over on his side, his mouth open, his eyes staring fixedly. And thus he died, and afterwards his legs jerked spasmodically.

Some twenty minutes later, two black cars braked hard one behind the other and stopped abruptly outside the hotel. With the same abruptness, three men in black raincoats, two bareheaded, the other wearing a felt hat pushed back, jumped out of the first car and rushed into the hotel. Two policemen got out of the second car and stationed themselves at the door of the hotel. Three, then four, then five passersby stopped to look. When they were five, the policemen dispersed them.

On the first floor, the three men found the hotel manager watching a street vendor of the kind who frequent the cafés in the Gran Via, showing off some toy parrots. The manager, delighted, had his hand in his pocket and was about to buy one. One of the bareheaded men addressed him.

"Police. Is there a man called Celestino Marcilla staying here?"

"Yes. On the second floor. Room 9." He made as if to telephone. "Shall I see if he's there?"

"No need. Come with us. Bring your pass-key."

"What's wrong?"

"A warrant for arrest."

The manager's face fell.

"What for?"

"Politics. A scoundrel!"

They went upstairs. The parrots went on whirling round their sticks without an audience. They had not yet reached the landing before they saw a pool of blood coming from under the door. The manager opened it, keeping his legs apart so as not to step in the blood.

"Murdered! Brutally murdered!"

The men stooped down and counted, between the nape of the neck and the base of the shoulderblades, four wounds, four thin, clean holes which might have been made by a knife or a sword, from which the blood still flowed, between the capsized chairs.

The service for the soul of Don Celestino Marcilla Hernandez was celebrated on the Tuesday in the church of San Isidro. The police had been discreet, and nothing had leaked out—except, of course, to Vicente and Pascualita. The notices in the papers had announced that the deceased had died after receiving the last sacraments. The congregation was small, and its embarrassment might well have been taken for sadness. The body was interred in sacred ground, in the cemetery of San Isidro, which is situated some two kilometres outside the town in the southwestern suburbs of Madrid. To this day the tombstone, above the usual *Here lies*, bears the inscription:

LAUS DEO.